P. C. Doherty was born in Middlesbrough and educated at Woodcote Hall. He studied History at Liverpool and Oxford Universities and obtained a doctorate at Oxford for his thesis on Edward II and Queen Isabella. He is now the Headmaster of a school in North-East London, and lives with his wife and family near Epping Forest.

P. C. Doherty's previous Hugh Corbett medieval mysteries are also available from Headline.

Also by Paul Doherty and available from Headline

The Rose Demon
The Haunting
The Soul Slayer

An Ancient Evil
Being the Knight's Tale
A Tapestry of Murders
Being the Man of Law's Tale
A Tournament of Murders
Being the Franklin's Tale
Ghostly Murders
Being the Priest's Tale

Hugh Corbett medieval mysteries
Satan in St Mary's
Crown in Darkness
Spy in Chancery
The Angel of Death
The Prince of Darkness
The Assassin in the Greenwood
The Song of a Dark Angel
Satan's Fire
The Devil's Hunt

Under the name of Paul Harding
The Nightingale Gallery
The House of the Red Slayer
Murder Most Holy
The Anger of God
By Murder's Bright Light
The House of Crows
The Assassin's Riddle

Under the name of Michael Clynes
The White Rose Murders
The Poisoned Chalice
The Grail Murders
A Brood of Vipers
The Gallows Murders
The Relic Murders

Murder Wears a Cowl

P. C. Doherty

HEADLINE

First published in 1992
by HEADLINE BOOK PUBLISHING

First published in paperback in 1993
by HEADLINE BOOK PUBLISHING

10 9 8 7 6 5

ISBN 0 7472 3991 6

Printed and bound in Great Britain by
Caledonian International Book Manufacturing Ltd, Glasgow

HEADLINE BOOK PUBLISHING
A division of Hodder Headline PLC
338 Euston Road
London NW1 3BH

To my daughter Vanessa Mary

Prologue

The creaking of the scaffold rope was the only sound to disturb the dark silence which hung like a cloud over the great open expanse outside St Bartholomew's in West Smithfield. During the day the area bustled with colour and noise but, at night, the ghosts would claim it for their own. The great scaffold with its out-jutting beams and yellow knotted ropes was a common sight, as were the corpses which dangled there, necks twisted, eyes protruding, swollen tongues clenched between yellow teeth. The city fathers decreed that executed malefactors should always hang for three days until their bodies started to rot and the sharp-beaked ravens began to gouge the eyes and soft flesh of the face.

No one ever approached that scaffold at night. The old hags claimed the Lords of Hell came to dance there. Even the dogs, cats and kites of the city left the place alone once darkness had fallen. Ragwort, the beggar, however, thought different. During the day Ragwort always sat at the corner of St Martin's Lane in West Cheap, his copper-begging bowl extended as he whined for alms from the faithful, the rich and the patronising as they crossed London's great market place to do business at St Paul's. At night, however, Ragwort moved back to

Smithfield, to sleep beneath the scaffold. He felt protected there. No one would dare accost him and he accepted the grisly corpses hanging above him as his companions, even protectors against the robbers, thieves and nightwalkers who plagued the narrow alleyways of London. Sometimes, when he could not sleep, Ragwort would crouch on the wooden slats he used as legs and chatter like a magpie to the corpses. He would wonder about their lives and what had gone wrong. They were the best, indeed the only listeners, to his own dismal tale: how he had been a soldier, born and bred in Lincolnshire, before becoming an archer in Edward of England's army in Scotland. How he had attacked a castle with scores of his companions, climbing the scaling ladders and then how God, aided and abetted by a red-haired Scotsman, had brought him low as hell. The ladder had been overturned, Ragwort had fallen into the dry moat and, when he had tried to crawl away, his legs had been drenched in sticky, burning, black oil. He had screamed for days, twisted in agony for months after the surgeons neatly chopped both legs off beneath the knee and strapped on wooden slats. Ragwort had been given a few coins, put on a cart and sent south to London to beg for the rest of his life.

Ragwort had come to terms with this. He had good custom and the great lords and the fat lawyers were generous patrons. He ate well, drank a flagon of red wine each day and, when the weather turned cold, the good brothers in the hospital of St Bartholomew's always allowed him to sleep in their cellars. Ragwort claimed he had visions, strange fancies which plagued his dreams: sometimes he was sure he saw red-horned demons walking the streets of London. On the evening of May 11th 1302, as Ragwort made himself comfortable beneath the swinging corpses, he had another premonition of impending evil:

the stumps of his legs ached, he had a prickling at the back of his neck and his stomach bubbled like a pot of seething fat. He slept fitfully for a while and woke just as a strong breeze sprang up to send the cadavers above him twisting and turning in some macabre dance of death. Ragwort tapped the soles of one of the corpse's feet.

'Shush!' he whispered. 'Let old Ragwort listen!'

The beggar crouched like a dog, his ears straining into the darkness. Then he heard it, the slap of sandals on the cobbles and the sound of heavy breathing: a dark figure hurried towards him. Ragwort drew back into the darkness, almost hiding behind the legs of the corpses hanging there. He peered at the approaching figure. Who was it? A woman? Yes, a woman. She was wearing a dark gown and her footfall was heavy. An old woman, Ragwort concluded, as he caught a glimpse of grey hair beneath the hood and the slightly hunched shoulders. She seemed in no hurry and posed no threat so Ragwort wondered why his heart kept pounding, his throat turned dry and a terrible coldness caught the nape of his neck, as if one of the hanged men had stooped down to stroke him gently. Then Ragwort knew the reason. He heard another footfall, someone was hurrying behind the woman. This person moved with speed and greater purpose. The first figure stopped as she, too, heard the pursuing footsteps.

'Who is there?' the old woman called out. 'What do you want?'

Ragwort tensed, pushing his fingers into his mouth. He felt the evil approach. He wanted to shriek out a warning. Something dreadful was going to happen. A second shape appeared out of the darkness and moved towards the old lady.

'Who are you?' she repeated. 'What do you want? I am on God's business.'

Ragwort moaned gently to himself. Couldn't the woman see? he thought. Couldn't she sense the malevolence creeping through the darkness? The second figure drew closer. All Ragwort saw was a hood and a gown. As the moon slipped from between the clouds, he caught the gleam of white flesh and saw that the second stranger also wore sandals. The old woman relaxed.

'Oh, it's you!' she snapped. 'What now?'

Ragwort couldn't hear the muttered reply. The two figures drew together. Ragwort saw a flash of steel and hid his eyes. He heard the gentle slash of a razor-edged knife cutting skin, vein and windpipe. A dreadful scream shattered the silence, cut off by a terrible gurgle as the old woman, choking on the blood which gushed up into her throat, crumpled to the cobblestones. Ragwort opened his eyes. The second figure had gone. The old lady lay in an untidy heap. She moved once but Ragwort sat transfixed by terror at the thin stream of blood snaking across the cobblestones towards him.

Later that same week in a garret at the top of a decaying mansion on the corner of Old Jewry and Lothbury, Isabeau the Fleming carefully counted out the coins in neat little stacks, the fruits of her hard night's work. She had accepted three visitors: a young nobleman, lusty and vigorous, a yeoman from the Tower garrison and an old merchant from Bishopsgate who liked to tie her up whilst he lay beside her. Isabeau grinned. He was always the easiest, so quickly pleased and so generous in his thanks. Isabeau drew the ribbons from her bright red hair and shook her locks loose over her shoulders. She shrugged off the dress of blue damascene and threw it, together with her undershift and gartered hose, into a crumpled heap. She stood and turned before the shining piece of metal which served as a mirror. She always went through the same ritual every night. Old Mother Tearsheet had advised her to do this.

'A courtesan who looks after herself, Isabeau,' the old beldame had cackled, 'stays younger and lives longer. Always remember that.'

Isabeau went over to the pewter bowl which stood on the lavarium and, using a sponge and a piece of Castillan soap, provided by a grateful Genoese captain, carefully washed her smooth, alabaster-white body. She jumped as a small bird, fluttering under the eaves of the old house, dashed itself against the shutters. A cat, hunting in the dark alleyway below, sang a screeching song to the moon. Isabeau stopped and listened to the old house creaking on its timbers. She must be so careful. The killer had already slain fourteen, or was it more, of her sisters? Their necks slashed so roughly, their heads dangled to the rest of the body only by strips of bone and muscle. She had seen one, the corpse of Amasis, the young French whore who used to trip so daintily up and down Milk Street looking for custom. Isabeau went back to her washing, enjoying the sensuous feel of the sponge against her skin. She cupped her full young breasts and ran her hand over her muscular, flat stomach. She heard a sound on the stairs but dismissed it as some foraging rat, seized a napkin and began to dry herself. She turned, moving the candle to a small chest next to the huge bed, covered with a swan-feather mattress, and donned a crumpled nightgown.

'Isabeau.' The voice was soft.

The whore turned, staring at the door.

'Isabeau, Isabeau, please I need to see you!'

The girl recognised the voice, smiled and tripped quietly to the door. She drew back the huge iron bolts, swung the door open and stared at the dark cowled figure cradling a small candle.

'What is it you want?' Isabeau stepped back. 'Surely not now,' she mocked, 'at this time of night?'

'Here,' her unexpected guest replied. 'Hold the candle!'

Isabeau stretched out her hand and, for a second, glimpsed the broad-bladed knife as it swept towards her soft, tender throat. She felt a terrible fiery pain and collapsed as her life-blood streamed down her freshly washed body.

In the Louvre Palace, which stood on the Ile de France under the towering mass of Notre Dame Cathedral, ran a maze of secret corridors and passageways. Some led to nowhere but blank walls. Others twisted and turned so much that any intruder soon became lost and disheartened. At the end of this maze, like the centre of some great web, was Philip IV's secret chamber. A room in the shape of an octagon, its walls were wood-panelled with only two small, arrow-slit windows high in the wall. The floor was carpeted from wall to wall in thick wool almost a foot deep. Philip IV liked this room. No sounds were ever heard. Even the door had been cunningly built into wood-panelled walls, so it was difficult to get in and, for the unwary, even more confusing to get out. The room was always lit by dozens of pure beeswax candles, the best the court chamberlain could provide. In the centre of the room was a square oaken table with a green baize top. Behind it a high-backed chair and, on either side of the table, two huge coffers, each with six locks. Inside each of these was another casket secured by five padlocks containing Philip of France's secret letters, memoranda and the reports of spies from all over Europe. Here, Philip sat at the centre of his web and spun his skein of lies and deceits to ensnare the other rulers of Europe, be they Prince or Pope.

Philip of France now lounged in his huge chair, staring at the gold and silver stars painted on the ceiling, gently drumming his fingers on top of the table. Across from him sat his Chancellor and Master of Secrets, the apostate William of Nogaret. This Keeper of the King's Secrets talked softly, yet rapidly, as he moved from one European court to another and all the time he watched this most impassive of kings. Philip, whom men nicknamed 'Beautiful', with his long, white face, pale blue eyes and hair the colour of burnished gold, looked every inch a king. He exuded majesty, as a woman would perfume, or a court fop an exotic fragrance, but Nogaret knew his master to be a cunning, sly fox who kept his face and his manner inscrutable, leaving others to guess his true intentions.

Nogaret paused and swallowed hard. He edged his stool slightly sideways for he knew that on his side of the desk was a dreadful oubliette, a trap door in the floor controlled by a lever under the rim of the King's desk. Nogaret knew what would happen if that trap door suddenly opened. He himself had seen a victim fall on to the steel-tipped stakes below.

'You have paused, William?' the King murmured.

'Your Grace, there is the matter of finance.'

Philip's blue eyes swung lazily at Nogaret.

'We have our taxes.'

Nogaret's dark hooded eyes blinked and he gently stroked his skin, a gesture which made his sallow, narrow face look even more drawn and pinched.

'Your Grace, a war against Flanders will empty the Treasury!'

'We can borrow.'

'The Lombards won't lend!'

'There are merchants who will.'

'They are taxed to the hilt.'

'So, what do you suggest, William?'

'There is the Church.'

Philip smiled slightly and gazed hard at his master of secrets.

'You would like that, wouldn't you? You would like us to tax the Church?' Philip leaned forward, lacing slender fingers together. 'Some men, William,' he continued, 'some men maintain you do not believe in the Church. You do not believe in God or Le Bon Seigneur.'

Nogaret gazed blankly back. 'Some men say the same of you, your Grace.'

Philip's eyes rounded in mock innocence.

'But my grandfather was the sainted Louis, whilst your grandfather, William, together with your mother, was condemned as a heretic, placed in a barrel of tar and burnt in the public market place.'

Philip watched the muscles in Nogaret's face tense with fury. He liked that. He relished it when others lost their calm and showed the true nature of their souls. The King leaned back and sighed.

'Enough! Enough!' he muttered. 'We cannot, we will not, tax the Church.'

'Then "we cannot, we will not",' Nogaret snapped back, mimicking the King's words, 'invade Flanders.'

Philip curbed the rush of fury within him and smiled. He gently smoothed the green-baized table top. 'Be careful, William,' he murmured. 'You are my right hand.' The King lifted his fingers, 'But if my right hand knew what my left hand was doing, I would cut it off!'

Philip turned, grasped the wine jug and filled a cup to the brim, watching the wine wink and bubble around the rim. He handed it to Nogaret.

'Now, my Master of Secrets, enough of this bandying of words. I need money, and you have a plan.'

Nogaret sipped gingerly at the wine and stared back.

'You do have a plan?' Philip repeated.

Nogaret placed the cup down. 'Yes, your Grace, I do. It will involve us in the affairs of England.' He leaned forward and began to talk quietly.

Philip listened impassively but, as Nogaret described his scheme, the King folded his arms, almost hugging himself with pleasure at the honeyed words and phrases which dripped from Nogaret's lips.

Chapter 1

Edward of England sat slumped in a window seat in the small robing chamber behind the throne room of Winchester Palace. For a while he watched one of his greyhounds gobble the remains of some sugared wafers from a silver jewelled plate, then gently lope across to a far corner to squat and noisily crap. Edward smiled to himself and gazed under bushy eyebrows at the two men seated on stools before him. The old one, John de Warrenne, Earl of Surrey, gazed blankly back. Edward studied the Earl's cruel face; his beaked nose, square chin and those eyes which somehow reminded Edward of the greyhound in the corner. De Warrenne, he mused, must have a brain in that close-cropped hair but Edward could not swear to it. De Warrenne never had an original idea, his usual reaction to anything would be to charge and kill. Edward secretly called de Warrenne his greyhound for, whatever Edward pointed to, de Warrenne would always seize. Now the Earl just sat there perplexed by the King's angry litany of questions, watching his master and waiting for the next order to be given. Despite the early-summer morning, de Warrenne still wore a thick, woollen cloak and, as always, a chain-mail shirt and the brown, woollen leggings of a soldier, pushed into loose riding boots, the spurs still attached. Edward chewed his lip. Did the Earl ever change his clothes? the King wondered. And what happened when he went to bed? Did his wife Alice bear the imprint of that mail on her soft, white body?

Edward glanced at the man next to de Warrenne, dressed simply in a dark-blue cote-hardie bound by a broad, leather belt. This man was as different from de Warrenne as chalk from cheese, with his dark saturnine face, clean-shaven chin, deep-set eyes and unruly mop of black hair which now showed faint streaks of grey. Edward winked slowly at his Master of Clerks, Hugh Corbett, Edward's special emissary and Keeper of the Secret Seal.

'You see my problem, Hugh?' he barked.

'Yes, your Grace.'

'Yes, your Grace!' Edward mimicked back.

The King's sunburnt face broke into a mocking smile, his lips curling so he looked more like a snarling dog than the Lord's Anointed. He rose and stretched his huge frame until the muscles cracked, then he ran his fingers through his steel-grey, leonine hair which fell down to the nape of his neck.

'Yes, your Grace,' the King jibed again. 'Of course, your Grace. Would it please your Grace?' Edward lashed out with his boot and caught the leg of his clerk's chair. 'So, tell me Master Corbett, what is my problem?'

The clerk would have liked to have informed the King, bluntly and succinctly, that he was arrogant, short-tempered, cruel, vindictive and given to wild bursts of rage which profited him nothing. Corbett, however, folded his hands in his lap and stared at the King.

Edward was still dressed in his dark-green hunting costume, his boots, leggings and jerkin stained with fat globules of mud. Moreover, every time the King moved he gave off gusts of sweaty odour; Corbett wondered which was worse, the King or the King's greyhound. Edward crouched before Corbett and the clerk stared coolly back at the red-rimmed, amber-flecked eyes.

The King was in a dangerous mood. He always was after hunting; the blood still ran hot and fast in the royal veins.

'Tell me,' Edward asked with mock sweetness. 'Tell me what our problem is?'

'Your Grace, you have a revolt in Scotland. The leader, William Wallace, is a true soldier and a born leader.' Corbett saw the annoyance flicker across the King's face. 'Wallace,' Corbett continued, 'uses the bogs, the fens, the mists and the forests of Scotland to launch his attacks, plan his sorties and arrange the occasional bloody ambush. He cannot be pinned down, he appears where he is least expected.' Corbett made a face. 'To put it succinctly, your Grace, he is leading your son, the Prince of Wales and commander of your forces, a merry jig.'

The King's lips parted in a false smile. 'And, Master Corbett, to put it succinctly, what is the rest of the problem?'

The clerk glanced sideways at de Warrenne but found no comfort there. The Earl sat as if carved out of stone and Corbett wondered, not for the first time, if John de Warrenne, Earl of Surrey, was in full possession of his wits.

'The second part of the problem,' Corbett continued, 'is that Philip of France is massing troops on his northern borders and, within the year, he will launch an all-out assault against Flanders. On the one hand, if God wills it, he will be defeated but, if he is victorious, he will extend his empire, destroy an ally, interfere with our wool trade and harass our shipping.'

Edward rose and clapped his hands slowly. 'And what is the third part of the problem?'

'You said you had a letter from the Mayor of London but, as yet, your Grace, you have not revealed its contents.'

The King sat down on a stool, dug inside his jerkin and pulled out the white scroll of parchment. He unrolled it and his face became grave.

'Yes, yes,' he spoke up. 'A letter from the Mayor and the Council of London, they require our help. There's some bloody assassin, some killer slitting the throats of whores, prostitutes and courtesans from one end of the city to the other.'

Corbett snorted with laughter. 'Since when have the city fathers been concerned about the deaths of some poor whores? Walk the streets of London in the depths of winter, your Grace, and you'll find the corpses of raddled whores, frozen stiff in ditches or starving on the steps of churches.'

'This is different,' de Warrenne spoke up, turning his head slowly as if noticing Corbett for the first time.

'Why is it different, my Lord?'

'These are not your common night-walkers but high-ranking courtesans.'

Corbett smiled.

'You find it amusing, clerk?'

'No, I don't! There's something else isn't there?'

Edward balanced the small scroll of parchment between his fingers. 'Oh, yes,' he replied wearily. 'There's something else. First, these courtesans know a lot of secrets. They have made it clear to the sheriffs and the great ones of the city that if something is not done, our ladies of the night may start telling everyone what they know.'

Now Corbett's grin widened. 'I'd give every penny I

have to be there when it happens. All our virtuous burgesses having their dirty linen washed in public.'

Edward smiled at the thought. 'I could say the same but these burgesses raise taxes for me. The city of London offers interest-free loans.' His voice became a snarl. 'Now you can see the problem, Corbett. I need silver to keep Philip out of Flanders and drive Wallace out of Scotland, otherwise my armies will melt away like ice before a fire.' The King turned, hawked and spat into the rushes. 'I couldn't give a damn about the whores, I couldn't give a damn about the burgesses. I want their gold. I also want vengeance!'

'Your Grace?' Corbett asked.

Edward just stared moodily at the greyhound, now getting ready to cock its leg against one of the wall tapestries. The King absent-mindedly took off a boot and threw it at the dog who yelped and scampered away.

'Some whores have died,' Edward answered. 'But there are two deaths I will not accept.' He took a deep breath. 'There's a guild of high-born widows in the city. They call themselves the Sisters of St Martha, they are a lay order dedicated to good works. To be specific: the physical and spiritual well-being of the young girls who walk the streets. Now, I gave these Sisters my personal protection. They assemble in the Chapter House at Westminster Abbey where they pray, meet and plan their activities. The Sisters do good work, their superior is the Lady Imelda de Lacey whose husband went with me on crusade. Did you ever meet him, Corbett?'

The clerk shook his head but watched the King carefully. Edward was a strange man. He could swear, be violent, treacherous, cunning, greedy and vindictive but he always kept his word. Personal friendship was as sacred as the Mass to him. The King especially remembered the companions of his youth, those knights who travelled with him and the now dead, but much beloved, Queen Eleanor, to fight in Outremer. If any of these companions or their interests were hurt, the King would act with all the speed and energy he could muster. Corbett felt a secret dread. He had promised his wife Maeve that he would return to London and take her and their three-month-old baby daughter Eleanor to visit her family in Wales. Corbett cringed at what the King might ask.

'Now, amongst the Sisters of St Martha,' Edward continued slowly, 'was the widow of one of my boon companions, Lady Catherine Somerville. Two weeks ago, Lady Catherine returned from Westminster along Holborn, her companion left her at St Bartholomew's and Lady Somerville took a short cut across Smithfield to her house near the Barbican. She never reached her home. The next morning her body was found lying near the gallows, her throat slashed from ear to ear. She died the same way as the whores she tried to help. Who,' Edward glared at de Warrenne, 'would kill an old lady in such a barbaric fashion? I want vengeance,' the King muttered. 'I want this killer seized. The city fathers are in uproar. They want their good names untarnished and the widows of high-ranking lords protected.'

'You mentioned a second death, your Grace?'

'Yes, I did. In the grounds of Westminster Abbey there's a small house. I persuaded the Abbot and monks to give it, as a stipend, a sinecure, a benefice, to an old chaplain of mine, Father Benedict. He was a saintly, old priest who loved his fellow man and was dedicated to good works. The night after Lady Somerville was killed, Father Benedict was burnt to death in his house.'

'Murder, your Grace?'

The King made a face. 'Oh, it looked like an accident

but I think it was murder. Father Benedict may have been ancient but he was careful, quick on his feet. I cannot understand why he reached the door of his house, even had the key in his hand but failed to get out.' The King spread out his fingers, carefully examining an old sword cut across the back of his hand. 'And before you ask, Corbett, there is a connection. Father Benedict was chaplain to the Sisters of St Martha.'

'Is there any motive for these murders?'

'In God's name, Corbett, I don't know!'

The King rose and hopped across the room to collect his boot. Corbett sensed his royal master was hiding something.

'Your Grace, there's something else, isn't there?'

Now de Warrenne began to pluck at a loose thread on his cloak as if he had discovered the most interesting thing in the room. Corbett's apprehension grew.

'Yes, yes, Corbett, there's more. One of your old friends is back in London.'

'Old friend?'

'Sir Amaury de Craon, personal emissary of His Most Christian Majesty, King Philip of France. He has rented a house in Gracechurch Street and brought quite a small retinue with him as well as letters of friendship from my royal brother the King of France. I have issued de Craon safe conducts but, if that bastard's here, then there's more trouble brewing in London than I would like to contemplate.'

Corbett rubbed his face in his hands. De Craon was Philip's special agent. Where he went, trouble always followed: treason, sedition, conspiracy and intrigue.

'De Craon may be a bastard,' Corbett answered, 'but he's not a common murderer. He cannot be involved in these killings!'

'No,' de Warrenne answered, 'but the flies which feed on shit are not responsible for it either.'

'Very eloquently put, my Lord.'

Corbett turned to the King, now leaning against the wall.

'Your Grace, what has this got to do with me? You gave me your word, once this royal progress in the West was finished, I was released from all duties for the next two months!'

'You are a clerk,' de Warrenne jibed out of the corner of his mouth.

'I am as good a man as you, my Lord!'

The old Earl gave a long rumbling belch and looked away.

'I want you to go to London, Hugh.'

'Your Grace, you gave me your word!'

'You can kiss my royal arse. I need you in London. I want you to stop these murders, find the slayer and see the bastard hanged at Tyburn. I want you to find out what de Craon and his companion Raoul de Nevers are up to! What mounds of shit they are turning over!'

'Who is de Nevers?'

'God knows. Some petty French nobleman with all the airs and graces of a court fop.' The King grinned. 'They have both shown an interest in you. They even paid a courtesy visit to the Lady Maeve.'

Corbett started and felt a shiver of apprehension. De Craon's meddling was one thing but de Craon under his own roof with his wife and child was another.

'You will go to London, Hugh?'

'Yes, your Grace, I will go to London, collect my wife, child and household and, as planned, go to Wales.'

'By God, you will not!'

Corbett rose. 'By God, Sire, I will!' He stopped by

de Warrenne and looked down. 'And you, my Lord, should drink more milk. It will relieve the wind in your stomach.'

The clerk walked towards the door and turned as he heard the hiss of steel. Edward now stood beside his throne, he had drawn his great sword from its sheath hanging on the back of the chair.

'Your Grace intends to kill me?'

Edward just glared back and Corbett saw the King was on the verge of one of his most spectacular outbursts. All the usual signs were there: pale face, the gnawing lips, the threatening gesture with the sword, the nervous kicking of the rushes. Like a child, Corbett thought, a spoiled brat who can't get his own way. Corbett turned back towards the door. The cup the King threw, narrowly missing Corbett's head, reached it before he did. Corbett was about to lift the latch when he felt a dagger prick the side of his neck. De Warrenne was now standing behind him; one word from the King and Corbett knew the Earl would kill him. He felt the hilt of his own dagger pushed into his belt.

'What now, my Lord Earl?' he murmured, looking over his shoulder at the King who now slouched on his throne, all signs of anger gone, his eyes pleading.

'Come back, Hugh,' he muttered. 'For God's sake, come back!'

The King threw his sword into the rushes. The clerk turned and walked towards him; he was shrewd enough to know when he had reached the limits of royal patience.

'Put your dagger away, de Warrenne! For God's sake we are friends not three drunken travellers in a tavern! Corbett, sit down!'

The King stared at his master clerk. Corbett saw the tears brimming in Edward's eyes and groaned inwardly.

He could deal with the King in one of his royal rages but Edward growing maudlin was both pathetic and highly dangerous. Corbett had attended the recent interview between the King and his eldest daughter who had secretly married someone whom the King considered beneath her. At first Edward had tried rage then tears and, when that did not work, beat his daughter, tossed her jewellery into the fire and banished both the hapless princess and her husband to the draughtiest manor house in England. The King's rages could be even more dangerous. Corbett had heard of certain Scottish towns who'd had the temerity to withstand his sieges, being taken by storm and no quarter given to woman or child.

The King clicked his fingers and de Warrenne, his dagger re-sheathed, served wine for them all. The old Earl then sat slurping noisily from his cup, now and again glaring at Corbett as if he wished to hack the clerk's head clean off his shoulders.

'Everyone leaves me,' the King began mournfully. 'My beloved Eleanor is dead. Burnell's gone – do you remember the old rogue, Hugh? Hell's teeth, I wish he was with me now.'

The King wiped his eyes on the back of his hand and Corbett sat back to admire Edward-the-player in one of his favourite roles – the old King mourning past glories. Of course, Corbett remembered Eleanor, Edward's beautiful Spanish wife. Whilst she had been alive, the King's rages had been held in check. And Chancellor Burnell, Bishop of Bath and Wells: he had been a shrewd old fox who had loved Corbett as his own son.

'Everyone's gone,' the King moaned again. 'My son hates me, my daughters marry whom they wish. I offer the Scots peace and prosperity but they throw it in my face whilst Philip of France dances round me as if I was some benighted maypole.' The King reached out and clasped Corbett's wrist. 'But I have you, Hugh. My right arm, my sword, my shield and my defence.'

Corbett bit his lip sharply. He must not smile or stare at de Warrenne who now had his face deep in his wine cup.

'I am begging you,' the King wheedled. 'Hugh, I need you. Just this once. Go to London, clear up this mess. You will see your wife, your baby child.' The King's grip tightened. 'You called her Eleanor. I'll not forget that. You'll go, won't you?' The grip tightened even further.

'Yes, your Grace, I'll go. But when this is finished and the game is over, you will keep your word?'

Edward smiled bravely though Corbett caught the mockery in his eyes.

'I am not a chess piece, your Grace,' Corbett murmured and glanced sideways. Was the Earl sniggering at him?

'De Warrenne!' Corbett snapped.

The Earl looked up.

'Next time you draw your dagger on me, my Lord, I'll kill you!' Corbett rose and walked towards the door.

'Hugh, come back.' The King was now standing, balancing the sword between his hands. 'You're no chess piece, Corbett, but I made you what you are. You know my secrets. I gave you wealth, a manor in Leighton. Now, I'll give you more. Kneel!'

Surprised, Corbett went down on one knee whilst the King with all the speed he could muster, touched his clerk once on the head then on each shoulder, slapping him gently on the face.

'I dub you Knight.'

The proclamation was short and simple. Corbett, embarrassed, knocked the dust from his tunic. Edward resheathed the sword.

'In a month the chancery will send your letter of ennoblement. Well, Corbett, what do you say?'

'Your Grace, I thank you.'

'Bollocks!' Edward snarled. 'If de Warrenne threatens you again and you kill him I'll have to execute you. But now you are a knight with a title and spurs, it will be a fight between equals.' The King clasped Corbett's hand. 'You'd best go, my clerks will draw up the necessary letters, giving you my authority to act on these matters.'

Corbett left as quickly as he could, secretly pleased about the honour shown to him but quietly cursing the King for getting his own way.

Back in the robing room, de Warrenne wiped his eyes as he shook with laughter at the King's duplicity. For a few seconds Edward basked in the Earl's admiration then suddenly he leaned towards him.

'John,' Edward whispered. 'I love you as a brother but if you ever draw your dagger on Corbett again, by my crown, I'll kill you, myself!'

Corbett returned to his own chamber and absent-mindedly began to collect his belongings, tossing them into saddle bags. Maeve would be furious, he thought. Her beautiful, placid face would become pinched with anger, her eyes would narrow and, when she found the words, she would damn the King, his court and her husband's duties. Corbett smiled to himself. But, there again, Maeve would soon be placated. She would be proud of the knighthood and pause a while before returning to her ripe description of Corbett's royal master. Then there was Eleanor: three months old and already showing signs of being as beautiful as her mother. A lusty, well-proportioned girl. Corbett had been teased that he wanted a son, but he didn't really care as long as Maeve and the child were healthy. He sat on the edge of his bed and half listened to the sounds from the castle bailey below. The child must be healthy! He thought of his first wife Mary and their daughter, dead so many years now. Sometimes their faces would appear, quite distinct in his mind, at others they would seem lost in a cloying mist.

'It can't happen again,' Corbett muttered to himself, tapping his boots on the floor. 'It can't happen again!'

He picked up the flute lying on the bed and gently played a few notes. He closed his eyes and, in the twinkling of an eye, he was back down the years. Mary was beside him, the little girl, so quickly gripped by the plague, tottering about in front of her. Other memories followed, the cunning, shrewd look of Robert Burnell; the beautiful, passionate face of Alice-atte-Bowe. Other faces appeared, many killed or trapped in their own terrible treasons or subtle murders. Corbett thought of the King's growing irascibility and dangerous swings of mood and he wondered how long he would stay in the royal service.

'I have enough gold,' Corbett muttered to himself. 'There's the manor in Essex.' He shook his head. 'The King will not let me go but how long will the King last?' Corbett stared at the floor, running the flute between his hands, enjoying the texture of polished wood. 'It's treason,' he whispered, 'to even consider the death of a king.' But the King was well past his sixtieth year and when he died what would happen then? The golden-haired Prince of Wales was a different kettle of fish with his love of hunting, handsome young men and the joys of both bed and board.

When the old King dies, Corbett wondered, what would his successor do? Would the new king need him, or would he be replaced? What would Maeve say? The thought of his wife recalled the King's words about de Craon.

'I wonder what that red-haired, foxy-faced bastard wants?' Corbett muttered. He got off the bed and crossed to the table littered with parchment. Two pieces caught his eye. First, a dirty thumbed piece of vellum; the writing on it was a mixture of numbers and strange signs which the cipher his spy had used in Paris. Next to it, neatly written out in green-blue ink was the translation of the cipher by one of the clerks of the Secret Seal. Corbett picked this up, read it quickly and cursed. He had meant to tell the King about this. The spy, ostensibly an English trader buying up wines in the Paris market, had seen the English fugitive and outlaw Richard Puddlicott in the company of Philip IV's Master of Secrets, William Nogaret, at a tavern just outside the main gates of the Louvre Palace. Puddlicott was a wanted man in England: a thief, a murderer who had killed a royal messenger but, above all, he was a trickster. No one had a clear description of Puddlicott but his fraudulent behaviour had wiped out the profits of many a merchant. He had been a clerk at Cambridge but now used his considerable wit and intelligence to separate people from their hard-earned wealth and kept reappearing either in England or France with his nefarious schemes. No law officer had managed to seize him or lay him by the heels. Corbett's spy in Paris had sent a description of a blond-haired man with ruddy cheeks and a slight limp. Yet the King's seneschal in Bordeaux had also described Puddlicott as black-haired, of sallow complexion, well proportioned in all his limbs.

Corbett re-read the letter. All the spy had learnt was that the Master of Secrets had been talking to Puddlicott, but about what, he could not tell except Nogaret had seemed most welcoming and attentive.

'I should have told the King this!' Corbett repeated to himself and, striding to the door, with the documents clutched in his fist, he bellowed for a clerk to take them immediately to the King.

Afterwards, Corbett stared round the untidy room. His agitation, caused by his recent meeting, had now subsided; it was best, he concluded, if he left immediately.

'The sooner gone, the sooner done,' he murmured. 'Now, where is the honest Ranulf?'

Corbett's manservant, the honest Ranulf, was in the great hall squatting in a corner with guardsmen of the royal retinue, slowly inveigling them into a game of dice. The red-haired, pale-faced manservant looked around solemnly, his green, cat-like eyes serious and unblinking.

'I have little skill in dice,' he murmured.

The soldiers smiled for they thought they had trapped a coney in the hay. Ranulf jingled his purse.

'I have some silver,' he said, 'as has my companion here.' He turned to Corbett's groom and ostler, the blond-haired, fat-faced Maltote who sat next to him like some innocent plough boy. Maltote smiled owlishly at the soldiers and Ranulf grinned as he drew them into his trap. The dice was thrown, Ranulf lost and then, amidst shouts of 'Beginner's luck!', he began to win. He was fully immersed in the game when he saw the soldiers look up fearfully just as he felt his master's iron grip on his shoulder.

'Ranulf, my dear man,' Corbett whispered sweetly. 'A word in thine ear.'

Ranulf glowered up at him. 'Master, I am in a game.'

'Ranulf,' Corbett said. 'So am I. A word, away from your friends.'

Ranulf clambered to his feet and Corbett led him away, still gripping his shoulder tightly.

'Master, what is wrong?' Ranulf winced as Corbett's fingers dug into his shoulder.

'First, Ranulf, I told you not to use those dice against

the King's soldiers. They are hard-working men and you are not here to fleece them of every penny they earn. Secondly,' Corbett released his grip, 'you are to return to London immediately.'

Ranulf dropped the look of mock innocence and grinned mischievously.

'Thirdly,' Corbett continued, 'we need to pack our belongings.'

'Master,' Ranulf whispered hoarsely. 'I am winning.'

'I know you are, Ranulf, and you'll give every penny back! Maltote?'

Ranulf wandered dolefully back, raising his eyes heavenwards as Maltote passed him. Corbett looked at the young groom anxiously.

'You are not carrying any weapons?' he asked warily.

The lad smiled.

'Good!' Corbett grinned back, marvelling at the innocence in the lad's cornflower-blue eyes. Never had Corbett met a soldier such as Maltote who knew so much about horses, was so skilled in their treatment and management but was so hopeless with weapons. If Maltote carried a knife he'd either cut himself or anyone about him. If he carried a bow he would trip himself up or poke the eye out of some innocent bystander, and he was as dangerous as any enemy if he carried spear or sword.

'Maltote! Maltote!' Corbett murmured. 'Once you were an innocent horse soldier, a good cavalryman and now you have met Ranulf.' Corbett flinched at the look of admiration in his retainer's eyes. 'Yes, yes, I know,' Corbett muttered. 'What Ranulf does not know about dice, women and drink is not worth knowing. But we are for London. We must leave immediately. Take two horses from the royal stable, ride as fast as you can and inform the Lady Maeve that Ranulf and I are following.' Corbett licked his lips. 'Tell her,' he concluded, 'we are not going to Wales but will stay a little longer in London.'

The young messenger nodded vigorously and scampered off, pausing only to watch a sorrowful Ranulf hand back the illicit gains of his crooked dice. Corbett watched him go, closed his eyes and hoped God and Maltote would forgive his cowardice. After all, the young messenger would be the first to receive the brunt of the Lady Maeve's anger.

Chapter 2

The figure in the shadows was waiting. Nothing could be seen in the poor light streaming through the narrow window except the glint of the brass bodkin which the figure was pressing into a small, waxen image. The image had been carefully made: only the purest beeswax had been used, culled from candles which stood on the altars of churches or in the silver and gold candle-brackets of the very wealthy. As an object of hate, the waxen image had been fashioned most lovingly. Only six inches high; its creator had used the skill of a carver to fashion the rounded face, the long legs and arms and the jutting firm tits. A piece of dyed orange wool had been pinned to the head, and red crepe had been tied round the middle so it looked as if the image was wearing a voluminous skirt. Sightless eyes, two small buttons, stared back at its maker who looked at it, chuckled and stuck the bodkin once more into the soft white body. The figure plucked out the bodkin then carefully slashed the waxen image's neck.

In her small chamber above a draper's shop in Cock Lane, Agnes Redheard was terrified. She dare not go out. She had not bought food for days and, because of the lack of custom, her small pile of pennies had dwindled. She was hungry, thirsty and so lonely she would have given her body for free just for the solace of someone to talk to or to listen to her chatter. The young girl dressed feverishly because she believed her salvation was at hand. She pulled her bright-red smock down about her voluptuous body, tightened the leather thongs of her wooden pattens and combed her straggling red hair with a steel comb which had seen better days. She looked round the garret.

'Oh, Lord!' she whispered. 'I wish to be free of here.'

The chamber had become a prison ever since that night when, finding herself deserted by a customer, she had slipped along the blackened alleyways hoping her friend, Isabeau, would allow her to sleep on the floor. Agnes Redheard cursed the baker who, instead of taking her home, had roughly used her in the shadowy corner of a street, had paid her only half of what he had promised, then had driven her away with curses, threatening to call the watch.

Agnes had gone along Old Jewry and stopped just as a cowled figure had slipped out of the house where Isabeau lived. She had thought it strange but, in the darkened doorway of the shop, she had glimpsed the face and smiled, then hurriedly climbed the stairs fully intending to tease Isabeau. She was only half-way up when the blood trickling down from her friend's slashed throat had made her slip on the stair. She had screamed and screamed until the entire street was roused. Nevertheless, Agnes had kept her mouth shut. She had seen the face but couldn't believe that someone so holy could perpetrate such an obscene act. So Agnes had bought a quill and a scrap of parchment and sent an urgent message to Westminster. Now her benefactor had replied, telling her to come to the small chapel near Greyfriars. Agnes picked up her tattered cloak and skipped down the stairs. Outside, the dirty-faced urchin she paid a penny to, to watch the door, grinned and waved.

'No strangers here, Mistress!' he called out.

Agnes smiled and the boy wondered what was wrong for the whore's face wasn't painted. He could not understand why she kept hidden in her chamber, paying him money to warn her of any strangers approaching the house. The boy watched her go then hawked and spat. Whatever was wrong, he hoped Agnes Redheard would not discover he had failed to deliver her message at Westminster. Instead, he had dropped the paper into a sewer and spent the penny she gave him on a basket of plums covered in sugar.

Meanwhile, Agnes slipped through the streets, brushing past white-eyed beggars who whined for alms, and a cripple on wooden slats who cried out that he had seen the devil in Smithfield – but no one listened. The booths were open, under the projecting stories of the great houses, and leather-clad apprentices screamed that they had hot mutton, spiced beef and soft bread for sale. Agnes caught the savoury smells from the cookshops and her stomach clenched with hunger. On one occasion she felt so giddy she had to stop and lean against a doorway, watching an old woman at the corner of the alleyway hitch her skirts and squat to pee. The old woman caught Agnes's eyes and she cackled with laughter in a display of reddened gums and yellow, rotted teeth. Agnes looked away hurriedly, clenched her fists and ran on.

She followed the line of the city ditch, full of offal and refuse, the dead bodies of cats and dogs now ripening under a strong, summer sun. She turned right, down Aldersgate Street into St Martin's Lane then through alleyways which would take her to Greyfriars. She stopped at a crossroads where the Bailiff of the Ward had piled high on a stool the goods stolen by a burglar now on his way to the scaffold at Tyburn. Different people claimed the same objects and a violent row ensued, blocking all paths. Agnes stopped; she hadn't the strength to push through. A costermonger came alongside her with a little handcart full of bread, chunks of cheese and cooked eels. Agnes's hand reached out; she needed to eat, she had to chew something. Suddenly a small urchin threw the dead, bloated body of a toad into the cart. The costermonger picked it up and threw it back, screaming abuse, and Agnes seized her chance. She picked up a small, hard loaf of rye bread, a chunk of cheese and, seeing a gap in the crowd, slipped through, down a narrow, fetid alleyway. Turning left, she saw the small church before her. Agnes, her mouth full of bread and cheese, could have cried with pleasure. She was here, she was safe. She went up the crumbling steps and slipped through a darkened doorway. The message pushed under her garret door had been quite simple: she was to go to the church just before the Angelus bell and wait until her benefactor arrived.

She crouched at the foot of a pillar and pushed the rest of the bread and cheese into her mouth, chewing the last morsel slowly, enjoying the juices the food started in both mouth and stomach. She felt stronger but, oh, so tired. Her eyes were closing when she heard the whispered voice.

'Agnes! Agnes!'

The girl stood up, peering into the darkness.

'Where are you?' she called.

No answer. The girl, frightened now, backed against the pillar. She thought if she stayed there, she would be safe.

'Please!' she called. 'What is the matter?'

She edged round the pillar, her face twisted sideways and her neck exposed: so vulnerable. The murderer on the other side of the pillar killed Agnes Redheard with one slash of a cut-throat knife. Agnes, eyes open, staring with terror, slumped to the hard, paved stone floor as the killer crushed the waxen image into a ball and pushed it up a voluminous sleeve. For a few seconds the killer stood over the girl's body.

'Goodbye, Agnes,' the voice whispered. 'You may have seen me but didn't you know I also glimpsed you?'

Corbett and Ranulf left Winchester the morning after Maltote's departure. The King himself came down to the outer bailey, to say goodbye, and stood for a while chatting to Corbett about a number of minor matters. The King, grasping the horse's bridle, drew close and stared up at Corbett.

'You will take care, Hugh. You will end these killings.'

'I shall do my best, your Grace.'

'The business of Puddlicott . . .' the King muttered.

'The man's a rogue, one day he'll hang.'

'It's not so simple.' The King patted the horse's neck. 'If he has the friendship of Master Nogaret, Puddlicott will soon figure largely in our affairs but,' the King smiled thinly, 'we shall see what we shall see.' He released the bridle and stepped back. 'Give my regards to the Lady Maeve and to little Eleanor. Keep me informed! I shall stay at Winchester for a while and then move north to Hereford.'

Corbett nodded, patted his horse and, with Ranulf behind him leading the pack pony, he followed the narrow, cobbled path out of the castle and down into the town. Within the hour, just as the bells of Winchester were ringing for Prime, they cleared the city gates, following the winding country tracks east to the old Roman road. The sky was cloudless and, as the sun climbed, Corbett slowed his horse to an amble, enjoying the warm sweet smell of the countryside. The peasants were out in the fields tending their strips of land and in the meadows cattle and sheep cropped, moving sluggishly through the lush green grass, overgrown with primroses, periwinkles and other wild flowers. Dew still dripped from the hedgerows and Corbett listened to cuckoos, wood pigeons and thrushes singing high in the velvet darkness of the trees. A fox, with a fat young rabbit in its jaws, trotted across the trackway and drew curses from a startled Ranulf.

They paused for a while to break fast on watered wine and white bread Ranulf had begged from the palace kitchens. Corbett's manservant was surly. He hated the countryside. If he had his way, he would ride blindfold until he entered Cripplegate and became lost in the bustle, colour and stench of the London streets. Corbett, however, was happy. He could count his blessings: he was free from the King, returning to London and, if Maltote had done his job properly, Maeve's temper would have lost its biting edge. Nevertheless, he saw Ranulf's unhappiness and, as they mounted and continued their journey, he gave his manservant the reason for their return. Ranulf lost his fear of the open countryside, listening round-eyed until Corbett finished then he whistled softly through gapped teeth.

'Hell's teeth!' he breathed, mimicking the King. 'Someone's slaughtering the whores of London. A murdered priest. And that bastard Frenchman searching like a rat for mischief!' Ranulf shook his head wordlessly.

'And don't forget Puddlicott.'

Ranulf-atte-Newgate made a face. 'Who could forget Puddlicott?' he replied.

'What do you mean, Ranulf?'

'Well,' the manservant shrugged, 'before I entered your service, Master—'

'You mean when you were a night-walker and a thief?'

'I wasn't a thief!'

'Of course not, Ranulf, but let's say, when you found it difficult to distinguish between your property and someone else's.'

Ranulf glared at his master. His past was a topic they rarely discussed, for if it hadn't been for Corbett, Ranulf would have hanged at Newgate and his strangled corpse would have been thrown into the limepits near Charterhouse.

Corbett winked. 'I am sorry, Ranulf, you were saying?'

'Well, amongst the stews of Southwark and in the thieves' kitchens around Whitefriars, Puddlicott was a legend. He could break into any house, rifle any coffer. They claimed he could even shave a man without waking him.'

'Does anyone know what he looked like?'

Ranulf stared at a hawk circling lazily above a field. 'No. Some said he was short and fat, others described him as tall and thin. One man said he had red hair, another said he had black. He can talk fluently in Latin and can convince you that black is white, that you are a rogue and I am an honest man. However, he can't be responsible for the whores' murders!'

'What do you mean?'

'When I was a boy, something similar happened in London. There was a man – my mother knew his name but I forget it now – he hated women, he used to buy the services of whores but the only way his dick could rise would be to beat upon them. Well, things went from bad to worse. Eventually, he could only have his joy by watching them as he choked their breath away.'

'A Bedlam man,' Corbett observed.

'Mad as a March hare. He used to haunt the streets of

Southwark dressed in a red robe. He killed a good score before his own family hunted him down.'

'What happened to him?'

'My mother watched him being boiled alive under the gallows near the Bishop of Ely Inn. She told me he screamed for hours. Such a man is our murderer, not Puddlicott.'

Corbett shivered and looked away. De Craon was one thing, but what about this lunatic? He thought of Maeve and his apprehension deepened. Once the hunt began, would she be safe? And why, Corbett wondered, did this madman now kill respectable ladies? Perhaps even the old chaplain himself?

They continued in silence, stopping at an ale house at noon and, later in the day, using their royal licences, gained clean beds and a square meal at a small monastery outside Andover on the edge of the great forest.

They entered London late the following morning, taking the Red Cross route into Cripplegate and down through the city streets. Ranulf immediately relaxed and beamed at the cooks outside the hot-pie shops offering bread, ale, wine and ribs of beef. On the corner of Catte Street, a group of singers, young boys from a local church, sang a carol. Between each verse a sunburnt traveller talked about the church at Bethlehem and a pillar the Virgin Mary had leaned against. 'Which,' the speaker shouted, 'remains moist since the time she rested there, for, after it is wiped, it always sweats again.'

At the corner of West Cheap, Corbett stopped to listen to a fiery preacher. 'Woe to this city!' the man bawled, his eyes glowing like coals. 'Woe to the whores who have died! They have brought this judgement on themselves!'

The preacher, his eyes alight with madness, glared at Corbett and Ranulf. 'Satan looks after his own!' he cried.

'First, he feeds them with tidbits from his own mouth as if they were his own dear darlings but, afterwards, he turns on them and rends them like a fierce hound, gulping them down his foul, black throat like so many juicy morsels.'

Corbett studied the man's skeletal face. Was a madman such as this, he wondered, responsible for the murder of whores, like those whose red wigs he could glimpse in the crowds ahead of him?

'Shall we arrest him, Master?' Ranulf joked.

The clerk stared at the fanatic. The fellow was as lean and lithe as a cat and as he screeched, his eyes bounced from his head like the very devil. His cheeks and jaw were as bare of flesh as any recluse who lived on bread and ditch water. Suddenly the preacher stopped his litany of denunciation, jumped down and did a strange, fantastical dance.

Corbett looked at Ranulf and shook his head. 'I doubt if that fellow could walk straight,' he commented. 'Never mind struggle with some sturdy wench and wield a sharp cutting knife.'

They passed on down an alleyway, dismounting to lead their horses around a group of ragged-arsed children who were dancing round the corpse of a yellow mongrel which had been crushed by a cart, the blue innards bursting from its sagging belly. On the corner the beadles had caught a man who had drained water illegally from the Great Conduit. They were now forcing him to carry a leaking bucket of water on his head which they gleefully refilled.

Corbett grinned at Ranulf. 'It's good to be back in London,' he commented sourly.

Ranulf nodded his head vigorously, staring round at the mass of colour: hoods, mantles and tunics of every hue. The murrey and mustard of the city officials, the golden silk of high-born ladies, the merchants' woollen cloaks thrown back to display heavy purses and broad, jewelled belts. A group of Templars rode by, the great cross on the shoulders of their cloaks, their pennants and banners snapping in the breeze. Corbett and Ranulf continued across Cheapside, forcing their way through a throng of young noblemen who were admiring a pack of slender, lean-ribbed hunting dogs for sale.

At last they entered Bread Street. They left their horses at the Red Kirtle tavern and crossed the street, stepping carefully over the slopping sewer, towards Corbett's town-house. Ranulf, carrying the heavy saddle-bags, wished his master would walk on, but Corbett stopped to admire the freshly painted front door, which now shimmered under the gloss, noting how the craftsman had also placed heavy steel bolts in serried rows to reinforce it. For the rest, Corbett grinned, Maeve had hired painters to refurbish the three-storied building and, being contrary as Maeve could be, instead of the plaster being painted white and the beams black, Maeve had ordered the plaster to be painted black and the beams white whilst above the door was a vigorous depiction of the Llewellyn coat-of-arms next to the Red Dragon Rampant of Wales.

They slipped down the alleyway at the side of the house and in through the back door. Two old servants greeted them. The Welshman Griffin and his wife Anna. The latter had served Maeve in Wales and faithfully followed her mistress into the 'Land of the foreigners', as she termed it, when Maeve moved to London after her marriage to Corbett. Both Griffin and his wife viewed England as alien as Outremer, and the inhabitants of London as demons in human flesh. Corbett, however, they accepted and now greeted him ecstatically, both gabbling away in Welsh. Corbett just smiled and kissed each of them on the cheeks, indicating by signs that he did not wish them to announce his arrival to Maeve. He turned to speak to Ranulf but his manservant had dropped the saddle-bags on the floor and promptly had disappeared. Ranulf was rather frightened of Maeve, considerably in awe of a woman who was not only beautiful but had the wit to match his own and a tongue which could cut like a razor. Griffin looked askance at Corbett and pointed to the bags.

'Yes, yes,' the clerk commented. 'I would be grateful if you would move them in. Ranulf will be back. He's probably gone to see his baby son.'

The old man shook his head and screwed up his eyes as if he could not understand what Corbett was talking about, though the clerk suspected different. He was sure Griffin understood every word he said but the old man insisted on his Welshness and quietly enjoyed the confusion it caused. Suddenly, Anna, Maeve's old nurse, grasped him by the hand, her face became serious and she kept repeating words, of which the only one Corbett could understand was 'Llewellyn'. The clerk just shook his head, clasped each of his servants affectionately by the hand, and crept quietly upstairs towards the solar.

At the top he stood peering through the half-open door. Across the room sat Maeve in a russet dress, fastened closely at the neck, with a blue belt round her waist and a white veil secured by brooches to her blonde hair. She was sitting on a stool next to the fire. Corbett quietly groaned, for his wife was stabbing furiously at a piece of embroidery – a sure sign that the Lady Maeve was not in the best of moods. She detested sewing, hated embroidery but liked to take her temper out on the nearest piece of cloth to hand. Nevertheless, she was singing softly to herself, some strange Welsh lullaby, whilst rocking the small cradle beside her with the tip of her slippered foot.

Corbett, fully aware of the furies to come, stood and

admired the peaceful domestic scene. He gazed round the room, admiring how Maeve had turned the solar into a luxurious, even opulent chamber. Carpenters had placed wooden panelling around the room which stretched half-way up the high walls whilst the brickwork above it had been covered in a thick white paint. Some of this was hidden by brilliant-hued tapestries or carefully painted shields depicting the armorial bearings of both Corbett's and Maeve's families. Red woollen rugs not rushes covered the floor and at the end of the solar, the windows had been filled by glass, some of it tinted in brilliant, contrasting hues. Stonemasons had refurbished the old hearth with an intricately sculpted fire mantel resting on two huge pillars with dragons, scorpions and wyverns carved there. Corbett leaned against the doorway and smelt the sweet warmth from the herb packets Maeve must have thrown on the small log fire. His wife suddenly raised her head as if she knew she was being watched.

'What is this, woman?' Corbett shouted, pushing open the door. 'To come home and find my wife sitting amongst the ashes!'

Maeve gave a cry, dropped the embroidery and fairly ran across the room, the white veil round her head floating out like a banner.

'Hugh! Hugh!' She threw her arms round Corbett's neck and pressed closely against him, clasping his face between her hands and kissing him passionately on the lips.

'You should have announced yourself,' she cried, stepping backwards. 'A gentleman recently knighted should observe such courtesies!'

'So, you have heard the news?'

'Of course, Maltote told me.'

Corbett swallowed hard. 'And the other news?'

Maeve made a wry smile. Corbett clasped her hands

and pulled her back to him. He was surprised she did not seem angry; the smooth, unblemished skin of her face was not drawn tight nor was there any furrow on her brow or round her lips – sure signs that his wife had lost her fiery temper. The lips he had just tasted were soft and warm and her eyes held a teasing look.

'You are not angry, Maeve?'

'Why should I be? My husband has returned.'

'About the news?'

'Sir,' Maeve answered in mock surprise. 'You have been knighted.'

'Madame,' Corbett rasped. 'We are not going to Wales. You will not see your uncle!'

Maeve slipped her arms round his waist.

'True, true,' she mocked. 'We will not be going to Wales.' Her face became serious. 'But I will see my uncle.'

'What do you mean?'

'He is coming here. I have already despatched Maltote with the invitation.'

Corbett steeled his face, though he would have dearly loved to have screamed. He hadn't thought of that: the Lord Morgan ap Llewellyn sweeping into his house like some wild wind from the mountains of Wales. Oh, Lord, Corbett thought, he'll be here, he'll drink and eat as if there's no tomorrow. His retainers will get drunk in the London taverns, be arrested by the watch and get thrown into gaol when they try to break their necks. There will be nights of song and roistering as the Lord Morgan sings some savage song before breaking into tears at the vanished glories of Wales. In the morning, however, the Lord Morgan will rise as fresh as a daisy to argue about Edward's policies in Wales. He will challenge Ranulf to gamble and the house will ring with their curses as they do their best to cheat each other. Corbett slumped down on a stool.

'The Lord Morgan is coming here?' he said weakly.

Maeve crouched beside him and grasped his fingers.

'Oh, Hugh, don't object. He may be wild but he's growing old!'

'Your uncle,' Corbett grated, 'will never grow old!'

'Hugh, he loves me and, beneath his temper, he deeply admires you.'

Oh, divine sweetness, Corbett thought. He was about to object when he glimpsed the tears brimming in his wife's eyes – one of her favourite tricks: either accept now, she was saying, or I'll wander round this house like some martyr about to be burnt.

'How long is he staying?'

'Two months.'

In other words, six, Corbett thought. He sighed. 'Let the Lord Morgan come.'

Maeve kissed him again. 'We'll all be together,' she whispered, her eyes alight with pleasure.

Yes, Corbett thought wearily, we'll all be together.

Maeve clapped her hands. 'He can have the chamber at the back of the house and his servants can use the hall below or perhaps stay in a tavern.'

Corbett rose and caught the tendrils of his wife's hair and grinned. 'I'll be busy,' he observed, then he suddenly grasped Maeve by the shoulders.

'The King told me you had visitors, Maeve. The Frenchman, de Craon and his companion, de Nevers.'

Maeve made a face. 'De Craon was charming. Oh, I know Hugh, he is a fox but he brought me a scarf, pure silk from the looms of Lyons and a silver spoon for Eleanor.'

'Get rid of them!' Corbett rasped.

'Hugh!'

'De Craon is a cruel bastard who wishes me nothing but ill.'

'Hugh, he was courteous.'

'And how was his companion?'

'De Nevers?' Maeve made a face. 'He was handsome, quieter than de Craon, diplomatic and affable. I liked him.'

Corbett glared at his wife, then realised how ridiculous he must look. 'I am sorry,' he muttered. 'But de Craon always makes me uneasy.'

Maeve grasped him by the hand. 'Then forget him like I have. Come and see your daughter.'

Corbett followed her and stared down at his baby daughter. At three months, Eleanor already looked like Maeve: beautiful soft skin, clear regular features. He touched one of her tiny fingers. 'So small!' he whispered. The baby's hand felt warm, soft as a satin cushion. He squeezed gently and, under her small quilted blanket, Eleanor moved and smiled in her sleep.

'She is well?'

'Of course.'

Corbett placed his hand gently against the baby's forehead and Maeve watched him guardedly. Her husband, usually so calm, even cold, harboured the most terrible fears of what might happen to the child. Maeve looked away. Much as she could try, her husband's mind was still plagued by ghosts. The most frightening, surprisingly enough for a man so detached, was of losing those close to him, of being left alone. She seized him by the hand.

'Let's go,' she whispered. 'Our chamber is ready. There is wine, bread and fruit, next to the bed.' Maeve grinned. 'A bed covered in red silk,' she whispered. 'And in the centre, two embroidered turtle doves.' Her face became serious. 'You may want to rest? Drink something sweet? You must be tired after your long journey.'

Corbett grinned back. 'Call Anna,' he murmured, pulling Maeve close to him. 'Let her sit with Eleanor and I shall show you, Madam, how tired I am!'

Chapter 3

The next morning Corbett rose early. He doused the light in its sconce holder and opened the small latticed window which looked out over the gardens and small orchard at the back of the house. The day was about to break, the sky already scored with gashes of bright light. He could hear the bells of St Lawrence Jewry clanging as dawn broke, the usual sign for the city gates to be opened and a fresh day's business to begin. He returned to his bed and kissed his still sleeping wife on the side of her face then stood over Eleanor's cradle for a while and watched his little daughter gaze solemnly back. Corbett was fascinated. The child was so placid, so even-tempered. Before he had risen he had heard her gurgling to herself, smacking her little lips and chatting to the wooden doll Maeve had placed on the small bolster beside her. Corbett reluctantly turned away and dressed hurriedly in the clothes Maeve had laid out over the chest the night before; leggings of dark blue, a soft white shirt, with a sleeveless cote-hardie with a cord to fasten round the waist. Corbett threw the latter aside. He knew the horrors which might confront him so he took his sword-belt off the peg on the wall and buckled it round his middle. He picked up his boots and cloak, tiptoeing gently out of the room just as Eleanor suddenly realised she was hungry and began to bellow as if she wanted to show her father some new aspect of her character.

'Her mother's daughter,' Corbett whispered to himself as he crept up the stairs and pushed open the door to Ranulf's chamber. As usual, the room looked as if a violent struggle had taken place. Corbett could only tell his servant was there by a series of loud snores. Corbett enjoyed shaking him awake, then went down to the buttery to wait. Scullions had not yet started the fire so he poured himself a jug of watered ale. Ranulf appeared, bleary-eyed and unshaven. Corbett let him quench his thirst before pushing the still half-sleeping manservant out of the house and across the street to the tavern. There was the usual commotion of mocking argument until a burly ostler brought out and saddled their horses. Ranulf splashed water over his face from the huge butt and gave the fellow the rough edge of his tongue, bluntly informing him that some people had to work and not just loll around in warm straw. This provoked a stream of abuse from the ostler which Ranulf thoroughly enjoyed. He was still throwing catcalls over his shoulder when they rode out into the Mercery and down towards the Guildhall.

The day would be a fine one and apprentices and traders were already pulling out their booths in front of the houses, fixing up poles, putting up the awnings and laying out their goods. The air was thick with the wood smoke of the artisans in their little huts behind Cheapside. Carts bringing their produce into the city crashed along the cobblestones, the drovers cracking the air with their whips and cursing their horses. Apprentices, wearing canvas and leather jerkins, kept a wary eye on the beggars moving about in the shadows between the houses. These were the upright men: not the real poor but the cranks and counterfeiters looking for easy pickings before the day's business began. Four of the city watch marched by, leading a line of night-walkers, drunkards, thieves, blowsy whores and roaring boys, towards the great water tank, or Conduit, where most of them would stand in a cage all day to be abused by the good citizens whose sleep they had disturbed.

Corbett looked up as the bells in the steeple of St Mary Le Bow began to chime and he saw the great night-light, the beacon which guided Londoners during the hours of darkness, being doused. Now other bells began to toll, calling the faithful to early-morning mass. Ranulf stared round and drank in these sights, then, glowering at Corbett, began to complain loudly about the lack of food and how he was starving. They stopped at a cook shop, the reins of their horses looped through their arms as they gulped small bowls of hot spiced beef. Ranulf chattered about his son, the illicit fruit of one of his many amours. Corbett listened attentively. Ranulf wished to bring the boy for a short stay at the house in Bread Street. Corbett smiled bravely but his heart sank with despair. Lord Morgan, Ranulf and Ranulf's young son would utterly destroy the peace and quiet of his household.

Corbett finished chewing the meat and washed his hands in a small bowl of rose water brought out by a thin-faced urchin. The lad looked half-starved, his eyes almost as big as his face. Corbett pressed a coin into the boy's hand. 'Buy some food yourself, lad.'

He dried his hands on a napkin and waited to make sure the boy did as he was told. Then, leading the horses, they walked down Cheapside. Corbett, half-listening to Ranulf's glowing description of his son, recalled the events of the night before: after their wild, passionate love-making, Corbett and Maeve had gone down for a meal in the kitchen before going back to bed. He recalled Maeve's teasing and his idle chatter about affairs at court. His wife, however, became anxious as Corbett described the reasons for his return to London.

'I have heard of these murders!' Maeve commented, sitting up and drawing the sheets round her body. 'At first no one noticed. In a city like this, girls are killed or disappear and no one cares but,' she shook her head, 'the deaths of these women, the manner of their dying – is it true?' she asked.

Corbett, lying flat on his back, suddenly stirred.

'Is what true?'

'They say the murderer—' Maeve shivered and brought her knees up under her chin. 'They say the killer mutilates the bodies of the girls.'

Corbett looked up in surprise. 'Who told you that?'

'It's common gossip. Most women are frightened to go out at night but that last death was during the day.' Maeve went on to tell him of the recent killing and the mutilated corpse of a whore being found in the porch of a church in Greyfriars.

Corbett gently stroked her bare arm. 'But why the fear? The women he has killed have all been whores and courtesans?'

'So what?' Maeve tossed her head. 'They are still women and Lady Somerville was certainly not an whore!'

Corbett had fallen silent. Somehow he believed that Lady Somerville's death was different from the rest. Had the old lady discovered something? Had she surprised the killer?

Corbett looked round as Cheapside began to fill. Already he could glimpse the whores in their bright clothes and garish wigs. Suddenly the day didn't seem so bright and as he recalled Maeve's words about mutilation he felt uneasy. His usual adversaries, be they de Craon or some calculating murderer, had reason and motive for their actions. But what now? Was he hunting – as Ranulf had described the previous day – some mad man, some lunatic with a twisted hatred of women who found it easier to prey upon poor street-walkers but who might change and strike at any woman, lonely and vulnerable enough. Corbett wished he could turn and go back home. He felt he was about to enter a very darkened house with shadowy labyrinthine passages and, somewhere, a killer lurked waiting for him to come. Oh, God, he prayed, bring me out of this safely; from the snare of the hunter, Lord, deliver me.

At the Guildhall, Corbett's sombre mood was not helped by a beadle standing on the steps auctioning the goods of a hanged felon: a battered table, two broken chairs, one ripped mattress, two thimbles, a set of hose, a shirt, a doublet and a battered pewter cup inlaid with silver. The man had apparently robbed a church but his accomplice had escaped so a rather shabby cleric, holding a candle in one hand and a bell in another, was loudly proclaiming his excommunication in a litany of curses.

'May he be cursed wherever he be found. At home or in the field, on a highway or a path, in the forest or on water. May he be cursed in living and in dying, in eating and drinking, whilst hungry and thirsty, sleeping, walking, standing, sitting, working, resting, urinating, defecating and bleeding. May he be cursed in the hair of his head, in his temples, brow, mouth, breast, heart, genitals, feet and toe-nails!' On and on the dreadful, sonorous declamation continued.

'I think,' Ranulf whispered to Corbett, 'that the poor bastard should get the message now!'

Corbett grinned and threw the reins of his horse at

Ranulf. 'Stable him in a tavern,' he ordered. 'I'll meet you inside.'

A beggar, his face hooded and masked, crouched in the doorway of the Guildhall whining for alms whilst, on the other side, a huckster sold pretty ribbons. Corbett stopped and indicated both to move out of his way.

'I know who you are,' he said softly. 'You're upright men, counterfeiters, and whilst I am busy with the beggar, the other will try and pick my purse.'

The two men fairly scuttled away and Corbett walked down the passageway, across a courtyard and into a small mansion. The Guildhall proper was merely a walled enclosure containing a number of buildings around a large, three-storied house. Corbett waited inside the doorway until Ranulf joined him. They went up a rickety wooden staircase into a spacious, white-washed chamber where clerks sat at a table scratching away at great rolls of vellum and parchment. Not one of them looked up as Corbett and Ranulf entered but a large fat man, seated at the head of the room, got up and waddled over. Corbett recognised the podgy, red face above the ill-fitting gown and food-stained jerkin.

'Master Nettler.' Corbett extended a hand which Nettler, Sheriff of the Wards in the north of the city, clasped, his watery blue eyes alight with pleasure.

'We expected you, Hugh. The King's letters arrived last night.' Nettler glanced at the scriveners and lowered his voice. 'No man can be trusted,' he muttered. 'The killer could be anyone in this room. I am not dealing with it. One of the under-sheriffs will advise you. Come! Come!'

He led them out along the passageway to a small, dusty chamber. A clerk sat at a high desk in the corner, copying letters. Beside him stood a tall, broad-shouldered, prepossessing man whom Nettler introduced as Alexander

Cade, Under-Sheriff of the city. Once the introductions were finished, Nettler brusquely left; the Under-Sheriff completed the letter whilst Corbett studied him. He had heard of Cade, an excellent thief-catcher with an astute eye who could spot a villain across a crowded tavern. The rogues of London's underworld rightly feared him yet, despite his size, Cade looked like a court fop in his gaudily trimmed gown, high leather riding boots, cambric shirt, and small skull cap which he wore on the back of his thick black hair. His forked beard was neatly trimmed which, together with his sallow features and lazy, good-natured eyes, gave Cade the appearance of a man who enjoyed the good things of life rather than the ruthless pursuit of villains and rogues. He waved Corbett and Ranulf to a window seat whilst he finished the letter. Once done he turned with a flourish.

'You're here about the murdered whores?' Cade made a face. 'Or should I be honest? Your presence here is not about them but about Lady Somerville's death as well as that of Father Benedict.'

Cade whispered something to his clerk, who got down from his seat, went over to one of the shelves and brought back a sheaf of documents.

'Thank you,' Cade muttered. 'You may go.'

He waited until the old man closed the door behind him then picked up a stool and sat opposite Corbett.

'There are three matters which concern me,' he announced. 'The deaths of the whores, the deaths of Lady Somerville and Father Benedict, and Puddlicott's arrival in London.'

Corbett's jaw dropped in surprise.

'Oh, yes,' Cade said. 'Our friend, that master of disguise, Richard Puddlicott of a dozen names and countless appearances, is back in the city.' Cade's eyes opened wide. 'This time I want to catch him! I want to see that clever bastard in chains.'

'How do you know he is here?'

'Just read these.' Cade handed the sheaf of documents over. 'Read them,' he repeated. 'Take your time, Master Corbett. Or should I call you Sir Hugh?' Cade smiled. 'We have heard the news. Accept our congratulations. The Lady Maeve must be pleased.'

'Yes. Yes,' Corbett murmured. 'She is.'

Cade went over, filled two goblets of wine and handed them to Corbett and Ranulf. 'I will leave you alone. When you have read them, then we will talk.'

Cade sauntered off, Ranulf turned to stare out of the window at a file of prisoners being led out into the yard below whilst Corbett studied the documents. The first two were letters informing the sheriffs of London how angry the King was that so many bloody murders had been committed in the city; in particular, the grisly death of Lady Somerville and the mysterious circumstances surrounding the fire which had killed Father Benedict. The next document was a memorandum drawn up, apparently by Cade himself, listing the number of women killed and, beside each of them, the date of their deaths. Corbett whistled under his breath. There were sixteen in all, excluding Lady Somerville. All the deaths had occurred within the city limits: as far west as Grays Inn; on the east Portsoken; Whitecross Street in the north; and as far south as the Ropery which bordered the Thames. Corbett also noticed how the murders had begun about eighteen months ago and were regularly spaced once a month, on or around the thirteenth day. The only exceptions were Lady Somerville who had been killed on the eleventh of May and the last victim, the whore found in a church near Greyfriars, murdered only two days previously. The whore was killed usually in her own chambers, although three, including the last, had been murdered elsewhere. All had died in the same gruesome manner: the neck slashed from ear to ear and the woman's genitals mutilated and gouged with a knife. Again, the only exception was Lady Somerville who had been killed in Smithfield by a swift slash across the throat. Cade had also written that there was no other mark of violence and each whore's dress was always neatly rearranged. Corbett stared at the memorandum then looked up.

'A death every month,' he murmured. 'On or around the thirteenth.'

'What's that, Master?'

'The whores: they were all killed around the same date, their throats slashed, their genitals mutilated.'

Ranulf made a rude sound with his lips. 'What do you think, Master?'

'Firstly, it could be some madman who just likes to kill women – whores especially. Secondly, it could be someone searching for a particular whore or—'

'Or, what?'

'Some practitioner of the black arts – magicians always like blood.'

Ranulf shivered and looked away. From his window he could see the towering mass of St Mary Le Bow, where Corbett had struggled and fought against a coven of witches led by the beautiful murderess Alice Atte-Bowe.

'I don't know,' Corbett murmured and went on to read the memorandum on the death of Father Benedict: a short, caustic report from the coroner's clerk. According to this, on the night of the twelfth of May, the monks at Westminster had been woken by the roar of flames and had rushed out to see Father Benedict's house, which stood in a lonely part of the abbey grounds, engulfed in flames. The brothers, organised by William Senche, steward of the nearby Palace of Westminster, had tried to douse the flames with water from a nearby well but their efforts had been fruitless. The building was gutted except for the walls, and inside they found the half-burned corpse of Father Benedict slumped near the door, key in hand and, beside him, the remains of his pet cat.

There was no apparent cause of the fire. The shuttered window high in the wall had been open and a light breeze may have fanned the blaze caused by some spark from the fire or candle flame.

Corbett looked up. 'Strange!' he exclaimed.

Ranulf, half-watching the line of felons being manacled in the courtyard below, jumped.

'What is, Master?'

'Father Benedict's death. The priest was an old man, Ranulf, and therefore a light sleeper. He gets up in the middle of the night, disturbed by a fire which has mysteriously started. He's too old to climb out of the window so he grabs the key, reaches the door but never opens it. What is stranger still, is that his cat dies with him. Now, a dog might stay with his master but a cat would leave, jump out, especially as the window was open, yet the cat also dies.'

'It could have been overcome by smoke,' Ranulf suggested.

'No.' Corbett shook his head. 'I can't understand how a man could reach the door, have the key in his hand, yet not struggle for a few seconds more to insert the key and turn it. Yet, it's the cat which really puzzles me more. The few I have known remind me of you, Ranulf. They have a keen sense of their own survival and a particular horror of fire.'

Ranulf looked away and pulled a face. Corbett went

back and studied Cade's scribbles on the bottom of the memorandum. According to the under-sheriff, earlier on the day he died Father Benedict had sent a short letter to the sheriff saying that he knew something terrible and blasphemous was about to happen but that no further details were available. Corbett shook his head and looked at the last, greasy, tiny scrap of parchment. A short report from a government informer about rumours of the master counterfeiter, Richard Puddlicott, being seen in Bride Lane near the Bishop of Salisbury's inn. Corbett tapped the parchment against his knee and stared at the dirty rushes on the floor. So many mysteries, he wondered, but Puddlicott really intrigued him. The King's messengers had been pursuing the villain all over Europe, so what was he doing in England? Was his presence linked to these deaths? Or was he in London for some other nefarious purpose? Either for his own or for Amaury de Craon's? Corbett sat lost in his own thoughts, sipping his wine until Cade returned.

'Did you find the papers interesting, Corbett?'

'Yes, I did. You have no clues to the murderer of the whores?'

'None whatsoever.'

'And Lady Somerville?'

'She was returning with a companion from a meeting of the Sisters of St Martha at Westminster. They went along Holborn and stopped for a while at St Bartholomew's Hospital. Lady Somerville then announced she would slip across Smithfield to her house near the Barbican. Her companion objected but Lady Somerville just laughed. She said she was old and, being involved in her good works, was well known to all the rogues of the underworld who, therefore, would not accost her.' Cade shrugged. 'Lady Somerville had one son who had been out roistering with friends. He returned in the early hours, discovered his mother had failed to return and organised a search. His servants found her body near the gallows in Smithfield, her throat cut from ear to ear.'

'But no other mutilations on the corpse?'

'None whatsoever.'

'Before her death was Lady Somerville distressed or anxious?'

'No, not really.'

'Exactly, Master Cade.'

The under-sheriff hid his irritation. 'Well, one of her companions claimed she was withdrawn and kept muttering a certain proverb.'

'Which is?'

'*Cacullus non facit monachum*; the cowl doesn't make the monk.'

'What did she mean by that?'

'I don't know. Perhaps it was a reference to another of her charitable duties.'

'Which was?'

'She often laundered the robes of the monks at Westminster. You see their abbot, Walter Wenlock, is ill. The prior is dead so Lady Somerville often supervised the abbey laundry.'

Corbett handed back the sheaf of parchments.

'And Father Benedict's death?'

'You know what we did.'

'Strange, he didn't unlock the door?'

'Perhaps he was overcome by the smoke, or his robe caught fire?'

'And the cat?'

Cade leaned against the wall and tapped his foot on the floor. 'Master Corbett, we have corpses all over London and you ask me about a cat?'

Corbett smiled. 'I just can't see why the cat couldn't escape through the open window?'

Cade raised his eyebrows then narrowed his eyes.

'Of course,' he murmured. 'I hadn't thought of that.'

'I would like to see the house or what remains of it. And the message Father Benedict sent to you?'

'We don't know what it meant, it could be anything. You know the scandals which can plague the lives of priests and monks. Perhaps it was something like that or it could be connected with Westminster.'

'In what way?'

'Well, the abbey and palace are deserted. All building work has come to a sudden halt because the King cannot pay his masons. The Exchequer and Treasurer now travel with the King, so the court has not been there for years. Wenlock the Abbot is ill and the community rather lax. Indeed, the only importance about Westminster is that the King has moved a great deal of his treasury to the crypt beneath the Chapter House.'

Corbett looked up startled. 'Why?'

'Because of the building work at the Tower. Most of the rooms there are now unsafe. The crypt at Westminster Abbey, however, is probably the safest place in London.'

'You are sure the treasury is safe?'

'Yes, on the very day Father Benedict died I went down to see him but he was absent so I checked on the treasury. The seals of the door were unbroken so I knew it was safe. You see, there is only one entrance to the crypt, the sealed door. Moreover, even if someone got in, the narrow flight of stairs down to the crypt have been deliberately smashed and the rest of the building protected by the thickest walls I've ever seen.'

'And Master Puddlicott?'

'All I can say,' Cade replied, 'is that the bastard has

been sighted in London, albeit the sighting is second-hand.'

'He must be here for mischief!'

Cade laughed drily. 'Of course, but what?'

Corbett nudged the now dozing Ranulf awake.

'Look, Master Cade, you know the French envoy, de Craon, and his companion, de Nevers, are in London? They are ostensibly here bearing friendly messages from their master to our King, but there's no real reason for their presence.'

'Are you saying they could be connected with Puddlicott?'

'It's possible. Puddlicott has been seen in the company of Master William Nogaret, Philip IV's Keeper of Secrets.'

Cade went across and filled a goblet of wine for himself, to which he added a generous drop of water.

'Oh, yes,' he replied. 'We know de Craon is in London. He attended a civic reception and presented his letters of accreditation to the Mayor. Since then, we have kept a quiet watch on his house in Gracechurch Street but we are now bored with him. He has done nothing untoward, apparently, being more interested in our shipping along the Thames than anything else. And, as there's no war with France, there's no crime in him doing that.'

Corbett rose and stretched. 'So,' he sighed. 'Where shall we begin?'

The under-sheriff spread his large hands. 'As my master said, I am at your service.'

'Then let's follow Master Cicero, *Et respice corpus*?'

'I beg your pardon, Master Corbett!'

'Let's look at the corpse.' Corbett picked up his own cloak. 'May I borrow the list of names of the women killed?'

Cade handed it over.

'This last victim, is she already buried?'

'No, she lies in the charnel house of St Lawrence Jewry.' Cade drained his cup and strapped on his sword-belt. 'If you wish to look at her, you must hurry. The good priest intends to bury her next to the others later this morning.'

'What's that?' Ranulf stuttered. 'You said, "next to the others"?'

'Well,' Cade replied. 'The dead whores are always brought in a cart from a small outbuilding in the Guildhall. We pay the priests of St Lawrence Jewry to bury them – a shilling a time, if I remember correctly.'

'And everyone,' Ranulf remarked, 'except Lady Somerville, has been buried there?'

'Yes. And for a shilling, they don't get much: a tattered canvas sheet, a shallow hole in the ground and remembrance at the morning Mass.

'Doesn't anyone ever claim the body?'

'Of course not. Some of these poor girls are from Scotland, Ireland, Flanders, towns and villages as far west as Cornwall and as far north as Berwick-on-Tweed.'

'And no one attends their funerals?'

'No. We thought of that and kept a careful watch.' Cade gave a shiver. 'They are buried like dogs,' he murmured. 'Not even their regular customers come to bid a fond farewell.'

Corbett finished his wine and handed the cup back to Cade.

'I'll ignore your blushes, Master Cade, when I say the King has high regard for you.'

The under-sheriff looked embarrassed and shuffled his great, booted feet.

'However,' Corbett neatly closed the trap. 'Isn't it strange that you have failed to draw up a list of customers of these whores? Who frequented them? After all, your informants can tell you about the emergence of a rogue like Puddlicott but not about the customers of dead whores.'

Cade's smile faded. 'Look,' the under-sheriff sat down on a stool and ticked his points off on stubby fingers. 'First, some of these whores were high-class courtesans. Oh, yes, they are poor in death but, when alive, they were favoured by some of the rich and powerful men of the city—'

'Wait,' Corbett interrupted. 'Some of these young ladies earned silver and gold. What happened to it?'

Cade pulled his mouth down. 'Most of them immediately spend what they earn. Once they die their property is plundered by people who should know better. Finally, they have no heirs or relatives so any remaining property is immediately confiscated by the Crown.'

Corbett nodded. 'Go on.'

'Well, as I was saying, the lords of the soil, the prosperous merchants, would not take too kindly to having their names linked with, what they now term, common street-walkers. Secondly,' Cade drew in his breath, his eyes turned away and Corbett sensed the under-sheriff was not telling the full truth. 'Secondly,' Cade repeated, 'it's the manner of their deaths which makes me guarded: most of them were killed in their own chambers, so they must know their killer or they wouldn't open the door. Master Corbett, I am an under-sheriff, my fees are paid by the wealthy burgesses, I do not want to be the official who finds that one of my pay-masters visited a whore on the night she died.' Now Cade *did* blush with embarrassment and he rubbed the side of his face with his hand. 'Yes, yes, I admit,' he continued, 'I am frightened. I'll catch any rogue – be he priest, merchant or lord – but, Master Clerk, this is different. I can discover that the Lord Mayor himself visited a whore but what does that prove?'

'You could search for a pattern, a name, common to all the killings.'

Cade jabbed a hand at Corbett. 'No, Master Clerk, you are the King's confidant, you were recently knighted by him. *You* find out! *You* point the finger! For God's sake, man, that's why you were sent here and I say that without intending any offence!'

Corbett chewed the inside of his lip, he stretched over and touched Cade gently on the hand.

'I understand,' he muttered.

In fact, Corbett did, and appreciated why an under-sheriff had been appointed to deal with something none of his superiors would touch with a bargepole. Corbett smiled to himself; he also understood why the King had sent him back to London.

He stared at the list Cade had given him. 'You are most observant, Master Cade,' he remarked. 'These whores must have known their killer; shown a great deal of trust. Even this last one, Agnes, whose corpse we are about to inspect. She was killed in a church,' Corbett continued, 'I suspect she was invited there by her killer.'

'Possibly,' Cade replied. 'But let's put the deaths of these poor girls to one side. How do you explain Lady Somerville's murder?'

'I don't know,' Corbett muttered. 'Perhaps the old woman knew something. But I tell you this, Cade, your anxieties are well founded. When we arrest this killer – and don't worry we will – I wager it will be some high-born bastard with a great deal to hide.'

'Sweet Lord!' Cade whispered.

Corbett stared at the far wall. 'What puzzles me,' he continued, 'is why the killings have increased. According to your list, Master Cade, a whore dies on or around the thirteenth of each month but in May the pattern changes: Somerville is killed on Monday the eleventh of May; the priest the following evening; a prostitute, Isabeau, on Wednesday the thirteenth of May and then, soon afterwards, the girl in Greyfriars. What crisis has forced the murderer to change his pattern?'

'Unless . . .' Cade interrupted.

'Unless what?'

'Unless there is more than one murderer.'

Chapter 4

Corbett and Ranulf waited for Cade to collect his belongings. They left the Guildhall and went down to Catte Street, the area round Old Jewry and the dark, looming mass of St Lawrence's Church. A crowd had gathered near the stocks placed outside the wicket gate of the cemetery. Most of the onlookers were city riff-raff who were baiting a man locked in the stocks for selling faulty bow-strings, whilst his shoddy merchandise was piled in a heap and burnt under his nose. The poor unfortunate, his head trapped in the wooden slats, was forced to breath in the acrid smoke which irritated his mouth, nose and eyes. Now and again he would yell abuse at his tormentors before falling into a fit of coughing which jarred his head against the slats.

Corbett and his companions pushed through the crowd into the derelict cemetery. Cade went across to the priest's house, he knocked at the door and talked to someone inside. A few minutes later a small, portly figure emerged, a huge bunch of keys in his hand. Corbett threw a warning glance at Ranulf to behave himself for the priest's broad girth, rosy face and womanish waddle indicated he was a man of the cloth more interested in the fruits of the earth than the salvation of souls. He wore a cloak of

Lincoln green, edged with bright squirrel fur, whilst cheap jewellery glinted on wrists and fingers. His beady little eyes glared at Corbett. There were no introductions. Instead the priest opened a small leather bag he was carrying and drew out three sponges soaked in vinegar and herbs.

'You'll need these,' he rasped, handing one to each of them. 'Now, follow me.'

He led them round to the back of the church to a long windowless shed. He opened the padlock on the door and waved them in.

'Feast your eyes!' he jibed. 'I bury the poor bitch in an hour. You'll find a candle on the ledge to the right of the door.'

Corbett went first into the darkness and immediately caught the stench of putrefaction. He was glad he had the sponge and that his stomach was strong. Ranulf, however, went a dull grey colour so, after he had used a tinder to light the candle, Corbett told him to wait outside.

'Ignore the rats!' the priest called out. 'The coffin is on trestles in the centre.'

Corbett held the candle high and, despite the discomfort, felt a tinge of compassion for the lonely, oblong box. Cade, muttering curses, lifted the loose lid and revealed the ghastly sight of the woman lying there. Apparently, she was to be buried as she had been found, no attempt being made to dress the body. Her face, white as chalk, looked even more garish in the flickering candle flame, her skin was already turning puffy, her body bloated with corruption. Corbett examined the long purple gash which had severed the windpipe. Cade, one hand cramming nose and mouth, lifted the poor girl's dress. Corbett took one look at the mutilation, turned away and vomited the wine he had just drunk. He staggered to the door, a white-faced Cade following him into the sunlight. Corbett threw both sponge and candle at the feet of the priest.

'God have mercy on her!' he muttered between bouts of retching. 'She was someone's daughter, someone's sister.' He suddenly thought of his young daughter, Eleanor. Once, the mass of mutilated flesh he had just glimpsed, must have been a young child cooing in a cradle.

'God help her,' Corbett repeated.

He sat in a half-crouch and cleaned his mouth with the back of his hand. Ranulf brought an ewer of water from the priest's house and, without a by your leave, he held it up for Corbett to wash his hands and face. The clerk then stood, glared at the priest and undid the neck of his purse.

Two silver coins went spinning in the priest's direction. 'Here, Father!' Corbett muttered. 'I want a Mass sung for her. For pity's sake, before you bury her, douse the coffin in a mixture of vinegar and rose water and place a white cloth over the corpse. She probably lived a wretched life, died a dreadful death. She deserves some honour.'

The priest tapped the silver coins with the toe of his high-heeled boot. 'I'll not do that,' he squeaked.

'Yes, you bloody well will!' Corbett roared. 'You'll get someone to do it and, if you don't – and I will check – I will make it my business to have you removed from this benefice. I understand His Grace the King needs chaplains for his army in Scotland.' He stood over the now frightened priest. 'My name,' he whispered, 'is Sir Hugh Corbett, Keeper of the Secret Seal, friend and counsellor of the King. You'll do what I ask, won't you?'

The priest's bombast collapsed like a pricked bladder. He nodded and carefully picked up the silver coins. Corbett didn't wait but walked back to the wicket gate, where they had tied their horses, and stood for a while drawing in deep breaths.

'Whoever did that,' he nodded back to the church, 'must be both evil and bad.'

Cade, who still appeared nauseous, just muttered and shook his head whilst Ranulf looked as if he had seen a ghost. They walked down the Poultry, their stomachs unsettled as they passed the stinking tables and shearing tubs of the skinners who sat, knives in hand, scraping away the dry fat from the inside of animal skins before throwing the finished pieces into tubs of water.

Ranulf, now revived, cat-called the apprentices who stood waist-deep in the large vats of water, kneading the soaking skin with their bare feet. The abuse was swiftly returned but most of the skinners' venom was directed at a man chained by the beadles to the pole of one of their stalls. A placard round the fellow's neck proclaimed how the previous night, whilst drunk, this roaring boy had moved amongst the skinners' houses mewing like a cat. A barbed insult, implying that some skinners tried to trade cat skin in the place of genuine fur.

At last, Corbett and his party reached the Mercery where tradesmen behind stalls shouted that they had laces, bows, caps, paternosters, boxwood combs, pepper mills and threads for sewing. They passed the great seld, or covered market, in West Cheapside, finding it difficult to manage their horses because of the cows being driven up the Shambles towards the slaughter houses at Newgate. The animals seemed to sense their impending doom and struggled at the ropes round their necks. The horses caught their panic and whinnied in fear. Further up near Newgate, the slaughterers had been busy, turning the cobbles brown with blood, gore and slimy offal. They passed through Newgate, the summer breeze wafting the fetid odours of the prison and the foul stench of the city ditch which ran alongside of it.

'A morning for bad odours,' Cade mumbled. He pointed to the city ditch, a seething cauldron of stale water, dead rats, the carcasses of cats and dogs, human waste and rotting offal from the markets. Cade nudged Ranulf playfully in the ribs.

'Keep on the straight and narrow,' he warned. 'From next Monday, the sheriffs intend to use all malefactors in the city gaols to clear the ditch and have the rubbish rowed out to sea to be dumped.'

Corbett, still thinking about the corpse he had just viewed, stopped at Fleet Bridge to buy a ladle of fresh water from tipplers selling it from stoups and water barrels. The others joined him and they washed their mouths before continuing down Holborn towards the Strand. They passed the church of St Dunstan's in the West, the Chancery record office, went under Temple Bar and on to the broad Strand leading down to Westminster. The great highway was lined by the freshly plastered and painted great inns belonging to certain nobles; the road was busy with judges, lawyers and clerks, dressed in their rayed gowns and white coifs, making their way to and from the courts.

Outside the hospital of Our Lady of Roncesvalles, near the village of Charing, Corbett stopped to admire the new beautifully carved cross erected by his royal master in memory of his beloved wife Eleanor. Moving on, they rounded a bend in the road and saw before them the gables, towers and ornately carved stonework of Westminster Abbey and Palace. Entering the royal precincts by a small postern gate in the northern wall, they saw, to the right, the great mass of the abbey and, nearer to them, wedged neatly between the abbey and the palace grounds, the beautiful church of St Margaret. Yet the splendour of both the abbey and the church was tarnished by rusting scaffold stacked haphazardly against the walls by the masons who had ceased work when the treasury had run out of money to pay them.

Cade pointed north, around the other side of the abbey. 'Over there,' he remarked, 'in the middle of a small orchard you will find the ruins of Father Benedict's house and,' he moved his arm, 'behind the abbey church is the Chapter House where the Sisters of St Martha meet. Shall we go there first?'

Corbett shook his head. 'No, first we will visit the palace and see the steward, he may be able to give us more information.'

Cade pulled a face. 'The steward is William Senche. He's usually half-drunk and can't tell you what hour of the day it is. You know how it is, Sir Hugh, when the cat's away the rats will play.'

They led their horses into the palace yard. The King had been absent from his palace for several years and the signs of neglect were apparent; weeds sprouted in the palace yard, the windows were shuttered, the doors locked and barred, the stables empty and the flower-beds overgrown. A mongrel dog ran out and, hackles raised, stood yapping at them until Ranulf drove it off. Near the Exchequer House, overlooking the overgrown riverside gardens, they found a glum-eyed servant and despatched him to search out William Senche. The latter appeared at the top of the steps leading from St Stephen's Chapel and Corbett muttered a curse. William Senche looked what he was: a toper born and bred. He had bulbous, fish-like eyes, a slobbering mouth and a nose as fiery as a beacon. With his scrawny red hair and beetling brow, he was a very ugly man. He had already sampled the grape but when he realised who Corbett was, he tried to put a brave face on it; his answers were sharp and abrupt but he kept looking away as if he wished to hide something.

'No, no,' he remarked in a tetchy voice. 'I know nothing about the Sisters of St Martha. They meet in the abbey and things there,' he added darkly,' are under the authority of Abbot Wenlock and he's very ill.'

'So, who's in charge?'

'Well, there are only fifty monks, most of whom are old. Prior Roger is dead, so the sacristan Adam Warfield is in charge.'

The man danced from foot to foot as if he wished to relieve himself. His nervousness increased as Cade moved to one side of him and Ranulf to the other.

'Come, come, Master William,' Corbett mildly taunted. 'You are an important official, not some court butterfly. There are other matters we wish to talk to you about.'

'Such as?'

'Well, one in particular, Father Benedict's death.'

'I know nothing,' the fellow blurted out.

Corbett plucked him gently by the front of his food-stained jerkin. 'That,' he said, 'is the last lie you will tell me. On the evening of Tuesday, May twelfth, you discovered Father Benedict's house on fire.'

'Yes, yes,' the fellow's eyes snapped open.

'And how did you do that? The house can't be seen from the palace yard.'

'I couldn't sleep. I went for a walk. I saw the smoke and flames and rang the tocsin bell.'

'Then what?'

'There's a small well amongst the trees. We brought buckets but the flames were fierce.' The man pulled his lips down which made him look even more like a landed carp. 'When the fire was out we examined the rooms. Father Benedict was lying just behind the door.'

'He had a key in his hand?'

'Yes, he did.'

'Anything else untoward?'

'No.'

'And do you know how the fire started?'

'Father Benedict was old, he may have dropped a candle, an oil lamp, or a spark from the fire could have been the cause.'

'And you noticed nothing suspicious?'

'No, nothing at all. I can't tell you any more than that. Adam of Warfield would be of more help.' With that the fellow turned and bolted like a rabbit who had suddenly seen a fox.

Corbett looked at Cade, raised his eyebrows and went back through the postern gate into the abbey grounds, the under-sheriff laughing loudly at Ranulf's mimicry of the steward's accent and strange antics.

Before them rose the great mass of the abbey church and its stone carvings: snarling gargoyles and visions of hell. Corbett studied the latter, fascinated by the horrors the sculptor had so subtly depicted. Beneath a triumphant Christ in Judgement, the damned were being led by ghastly demons to be cooked in a great vat of bubbling oil where devils poked the unfortunate lost souls with spears and swords like cooks would do when boiling pieces of meat. Corbett heard a noise and looked to his left across the great empty vastness of the old cemetery. The grass and hemp were almost a yard and a half high but Corbett glimpsed an old gardener doing his best to clean the area around the graves.

'Sir,' Corbett called out. 'You have a task and a half there.'

The man half turned and faced Corbett with watery eyes and dirt-stained cheeks.

'Oh, aye,' the gardener replied in a thick rustic accent, tapping a derelict headstone. 'But my customers don't object.'

Corbett smiled and looked away at the great rounded buildings overlooking the cemetery.

'Is that the Chapter House?'

Cade nodded.

'And the crypt lies beneath it?'

'Yes.'

Corbett studied the thick buttresses and heavy granite wall. 'Tell me again, how the crypt can be entered.'

'Well, behind the Chapter House,' Cade said, 'lies the cloister but the crypt can only be entered by a door in the south-east corner of the abbey church. As I have said, the door is sealed. Behind that door there's a low vaulted passage which descends by a steep flight of steps. These steps are broken and, to get down into the crypt, where the treasure lies, special ladders have to be used.' Cade narrowed his eyes. 'I have already told you this so why the fresh interest?'

'I am just thinking of Father Benedict's cryptic message.' He smiled at the pun. 'I wondered if his warning was about the treasury? Perhaps he saw something?'

Cade shook his head. 'I doubt it. The treasury door is sealed, barred and locked, and even if you could get in, you would need siege equipment to reach the heart of the crypt. Moreover, I doubt if the good brothers would allow someone to climb out of their crypt with bags of treasure.'

Corbett reluctantly agreed and they crossed the grounds towards the main abbey buildings. A bleary-eyed, shuffling lay brother took care of their horses, then led them down paved passageways to Adam of Warfield's chamber. Corbett took an immediate dislike to the sacristan. He was tall, angular, very precise, and had a long crooked nose and a prim, pursed mouth. Corbett thought his eyes, under their shaggy brows, were shifty and uneasy. Warfield, however, made them welcome enough with dainty flutterings of his long boned fingers; he offered them ale and bread which Corbett refused, despite Ranulf's mutterings. All three of them sat on a bench feeling rather awkward, like boys in a school room, with the sacristan perched opposite them on a high stool, hiding his hands in the voluminous sleeves of his brown robe. Too composed, Corbett thought, too placid: not the sort of man you would put in charge of a great abbey. At first their conversation was desultory; Corbett asked after the old abbot who was virtually bed-ridden and expressed his condolences at the recent death of Prior Roger. Adam of Warfield seemed unmoved.

'We have sent word to Rome,' he rasped. 'But we have not yet received the authority to hold fresh elections for a new prior.' He smiled deprecatingly. 'But I do what I can.'

'I'm sure you do!' Corbett replied.

He could hardly abide the sanctimonious smile on the man's face so he stared round the austere chamber with its few sticks of paltry furniture. He sensed Warfield was a hypocrite, noticed the crumbs of fine sugar on the monk's dark robe and glimpsed the rim stain left by a wine goblet on the table. The clerk was sure that this monk liked his stomach as much as the priest at St Lawrence Jewry did his.

'Father Benedict's death?' he asked abruptly.

Adam of Warfield stiffened. 'I have told Master Cade already,' the monk whined. 'We were roused from our dormitory by Master William, the palace steward. We did what we could but the house was gutted by flames.'

'Don't you think it was strange,' Corbett continued, 'that on the day Father Benedict died, he sent a message to Cade saying something terrible, something quite blasphemous, was happening? I ask you now, Adam of Warfield, what is happening in the King's abbey which so disturbed that old, saintly priest?'

The sacristan let out a deep breath. Corbett caught the stench of wine fumes.

'Our Lord the King,' Corbett continued, 'had a deep love of Father Benedict and whatever was worrying him now intrigues me. Believe me, I will satisfy my curiosity.'

The sacristan was now agitated, his fingers fluttering above his brown robe. 'Father Benedict was old,' he stammered. 'He imagined things.'

He strained his scrawny neck and Corbett suddenly noticed the faded purple mark on the right side of the sacristan's throat. How, Corbett wondered, did an ordained priest and monk of Westminster get a love bite on his neck? He looked again and was sure the mark was not some cut or graze caused by shaving. Corbett rose and stared through the small, diamond-shaped window.

'The Sisters of St Martha, Brother Adam, what do you know of them?'

'They are a devoted and devout group of ladies who meet in our Chapter House every afternoon. They pray, they do good works, especially amongst the whores and prostitutes of the city.'

'You support their work?'

'Of course I do!'

Corbett half turned. 'Were you shocked by Lady Somerville's death?'

'Naturally!'

'I understand she did work in the laundry? What

work, exactly?' Corbett peered over his shoulder at the sacristan and noticed how pale the man's face had become. Were there beads of sweat on his forehead? Corbett wondered.

'Lady Somerville washed and took particular care of altar cloths, napkins, vestments and other liturgical cloths as well as the brothers' robes.'

'Do you know what Lady Somerville meant by the phrase "*Cacullus non facit monachum*"?'

'The cowl does not make the monk?' The sacristan smiled thinly. 'It's a phrase often used by our enemies who claim there's more to being a monk than wearing a certain habit.'

'Is that so?' Ranulf spoke up. 'And would you agree, Brother?'

Warfield threw him a look of contempt, and Corbett drummed his fingers on the window sill.

'So you don't know what she was referring to?'

'No, my relationship with the Sisters of St Martha is negligible. I have enough matters in hand. Sometimes I meet them in the Chapter House but that is all.'

'Well, well, well!' Corbett walked back to the bench. 'Nobody at Westminster seems to know anything. Am I right, dear Brother? Well, I wish to see three things: first, Father Benedict's house; secondly, the door to the crypt and, finally, the Sisters of St Martha. You say they meet every afternoon?'

The sacristan nodded.

'Then, my dear Brother, let's go. Let's begin.'

They walked out of the abbey buildings, Warfield leading them through overgrown gardens into a small orchard.

'What has happened here?' Ranulf whispered loudly. 'This is the King's abbey, the King's house, yet nothing has been attended to.'

'The fault is really the King's,' Corbett murmured. 'He is too busy in Scotland to press Pope Boniface for the right to hold elections. He has withdrawn his household from Westminster; his treasury has no money to pay masons or gardeners. I do not think he knows how bad the situation is. When this matter is over, he will be enlightened.'

'And the others don't care,' Cade added. 'Our wealthy burgesses regard Westminster as a village, whilst the bishops of Canterbury and London are only too happy to see it decline.'

The orchard thinned and before them, in a small enclosure with its fence broken down, stood the blackened ruins of Father Benedict's house. Corbett walked slowly around the building. It had not been built with wattle and daub but bricks quarried by the stone cutters, otherwise it would have been reduced to a smouldering heap. Corbett studied the wooden-framed window high in the wall, well over two yards above the vegetable garden.

'That is the only window?' he remarked.

'Yes.'

'And was the roof thatched, or tiled?'

'Oh, tiled with red slate.'

Corbett walked up to the front door which still hung askew on its steel hinges. The door was oaken, about two inches thick and reinforced with steel strips.

'And was there only one door?'

'Yes! Yes!'

Corbett pushed it to one side and they entered the blackened, ruined house, wrinkling their noses at the stench of burnt wood and stale smoke. The inside of the building had been totally gutted, the white-washed walls blackened and scorched. The stone hearth at the far end had been reduced to crumbling brick.

'A simple place,' Corbett murmured. 'Father Benedict's

bed must have been in the far corner? Next to the hearth? Yes?'

Warfield nodded.

'He probably ate, slept and studied here?'

'Yes, Master Corbett, there was only one room.'

'And on the floor?'

'Probably rushes.'

Corbett walked over to the near corner and sifted amongst the ashes on the floor. He pulled up a few strands and rubbed them between his fingers; yes, they were rushes and had probably been very dry and would have soon caught fire.

Corbett walked into the centre of the room and stared at the wall underneath the window, where the fire had burnt fiercely, turning the wooden window frame into black feathery ash; the flames had gouged deep black marks on the wall and reduced everything on the floor to a powdery dust. Corbett walked over to the hearth and to the remains of the wooden bed. He stood for a while, ignoring the impatient mutterings of his companions, and scraped his boot amongst the ashes.

'Bring me a stick, Ranulf!'

The manservant hurried out to the orchard and brought back a long piece of yew which he pruned with his dagger. Corbett began to sift amongst the ashes, digging at the packed earth, concentrating on a line which ran directly from the window; then he went over to where they stood near the door.

'Father Benedict was murdered,' he announced.

The sacristan gasped.

'Oh, yes, Brother Adam. Tell me again what happened when you tried to douse the flames?'

'Well, we couldn't get near the door, the heat was so intense. We threw buckets of water at the walls and through the window. It was the only thing we could do.'

'And then?'

'Well, the flames died and we forced the door.'

'It was still locked?'

'Oh, yes, but loose on its hinges.'

'And you found the half-burnt body of Father Benedict?'

'Just inside; the corpse of the cat beside him.' The sacristan shook his head. 'I can't see how he was murdered. The door was locked, there was only one key. Father Benedict would hardly open the door for someone to come in, start a fire, leave and then lock the door behind him!' The sacristan smiled in triumph as if he had presented some brilliantly lucid syllogism.

'The murderer didn't get in,' Corbett replied. 'If the fire had started near the hearth, the flames would have been the fiercest there. But look at the wall under the window and the wall directly opposite. Both are very badly burnt, as is the line of floor between. The fire started in the middle of the room. What happened was this; somebody tossed a jar, or skin, of oil, very pure oil because it is hard to detect, through the window into the middle of the room. The jar or skin burst, a tinder or candle was thrown and the dry, oil-drenched rushes soon turned into a raging inferno.'

'Of course!' Cade exclaimed. 'That's why the cat couldn't jump through the window, it was too high for it and the floor beneath the window had been saturated by oil.'

'And the far wall?' Ranulf explained. 'It's badly burnt because of the breeze from the window, which would waft the flames that way.'

'Nonsense!' the sacristan exclaimed.

'No, no,' Corbett replied. 'I have examined the floor in the centre of the room beneath the rushes. There's nothing but packed earth yet the clay there is stained with oil, some of it slightly less burnt.'

'But,' the monk protested, 'Father Benedict reached the door.'

'Oh, yes,' Corbett replied. 'The sound of the oil hitting the floor, and the roar of the flames would have roused him. He seizes his cloak and the key by his bed and, holding the cat, runs towards the door.'

'What about the wall of flames across the floor?'

'They would be fierce but, probably, still not fully fanned. Father Benedict would be desperate, he had to brave them before they grew, roaring to the rafters.'

'How do you know the key was not in the lock?' Cade asked.

'Because if it was, Father Benedict would have survived and the murderer would have chosen another scheme.' Corbett looked at the under-sheriff's sword belt. 'Your dagger, Master Cade, it's of the Italian mode, thin and slender. Can I borrow it?'

Cade shrugged and handed it over.

'Now,' Corbett said. 'Would you all stand outside? Ranulf, cup your hand beneath the keyhole.'

Corbett's companions, rather bemused, stepped outside the burnt building. Corbett heaved the door closed, holding it fast with one hand before slipping Cade's thin stiletto through the keyhole. At first it was blocked so Corbett carefully pushed until he heard Ranulf's exclamation of surprise. The clerk pulled the door open and handed the dagger back.

'Well, Ranulf, what do you have?'

His manservant showed him a thin strip of half-burnt wood, long and rounded as if cut by a master carpenter.

'You see, what happened,' Corbett concluded, 'was that

the murderer knew where Father Benedict kept his key. On the night he murdered the priest, he slipped this piece of wood through the keyhole, went quietly round to the window, threw in the oil and lighted torch then slipped away. Father Benedict reaches the door, the fire raging all around him; he inserts his key but the lock is blocked. He takes it out, perhaps tries again but it is too late.' Corbett stared at the sacristan. 'It couldn't have been there earlier, otherwise Father Benedict wouldn't have locked the door behind him. On, no, Master Sacristan, Father Benedict was cold-bloodedly murdered. I intend to discover why and by whom!'

Corbett turned at the sound of footsteps. A small, fat monk, the folds of his pasty face betraying both anxiety and self-importance, hurried out of the trees and across to the priest's house.

'Brother Warfield! Brother Warfield!' he gabbled. 'What is going on here?' He stopped, his head going back, like that of a small sparrow, lips pursed, little black eyes darting round the group. 'Who are these people? Do you need help?'

'No, Brother Richard, I don't!' Warfield replied.

The portly monk stuck his thumbs inside the tasselled cord round his waist. 'Well!' he exclaimed, staring round the room. 'I think you do!'

'Go away, little man!' Ranulf answered. 'This is Sir Hugh Corbett, Keeper of the Secret Seal, Special Emissary of the King!'

'I am sorry, so sorry,' the portly monk stuttered, his eyes pleading with Warfield.

'Don't worry, Brother Richard.' The sacristan clapped him hard on the shoulder. 'Everything is well here!' Warfield smiled at Corbett. 'Brother Richard is my assistant and most zealous in his duties.'

'Good,' Corbett snapped. 'Then both of you can show me the entrance to the crypt.'

Corbett turned away but not before he glimpsed the quick, warning glances which passed between Warfield and his portly assistant.

Chapter 5

Adam of Warfield took them over to the abbey church; the stone pillars and passageways stretched before them as silent as the grave. The air was musty and Corbett caught the bitter-sweet smell of incense and rotting flowers. The dappled shadows were broken by bursts of sunlight which poured through stained-glass windows high in the walls. They walked along a transept, their footsteps ringing hollow, even their breath seemed to echo in the vastness of the vaulted roof. At last they came to the south transept which was barred by a great oaken door reinforced with strips of steel and iron studs. The edge of the door, where it met the lintel, had been sealed with great blobs of scarlet wax and bore the imprint of the Treasurer's seal. The door was fastened by three bolts and each of these was secured with two padlocks.

'To each padlock,' Adam Warfield explained, 'are two keys. One is held by the King, the other by the Lord Mayor.' He pointed to the keyhole. 'This, too, has been sealed.'

Corbett crouched and stared at the great disc of purple wax which had been sealed by the Chancellor. Corbett examined everything carefully.

'Nothing is broken,' he said. 'But what happens if the King wishes to enter?'

'I asked that myself,' Cade replied. 'The barons of the Exchequer have made it very plain: the door is not to be opened except in the presence of the King himself. So far he has sufficient silver and gold and, if more is needed, he will melt down bullion still stored in the Tower.' Cade made a face. 'The peace with France,' he continued, 'has meant the King need not make a run on his treasury.'

Corbett nodded. Everything appeared secure and what Cade said nudged his memory about gossip at court: the treasury officials had boasted to him how the King, as yet, had no need to melt down cups of plate to pay his troops.

Corbett tapped on the door.

'And beyond this there are the steps?'

Adam Warfield sighed in exasperation. 'Yes, and they're broken. Anyone who tried to force that door would soon be discovered. You did say you wished to meet the Sisters of St Martha?'

And, without waiting for an answer, the sacristan and Brother Richard led them out of the abbey and into the cloisters. A square, porticoed walk bounded the garth, a green island of lush grass with a fountain splashing in the centre around which birds sang and swooped. They went through a small doorway, down more passageways and into the Chapter Room.

Corbett heard the mumble of voices which stilled as soon as they crossed the threshold. He blinked as they entered. Although the windows were unshuttered, the room was dark and candles glowed in the shadowy recesses and along the oaken table where a group of women sat. Corbett sensed an atmosphere of sadness as they all stopped talking and looked towards him. At first they were indeterminate, indistinct in the poor light so he peered closer: all the women were dressed in dark blue head-dresses, fastened with pieces of gold braid. They were wearing dresses and smocks of different hues but these were covered in tabards which matched their head-dresses. He stared hard at the livery depicted on them and made out the figure of Christ with a woman kneeling beside him, presumably St Martha. He caught a glimpse of bare ankles beneath the table and realised these ladies, however high-born, were similar to many noble widows who followed a monastic rule in their spiritual lives. Self-conscious of his own boots thudding on the wood-panelled floor, Corbett led the rest of his group across the room though he noticed how both Cade and the monks hung back as if trying to hide themselves.

'Do you think they always dress like this?' Ranulf whispered.

'I doubt it,' Corbett murmured. 'Just at meetings.'

'Why are you whispering? What are you doing here?' An old, white-haired lady at the top of the table stood cupping her hand to her ear. She challenged them again and a tall lady on her right repeated the question.

'Gentlemen, this is a meeting of our Sisterhood. You did not knock or ask for entrance.'

'My lady,' Corbett answered. 'We are here on the King's orders.'

The rest of the seated group began to murmur amongst themselves but the old lady at the top of the table clapped her hands for silence whilst the tall woman on her right rose and swept down to meet them. Corbett glanced round quickly at her companions and counted seventeen in all.

'I am the Lady Catherine Fitzwarren,' the tall woman announced. 'My superior, the Lady Imelda de Lacey, asked you a question. Who are you?'

Corbett studied her, noticing the grey hair escaping from beneath the coif yet the woman was not old; her face was smooth and clear without a wrinkle, high cheekbones emphasized eyes as grey as slate though her prim, pursed lips gave her a sour look. Corbett stood his ground; he was used to the domineering airs and graces of courtiers and the least said the better.

'Well, I know who you are,' Lady Fitzwarren's eyes flickered her contempt at the monks. 'And you,' she pointed a long, bony finger at Cade, 'are the under-sheriff who seems incapable of capturing the red-handed slayer of poor unfortunate girls!'

As she talked, Corbett stared at the lady seated at the top of the table. I have to be careful here, he thought. The de Lacey woman must be at least seventy summers old, the widow of one of Edward's great mentors, whilst Fitzwarren's husband had been one of the King's most successful generals in Wales. Corbett drew in his breath and glanced warningly at Ranulf.

'My Lady,' he stepped forward. 'I am Sir Hugh Corbett, Keeper of the Secret Seal and Chief Clerk of the Chancery.'

Lady Catherine immediately extended a white, thin hand for Corbett to kiss, which the clerk did, choosing to ignore Ranulf's muffled snigger.

'The King himself has sent me here to investigate the deaths of Lady Somerville and,' Corbett stammered, 'the other unfortunates you mentioned.'

'Well, Sir Hugh,' she snapped, 'you are welcome but do we really need the monks?'

Adam of Warfield and Brother Richard needed no second bidding but fled from the room like frightened rabbits.

'Well?' Lady Catherine turned with a prim smile on her face. 'We need more chairs.' She clapped her hands and serving women, seated in a darkened window recess, scurried to do her bidding. Corbett had to keep a straight face as the serving women, mumbling and muttering, dragged three high-backed chairs away from the wall to the near end of the long, oval table. Corbett ordered Cade and Ranulf to help. Lady Catherine swept back to her place whilst the three self-conscious men took their seats.

'Perhaps it's best,' old de Lacey announced in a surprisingly clear voice, 'if we tell the King's Emissary,' the words were tinged with sarcasm, 'something about the Sisters of St Martha. We are a group of lay women,' she continued heartily. 'Widows who, following the counsels of St Paul, now devote ourselves to good works. We take a solemn vow of obedience to the Bishop of London and our work is amongst women who walk the streets and alleyways of London. Women,' her gimlet eyes glared down at Corbett, 'who have to sell their bodies to satisfy the filthy lusts of men.' She paused and stared at Corbett as if he was personally responsible for every whore in London.

Corbett chewed the inside of his lip to avoid a smile. Ranulf lowered his head and received a kick from beneath the table.

'Ranulf, if you laugh,' Corbett hissed out of the corner of his mouth, 'I'll personally break your neck!'

'What was that? What was that?' de Lacey cupped her ear again.

'Nothing, my Lady. I wanted to make sure my servant had stabled the horses correctly.'

The old woman rapped the top of the table with a small mallet.

'You'll bloody well listen when I address you!'

Corbett steepled his fingers before his face, his lower lip clenched firmly between his teeth as he recalled stories of de Lacey: how this woman had often campaigned with her husband and was not averse to using language which would make a hardened mercenary blush. He glanced quickly around the table. Surprisingly enough, except for Lady Catherine Fitzwarren, the rest of the group were now sitting, heads bowed; a few shoulders were shaking and Corbett was relieved that he was not the only one to see humour in the situation. He sat motionless as Lady Imelda finished her caustic description of the Order's work.

'At the end of this meeting and only when we have finished,' Lady Imelda announced imperiously, 'our sub-prioress, the Lady Catherine, will provide you with any further help. She and her companion the Lady Mary Neville.' De Lacey clicked her fingers and pointed down the table at one of the women who now lifted her head and gazed straight at them.

Corbett and Ranulf looked at the petite, olive-skinned features of the Lady Mary. Ranulf took one glimpse of the dark blue eyes and gulped as his throat went dry and his heart beat faster. He had never seen anyone so beautiful and, although Ranulf had been with many women, he knew, sitting in this strange Chapter House, that for the first and possibly the last time in his life, he had fallen deeply in love. The woman smiled gently then looked away. Ranulf just gazed back hungrily and, for him, the rest of the meeting was a distant hum.

Corbett also watched the young widow turn away. It can't be? he wondered. No, it couldn't be! He felt shocked, his hands turning cold as ice. The Lady Mary bore the same Christian name, the same looks, the same demeanour of his own first wife, now years dead. Corbett couldn't believe it, he was so shocked he lost his usual alertness and didn't realise that the Lady Mary had had a similar effect on his manservant. Cade, however, glanced at both suspiciously and nudged Corbett gently with his elbow.

'You, sir,' Lady Imelda shouted down the table. 'Are you, Master Corbett, some coxcomb, some cloth-eared knave? I am speaking to you!'

Corbett smiled thinly and bowed. 'My Lady, my apologies, but my ride from Winchester was a harsh one.'

He studied the old, imperious face, the firm cheeks and hawkish look and resisted the urge to give this lady as good as he got. He forced himself to concentrate and, despite the eerie atmosphere of the room, began to quietly admire these courtly bred ladies; the only people in London who seemed to care about the droves of young women forced into prostitution.

The meeting moved from one item of business to another. The Lady Imelda described how they divided the city amongst them; each had a certain quarter to look after; how they had established refuges near St Mary of Bethlehem, in Mark Lane near the Tower; in Lothbury and at the junction of Night Rider and Thames Street. How they provided money and clothing, arranged marriages for some of the younger girls whilst others were clothed, given food, a few pennies and sent back to the villages and hamlets from whence they came.

Corbett sensed the sheer compassion beneath de Lacey's curt description, a genuine concern for others less fortunate then her. He gathered the Order had been in existence for at least twenty years and already the ladies had established close ties with the hospitals at St Bartholomew's and St Anthony's where the physicians gave their services free whilst the Guild of Apothecaries sold them herbs and medicines at much reduced prices. Better this, Corbett thought, than the dizzy-headed butterflies at court, dripping with jewellery, clothed in satin, with no thoughts in their empty noddles other than how their faces looked and their bellies were filled.

The meeting eventually finished with a prayer and, whilst the other sisters made to leave, smiling shyly at the men and whispering amongst themselves, the Ladies Catherine and Mary led them across to a small deserted chamber just off the Chapter Room. Lady Imelda suddenly bellowed at Corbett, how she hoped the King kept his shoulders warm and drank the herbal potions she sent to him.

'The King always suffered from rheums,' the old lady trumpeted for half of Westminster to hear. 'And as a boy he was always sniffing with colds. By the Mass, I wish I was back with him! A good strong horse between my legs and I'd teach those bloody Scots a lesson!' Her voice faded as the door closed behind them.

Lady Catherine smiled wanly but her companion leaned against the wall, hand to her face, giggling uncontrollably.

'You really must excuse the Lady Imelda,' Lady Fitzwarren murmured as they sat down on stools around a low, rickety table. 'She's going as deaf as a post, her language can be ripe but she has a heart of gold.' Lady Catherine blew her lips out. 'Well, I am afraid we have no wine.'

Corbett shrugged and said it didn't matter. He was now more interested in his servant who was staring fixedly at the Lady Mary. He followed Ranulf's gaze. She is beautiful, Corbett thought, and seems gentle as a dove. He clenched his fists in his lap, he had to forget the past as well as warn Ranulf that Lady Mary Neville was not some trollop to be teased and flirted with.

'Well,' Lady Catherine leaned forward. 'Your questions, Clerk?' She coughed and glanced at her companion. 'We knew you were coming,' she continued. 'The King informed us but the Lady Imelda always acts like that.' Fitzwarren smoothed the blue tabard over her knees. 'You want to ask us about the deaths of the girls?'

'Yes, My Lady.'

'We know nothing. Oh, we have tried to find out but even amongst the women we work with there's not a hint, not a whisper, not a suspicion of who the killer could be.' She licked her dry lips. 'You see, we work amongst the unfortunates, those who, by appearances anyway, even God has forsaken. Of course, we believe He has not. Now, we are not interested in what they do or who they know, where they go, which men have used their bodies. We are not even interested in their souls. We care for them as people, as women caught in a trap of poverty and ignorance, then lured to false wealth by empty promises. We believe that if we rescue them from that then all will be well.'

Corbett studied the woman. He could not understand her. She was harsh, yet gentle; idealistic but at the same time pragmatic. He glanced sideways and wished Ranulf would stop staring at the Lady Mary and that she would stop looking at him with those dark, doe-like eyes which stirred such memories in his own soul.

'So, you know nothing?' he asked.

'Not a jot, not a tittle.'

'Lady Mary, is that true?'

Corbett turned, ignoring Fitzwarren's hiss of annoyance. The young woman cleared her throat.

'The Lady Catherine is correct.'

Her voice was soft but Corbett caught the burr, the musical trace of an accent. It almost sounded Scottish and Corbett remembered the Nevilles were a powerful family owning vast tracts of land in Westmorland and along the Northern March.

'We know nothing, except that someone with a soul

as black as night is slaying these unfortunates,' she murmured. 'At first I used to attend their funerals at St Lawrence Jewry, the first three or four, but then I stopped. You can understand, Sir Hugh? Surely there must be more to the end of life than being wrapped in a dirty sheet and tossed like a bundle of refuse into a hole in the ground?'

Corbett remembered what he had seen at the church earlier in the day and nodded.

'Then let us talk of something else.' Corbett paused as the great bells of the abbey began to ring out for afternoon Mass though he idly wondered if the monks bothered to carry out their spiritual duties.

'What else is there to talk about?' Lady Catherine snapped.

'Lady Somerville's death. One of your sisters who was killed on Monday, May eleventh as she crossed Smithfield.'

'I can help you there,' Lady Mary spoke up. She leaned forward, her hands in her lap. 'We had a meeting here the very day she died and we finished late in the afternoon. Lady Somerville and I then left Westminster. We chose to walk because of the fine weather. We went along Holborn and visited patients at St Bartholomew's. Lady Somerville left the hospital but never reached her home; her murdered corpse was found in the early hours of the next morning.'

'Did anyone have a grudge against her?'

'No, she was quiet, austere and self-contained. She had a great deal of sadness in her life.'

'Such as?'

'Her husband died years ago whilst fighting in Scotland. They had one son Gilbert, I think he is a disappointment to her.' Lady Mary looked distressed. 'Sir Gilbert Somerville is more interested in the pleasures of life; he constantly reminded his mother that his father achieved nothing in his life, as the King's general, except an arrow in the neck.'

Corbett sat and stared at the wall behind her. So many players in this, he thought. The killer could be anyone.

'Before Lady Somerville died,' he asked, 'did she say anything strange or untoward?'

'No,' Fitzwarren tartly replied.

'Oh, come.' Corbett's voice became harsh. 'I have heard she kept repeating a phrase "*Cacullus non facit monachum*": the cowl does not make the monk?'

'Oh, yes,' Lady Mary's fingers flew to her lips. 'She did keep saying that. Indeed, she repeated it to me the day she died.'

'In what circumstances?'

'We were here, watching the brothers file out of the abbey church. I said something about them looking alike, how difficult it was to tell one from another in their hoods and cowls. She just repeated that phrase. I asked her what she meant, but she smiled and walked away.'

'Is that all? Was there anything else?'

'Yes. Yes, there was.' Fitzwarren tapped the side of her face with her hands. 'In the week before she died she asked me if I thought our work was worthwhile. I asked her why, and she replied what was the use in such a wicked world? Then the Friday before she died, you must remember it, Lady Mary, she came here rather late, looking very worried and agitated. She said she had been to see Father Benedict.'

'She didn't give the reason why?' Cade asked.

Corbett turned as Lady Mary clapped her hands together excitedly.

'Oh, I remember something!' she declared, her eyes

sparkling with excitement. Corbett reflected how truly beautiful she became when she threw off her air of subdued piety. 'Just before we reached St Bartholomew's she murmured something about leaving the Order. I objected but she maintained the abbey contained evil.' Lady Mary shrugged. 'I know it sounds strange but that's what she said.'

'Was Lady Somerville deeply involved in your work?'

'No,' Fitzwarren replied. 'And that makes what she said to Lady Mary even stranger. You see, Somerville suffered from rheumatism in her legs, she found walking the streets painful, even though the physicians claimed it was good for her. Her real work was in the abbey laundry, or rather the vestry on the other side of the Chapter House. She was responsible for keeping the altar cloths, napkins and robes clean.'

'And Father Benedict's death?'

'Sir Hugh,' Lady Fitzwarren replied. 'He died in a fire. We were bitterly sorry. He was not only our chaplain but an old, very gentle priest. Why do you ask?'

'How was he before he died? Did he say anything untoward?'

'Strange that you mention it, Sir Hugh,' Lady Mary interrupted. 'Oh,' she said, shaking her head, 'he didn't say anything but he was very quiet, distant.' She shrugged. 'But I don't know why. God rest him!'

'You noticed this after Lady Somerville visited him?'

'Yes, but I don't know what was said. Lady Catherine had her own problems and Father Benedict was our chaplain.'

Corbett rose. 'My Ladies, is there anything else?'

Both shook their heads in unison.

'Perhaps,' Corbett ventured, 'I could see your work.'

'We are going out tonight,' Lady Catherine replied.

Corbett suddenly remembered Maeve's face and shook his head. 'No, no, that's impossible!'

'Where do you actually work?' Ranulf asked.

'In our own ward,' Lady Mary answered. 'Farringdon.'

Corbett felt a twinge of jealousy at how the young woman smiled at Ranulf.

'We think it's best if we work,' she explained, 'in an area where we are known and safe, where we can always count on the local beadles for support. Perhaps tomorrow evening?'

Corbett smiled and bowed. 'Perhaps.'

The two women rose and led them back to the Chapter House. Corbett glanced suspiciously at his two companions; Cade had a reputation of being a taciturn man but since he had entered the Chapter House, he had been very withdrawn, a shadow of himself whilst Ranulf had ceased to snigger and mutter quips.

Halfway down the deserted Chapter House, Corbett stopped.

'May I look at the vestry room? You said it was here?'

Lady Fitzwarren led him across, opening a door in the far wall. Corbett looked inside; the vestry was nothing more than a long, oblong room with cowls, hoods and other monks' attire hanging on pegs driven into the wall. On the shelves were neatly piled altar cloths, napkins for the lavabo, amices, stoles and chasubles. Corbett could see nothing suspicious, certainly nothing to explain Lady Somerville's deep unease. He left and, outside the Chapter House, bade the ladies adieu, kissing both their hands. Corbett blushed as he turned away for he was sure Lady Mary had pressed his hand more firmly than perhaps she should have done.

They went back round the abbey and collected their horses. Ranulf was still silent but now Cade became talkative, he seemed fascinated by the Lady Imelda and made even the withdrawn Ranulf smile at his graphic description of how the old noblewoman would not think twice about walking into the Guildhall to harangue the Mayor and aldermen on whatever caught her fancy. They mounted their horses and left by the northern gate. On the road outside Corbett stopped and looked back at the darkened mass of Westminster Abbey. He clenched the reins tightly. What evil lurked in that great abbey which had so frightened Father Benedict and the Lady Somerville? What had they known which had caused their savage deaths? Corbett stared up at a gargoyle and the stone creature seemed to lunge towards him.

'When this business is finished,' Corbett said, 'the King needs to intervene here. There's something rotten in our great abbey.'

He turned and spurred his horse into a canter. The cowled, hooded figure hiding in one of the abbey's rooms above the Chapter House watched the three men ride off along Holborn. The watching figure clenched a set of rosary beads, smiled, then hissed with all the venom of a snake.

At The Bishop of Ely's inn Corbett and his party stopped and dismounted. Cade left, dourly excusing himself for other duties. Corbett watched the under-sheriff turn right, into Shoe Lane.

'What is wrong with Cade?' he murmured. 'Why is he so silent? What does he have to hide?'

Ranulf merely shrugged, so the clerk decided to move on. They joined the crowds pushing through Newgate as the road narrowed and became blocked with carts trundling into the city loaded with produce, fruit, rye, oats, slabs of red meat, squawking geese and chickens penned in wooden cages. The noise grew deafening as the huge dray horses plodded by, the wheels of the carts rumbling like claps of thunder and raising great clouds of dust. The air rang with strange oaths, sudden quarrels, the lash of whips and the jingle of harnesses. Corbett turned left just within the city gate, leading Ranulf down an alleyway strewn with broken cobbles which filled and blocked the sewer running down its middle. They had to walk slowly for sometimes the ground was broken by wide gaps and deep holes. Some were filled with bundles of broom and wood chip, others were cesspits full of night soil thrown out from the houses on either side.

'Master, where are we going?'

'St Bartholomew's. I want to look into the soul of a murderer.'

Chapter 6

They crossed a street and went down another alleyway dark as night with the houses tightly packed together. The gables of the upper stories jutted out so far that they met each other and blocked out the sunlight. At last they reached Smithfield, the great open expanse still thronged with people attending the horse fair, particularly the rich, eager to bid in an auction for Barbary mares. Young gallants in thick doublets with fiercely padded shoulders and tight waists, their sleeves were puffed out in concoctions of velvet, satin and damask, their legs covered in tight, multi-coloured hose which emphasized the shape of the calf and the grandeur of their codpieces. On the arms of these fops rested ladies equally splendid in rich tapestry dresses, square-cut at the breast and gathered high with cords of silk; their head-dresses were ornate, billowing out above eyebrows and foreheads severely plucked of hair. Corbett smiled when he compared these with the Sisters of St Martha, with their sober attire and unpainted faces.

They struggled through the crowd, past the great charred execution stake where criminals were burnt to death, and entered the arched doorway of St Bartholomew's hospital. They crossed an open yard, past stables, smithies and other outhouses to the hospital's long, high vaulted hall which ran parallel to the priory church. An old soldier, now turned servant, basking in the warm afternoon sun, offered to guide them in. They went along corridors, past chambers, clean and well swept, the windows thrown open, the rushes on the floor fresh and sprinkled with herbs. In each chamber there were three or four beds and Corbett glimpsed sick men and women, heads pressed against crisp linen bolsters. In the main, these were the poor unfortunates of the city whom the brothers took in to tend, cure or at least provide their deaths with some dignity. The old soldier stopped and knocked at a door. A voice cried 'Enter!' and Corbett and Ranulf were ushered into a sparsely furnished chamber. The air was fragrant with the smell from pots and bowls of crushed herbs and other concoctions. The apothecary, Father Thomas, sat with his back to them, crouched over a table under the window.

'Who is it?' he asked; his voice testy at being disturbed from the root he was dissecting with a small, sharp knife.

'We'll go if you don't want us, Father!'

The monk turned, a tall, ugly man yet his face was friendly.

'Hugh! Ranulf!' Father Thomas's long horsey features broke into a smile. He rose and clasped the hand of the clerk he had known since their days at Oxford. Corbett gripped the monk's hand tightly.

'*Sir* Hugh, now, priest.'

Father Thomas bowed mockingly, greeted Ranulf and asked after Maeve. He then turned back to taunt Ranulf, who smiled but did not indulge in the usual banter he so characteristically directed at close friends and acquaintances. Father Thomas pulled stools out.

'Are you hungry?' he asked.

'Yes,' Corbett replied. He hadn't eaten since the small bowl of meat earlier in the day and he had vomited most of that in the cemetery of St Lawrence Jewry. Father Thomas went to the door, opened it and shouted down the corridor. A few minutes later a lay brother entered with small freshly baked loaves wrapped in linen and two blackjacks of brimming frothy ale.

'I brewed it myself,' Father Thomas announced proudly.

Corbett tasted the cool, tangy ale and smiled appreciatively whilst Ranulf murmured his approval.

'Well,' Thomas sat opposite him. 'How can I help, Hugh? More murder? Some rare poison?'

'No, Thomas, I want you to let me look into the soul of a killer. You have heard of the prostitutes being killed and Lady Somerville's murder?'

'Yes, yes, I have.'

'I understand Lady Somerville called here on the night she died?'

'Yes, she did that.'

Corbett leaned forward. 'So, Father, what kind of man haunts whores, slits their throats then mutilates their sexual parts?'

Father Thomas made a face. 'Hugh, I know digitalis affects the heart, but how . . . ?' He shook his head. 'I know red arsenic in minor doses will ease stomach complaints but, if large doses are administered, it rips the stomach out. How and why, I cannot tell you. So, when it comes to the mind, the brain, the spirit, I am ignorant.' He drew in his breath, turned and picked up a yellowing skull from his desk. He held it out in the palm of his hand. 'Look, Hugh, this skull once housed a brain. In the palm of my hand I hold a receptacle which once had the power to laugh, cry, tell stories, sing, perhaps plumb divine mysteries or plan the building of a great cathedral.' Father Thomas put the yellowing skull on the ground beside him. 'When I studied at Salerno I met Arab physicians who claimed the human mind, the contents of the skull I have just shown you, the working of the brain, are as much a mystery as the nature of God.'

He rearranged his gown as he warmed to his theme. 'To put it bluntly, Hugh, these physicians had a number of theories. First, all physical disease comes from the mind. They even argue that people who are cured by miracles actually heal themselves. They also point out that, as the body is affected by what it eats and drinks, the mind is influenced by what it experiences. Some men are born with cleft palates or malformed limbs. Perhaps some men are born with twisted minds with a desire to kill?'

'Do you believe that, Father?'

'No, not really!'

'So, what explains our killer?'

Father Thomas stared at his hands. 'Let us go back a step. These Arabs maintained the brain, the mind, is moulded by its own experiences. If a person as a child, for example, is brutalised, he will become a brutal man. Now some priests would reject that. They will claim that all evil is the work of Satan.'

'And you, Father?'

'I believe it is a combination of the two. If a man drinks wine inordinately,' Father Thomas grinned at Ranulf, 'his belly becomes bloated, his face red, his mind hazy. Now, to continue the analogy, if a mind is fed on hatred and resentment, what would happen then?'

'I am sorry, Father, I don't know!'

'Well, the killer of these girls could be someone who has satiated every sexual desire and now wishes to expand his power. He acts as if he has the power of life and death.'

'So the cutting of their throats is part of the sexual act?'

'Perhaps.'

'Then why the mutilation?'

'Ah.' Father Thomas raised his eyebrows. 'That might contradict my theory. Perhaps the killer is someone who has lost his sexual potency or, indeed, can only achieve it by such a dreadful act.' Father Thomas ran his fingers through his thinning hair. 'I do not know all the details but I suspect the latter theory is the more correct. Your killer, Hugh, hates women, prostitutes in particular. He blames them for something, holds them responsible and feels empowered to carry out sentence against them.'

'So the killer is mad?'

'Yes, probably, driven insane by the canker of hate growing within him.'

'Would such a person act insane all the time?'

'Oh, no, quite the opposite. Indeed, such killers possess tremendous cunning and use every trick and foible to draw a curtain over their evil deeds.'

'So, it could be anyone?'

Father Thomas leaned closer. 'Hugh, it could be you, it could be me, Ranulf, the King, the Archbishop of Canterbury.' Father Thomas saw the puzzlement in Corbett's eyes. 'Oh, yes, it could be a priest, even someone living an apparently saintly life. Have you ever heard of the Slayer of Montpellier?'

'No, no, I haven't.'

'About ten years ago in France in the city of Montpellier, a similar killer was at large. He slew over thirty women before being captured and you know his identity? A cleric. A brilliant lecturer in law at the university. I do not wish to frighten you, Hugh, but the killer could be the last person you suspect.'

'Father Thomas,' Ranulf leaned forward, his inertia now forgotten as he listened to the chilling words of the priest.

'Father Thomas,' he repeated, 'I can understand, perhaps, such a man killing whores; but why Lady Somerville?'

Father Thomas shook his head. 'Ranulf, I cannot answer that. Perhaps she was the only woman available at the time.'

'But she wasn't mutilated?'

'Perhaps the killer felt angry at the way she helped the victims of his malice or . . .'

'Or what, Father?'

'Perhaps she knew the true identity of the killer and had to be silenced.'

Corbett put his tankard down. 'It's strange you say that, Father, because Lady Somerville kept repeating the phrase, "The cowl does not make the monk".'

'Ah, yes, quite a popular one now and rather fitting to your task, Hugh. No one is what he or she may appear.' Father Thomas rose and tightened the cord round his middle. 'I cannot help you with Lady Somerville's death, but wait.' He went to the door, summoned a lay brother and whispered instructions to him. 'I have sent for somone who might be able to assist you. Now, come, Hugh, what do you think of the ale?'

They were halfway through a discussion on brewing when a knock on the door disturbed them and a young monk, sandy haired and fresh faced, entered the room.

'Ah, Brother David.' Father Thomas made the usual introductions.

The monk gave Corbett a gap-toothed smile which made his freckled face look even more boyish. 'Sir Hugh, how can I help you?'

'Brother, on Monday, May eleventh, two women came here, Sisters of the Order of St Martha. Lady Somerville and Lady Mary Neville.'

'Oh, yes, they came to visit two sick patients, women we had taken in.'

'And what happened?'

'They stayed about an hour, chatting and talking, then Lady Somerville said she had to go. Lady Mary tried to stop her, offered to accompany her across Smithfield but the older one, Lady Somerville, said no, she would be safe. She left and that was it.'

'When did Lady Mary Neville leave?'

'Oh, shortly afterwards.'

'And what route did she take?'

The young brother smiled. 'Sir Hugh, I cannot help you with that.'

Corbett thanked him and Brother David was halfway out of the room when he suddenly turned.

'I heard about Lady Somerville's murder,' he remarked. 'Her body was found near the scaffold in Smithfield?'

'Yes, yes, that's correct.'

The monk nodded towards the window. 'It's growing dark, the horse fair is now ended. If you wish, and this may help, I know there's a beggar, a half-crazed man, who lost his legs in the King's war. At night, he sleeps beneath the scaffold; he feels he is safe there.' The young monk shrugged. 'He may have seen something. I heard him one night, as he passed the priory gates, screaming that the devil was stalking Smithfield. I asked him what he meant but he lives in a world of his own. He is always claiming to see visions.'

The young monk closed the door behind him and Corbett stared first at Father Thomas then at Ranulf.

'Chilling,' he murmured. 'The killer could be anyone but somehow I believe that Lady Somerville's death does lie at the root of it all.'

They took their farewells of Father Thomas. Corbett

paused awhile in the hospital to visit the wizened crones whom the Ladies Neville and Somerville had visited on the night of May the eleventh. These, however, proved witless, their minds wandering, their speech rambling so Corbett let them be. In the hospital courtyard he readjusted his cloak and looked at Ranulf who still appeared subdued, lost in his own thoughts.

'Ranulf,' Corbett teased gently. 'What is the matter?'

'Nothing, Master.'

Corbett linked his arm through his companion's and pulled him closer. 'Come on, man, you've been quiet as a nun!'

Ranulf shook himself free, stepped away and stared up into the gathering darkness; the blue sky was tinged with the dying rays of the setting sun and a faint breeze carried the fading sounds of the city towards them.

'There's something,' he muttered. 'But I don't want to talk about it.'

'And the rest?'

Ranulf sighed. 'Perhaps I am growing old, Master. I go out drinking and roistering in the taverns. I rub shoulders with the kind of girls this killer has slain. I see their eyes dance with merriment. I tease them and pay them gold.' He blew his cheeks out. 'Now I see another side to their lives and . . .'

'And what?'

'What really frightens me, Master, is what Father Thomas said. The killer could be anyone. If you and I hadn't been in Winchester, like every other man in the city, we'd be under suspicion and that includes our friend Alexander Cade.'

Corbett's face hardened. 'What do you mean, Ranulf?'

'Well, Cade's a good law officer. He never takes bribes. He is thorough and ruthless. So why was he so quiet at the abbey? And I noticed that at St Lawrence Jewry he soon left the death house, he kept his distance. Perhaps I am wrong, Master, yet, I agree with you, he is hiding something.'

'I suggest everyone is hiding something,' Corbett answered. 'You have heard Father Thomas. We are dealing with a man who leads two lives; an upright life in the daylight but, at night, he crawls the streets and alleyways hell bent on murder. Well, Ranulf, hold your nose and harden your stomach. It's time we visited the scaffold.'

They left the priory and crossed the now deserted ground of Smithfield market. A few people still tarried; a horse coper, desperately trying to sell two old nags who looked so exhausted they could hardly stand; a huckster with his barrow almost empty of apples; two boys kicked an inflated pig's bladder, whilst a drunk leaned against one of the elms and chanted some ribald song. The darkness was now gathering. They passed the spot where criminals were burnt and climbed the gently sloping hill where the great three-branched scaffold stood. The night breeze wafted down the bittersweet smell of corruption. Corbett and Ranulf immediately lifted the hems of their cloaks to cover their mouths and noses for in the poor light they could see the bodies still dangling from their ropes. Corbett told Ranulf to stay and went ahead to inspect. He kept his eyes away from the lolling heads, tried not to glimpse the bloated stomachs, the bare feet dangling as if still trying to grasp the earth. He looked round the scaffold: nothing. But then he heard the clatter of wooden slats so he stopped and waited. A strange-looking creature was making his way up the beaten track towards the scaffold. In the gathering dusk he looked like some dwarf swathed in rags. He stopped when he saw Ranulf, one hand went out, followed by a whine for alms. Then he glimpsed Corbett striding purposely down the track towards him. The hand fell away and the fellow turned as quick as a rabbit, despite the wooden slats fastened to the stumps of his knees.

'Don't go!' Corbett called.

Ranulf seized the man by the shoulder. The beggar whimpered; his twisted, lined face contorted into a pitying plea.

'For pity's sake, let me go!' he cried. 'I am a poor beggar man!'

Corbett came up and crouched before him. He stared into the bright half-mad eyes, noting the unshaven cheeks and jaw, the lines of saliva from toothless gums running down either side of the mouth.

'You come here every night, don't you?'

The fellow still tugged at Ranulf's hand.

'We mean you no harm.' Corbett added soothingly. 'Indeed.' He stretched out his hand where some pennies and two silver coins caught the beggar's eyes. The man relaxed and grinned.

'You mean well,' the fellow said. 'You come to help old Ragwort.'

He sat rocking on his wooden slats and Corbett felt uneasy as if he was talking to someone half buried in the dark earth.

'You mean me no harm,' he repeated and Corbett saw the fellow's dirty hand come up for the coins.

'These are yours,' Corbett whispered, 'if you tell us what you saw.'

'I sees visions,' the beggar replied, more composed now, settling down as Ranulf released his grip. 'I sees the devil walk. That's why I hide with the dead. They protect me. Sometimes I talk to them. I tell them what I know, what I see and sometimes they talk to me. They say how sorry they are.' The fellow grinned slyly. 'Never alone am I. Even in winter.' He pointed to the lights of St Bartholomew's. 'When the sun goes, so do I. I sleep in the cellars but I don't see my visions there.'

'And what did you see?' Corbett persisted. 'The night the old lady died?'

The fellow screwed up his eyes. 'I forgets now.'

Coins exchanged hands.

'Now I remember!' he yelled, almost deafening Corbett with his shout.

'Hush!' Corbett raised a finger to his lips. 'Just tell me, and the rest of the money is yours.'

Ragwort twisted his neck and nodded towards the scaffold. 'I am sitting there talking to my friends.'

Corbett suddenly realised he meant the people hanging from the ropes.

'When suddenly I hears footsteps and sees a figure coming out of the darkness. It's the woman.'

'Then what?'

'I hears other footsteps.'

'What did they sound like?'

'Oh, heavy. The devil is heavy, you know.'

Corbett glanced in exasperation at Ranulf. The beggar was half mad and the clerk wondered how much of what he was saying was true and how much the product of a fevered imagination.

'What happened then?' he muttered.

'I knows it's the devil,' the fellow repeated. 'I wants to warn the woman but she stops. She looks back into the darkness and cries out, "Who is it?" The devil draws closer and the woman says, "Oh, it's you".'

'Repeat that.'

'The old woman says, "Oh, it's you".'

'Then what happened?'

'The devil draws near. I hear the slash of the knife and the devil has gone.'

'What did the devil look like?'

'Oh, he wore a cloak and great black sandals on gnarled feet.'

'Sandals?' Corbett exclaimed and looked at Ranulf. 'One of our monkish friends!'

'Oh, no!' the beggar cried. 'It was the Lord Satan for he flew off, his great bat wings beating the night air.'

Corbett sighed and handed the rest of the coins over.

'Too good to be true,' he murmured. 'Come on, Ranulf, we've done enough!'

Corbett and Ranulf walked back through the darkened city to Bread Street. They found the household in turmoil. Maltote had returned and he and Ranulf fell on each other's necks like long-lost brothers. Corbett, raising his eyes heavenwards, kissed Maeve and baby Eleanor now staring up at him, round-eyed in excitement, and went upstairs to his bedchamber. Maeve followed with a cup of wine and sat beside him on the bed.

'It's dark out there!' Corbett said wearily. He looked at the lattice window. 'Dark as hell,' he added. 'There's something evil, nasty, brutish. Not human evil, not like de Craon who likes power, or Edward who wants to be seen as the new Justinian of the west!' Corbett grasped his wife's wrist. 'You are never to go out by yourself, certainly not at night, not until this business is finished!'

Then he put the wine cup down and hugged his wife, kissing her gently on the neck but, when he looked up, the darkness still pressed against the window.

Corbett rose early the next morning, broke his fast in the buttery, told Griffin, who was stumbling about the kitchen, that he was not to be disturbed and went to his small writing office at the back of the house. He took out a small piece of parchment, smoothed it with pumice stone and began to list everything he knew.

First: sixteen prostitutes had been killed. One dying every month, usually on or around the thirteenth of the month. They were all killed in the same way: throats slit and bodies mutilated. Most had been killed in their own chambers, though the last one had been in a church. Corbett bit the end of his quill. What else did he know? According to Cade the victims were all young, more courtesans than common street-walkers. So why did the killer select just these rather than the old hags and raddled whores who slept in the stinking alleyways? Corbett threw back his head. If most were killed in their chambers they must have opened their doors, allowing their killer to get close, so it must be someone they trusted? And who could that be? Someone rich? A customer common to them all? Or a city official? Or a priest? Corbett scratched his brow. Yet Cade had reported that no one had seen anything. Who was this killer? Who could slip like the shadow of death, stab, hack and disappear like some demonic will-o-the-wisp? And why the thirteenth? Was it some Satanic feast? Was the date significant? And why just one a month? What motive was there? Corbett recalled Father Thomas's words and shivered. He dipped his quill in the ink and continued writing.

Second: Lady Somerville's death. She had been killed out in the open. If the mad beggar could be believed, and Corbett distrusted the fellow's ramblings, Lady Somerville must have known her killer for she called out in the darkness to him. Did this provide any clue to the murderer? Again, Corbett was brought to the common denominator. Whom would Lady Somerville know? Whom would she stop for in the darkness? A priest? A monk? A city official? Someone from her own class? Someone she could trust?

Third: what did Lady Somerville mean by the phrase 'the cowl does not make the monk'? Was this a reference to the double life of the killer? Was it the murderer she was talking about? Or did it refer to the private life of some priest or monk? Corbett bit his lip and shook his head. Lady Somerville could have been talking about some other scandal, perhaps something she had seen at Westminster? And was her murderer the same red-handed slayer of the prostitutes? Or someone else who wished to make it look that way?

Fourth: Father Benedict. What troubled him? Why did he send that cryptic message to Cade? Wasn't it strange that Cade never managed to find him and discover the truth behind the priest's concerns? And was Father Benedict's murder linked to the death of the prostitutes?

Fifth: Richard Puddlicott? Was this master trickster involved in one of de Craon's subtle schemes? Did this have anything to do with the deaths Corbett was investigating? Corbett leaned back in his chair, his mind whirling with the different possibilities.

'How many mysteries here?' he murmured to himself. 'One, two or three? Are they separate or connected?'

'Hugh!'

Corbett whirled round. Maeve, sleepy-eyed, stood in the doorway. She looked like a ghost in the white, woollen blanket wrapped round her. She tiptoed over and kissed him gently on the head.

'You're talking to yourself,' she murmured.

'I always do.' He looked up at his wife. 'Is Ranulf up and about?'

'Sleeping like a pig, I heard him snoring from the foot of the stairs. He and Maltote were out last night.

Don't say anything, Hugh, but I think our Ranulf's in love.'

Corbett smiled, though his stomach lurched.

'Hugh, do you know who it is?'

'No,' he lied. 'You know Ranulf, Maeve. His love-life is as intricate and complex as a piece of your embroidery.'

Maeve spun on her heel. 'Oh, by the way,' she called out over her shoulder, 'Maltote brought me news. Dearest Uncle, the Lord Morgan, will be with us within a week!'

Corbett waited until the door closed behind her. 'Oh, God,' he sighed. 'Ranulf loves the Lady Mary Neville and will do something foolish and Uncle Morgan will only make matters worse!'

'I told you not to talk to yourself. So, it's the Lady Mary Neville!'

Corbett spun round. 'You fox!' he shouted. 'I thought you were gone!'

'The Lady Mary Neville.' Maeve's eyes rounded. 'I have heard of her. Ranulf aims high. Who knows,' she slipped behind the door before Corbett could throw something, 'next he will be wooing some Welsh princess!'

Corbett smiled and went back to his notes. He remembered his conversation with Cade and angrily scratched his head. He had searched for a pattern but, if there was one, why did it break down? He picked up his quill.

Item One: De Craon, what was his role?
Item Two: Where was Puddlicott? Why did he appear in Paris then in London? What was he doing? Was there some connection between him and de Craon? Did either or both have anything to do with the murders?
Item Three: What was Cade hiding?
Item Four: What was Warfield hiding?

Item Five: What did Somerville mean by her cryptic remarks about monks and something evil at Westminster? Did Father Benedict become her confidant? Was the same person responsible for their deaths?
Item Six: Was their murderer also the slayer of the prostitutes? If so, he must have been busy in the week beginning May 11th. Killing Somerville, Father Benedict and the whore Isabeau on subsequent evenings.
Item Seven: The last murder victim, Agnes, whose corpse he had viewed. She had been killed two days ago, just as Corbett was travelling back to the city. Her death had occurred on the 20th, not on the 13th. Why?

Corbett shivered. Was Cade correct? Was there really a pattern? Or were they hunting one, two or even three killers?

Chapter 7

An hour later a disgruntled, uneasy Corbett left the house quietly vowing he would have words with Ranulf who was still sleeping off the after-effects of last night's drinking. Maeve was now engrossed in the preparations for 'dear' Uncle's arrival and Corbett was determined to untangle the web of mysteries confronting him. He crossed the thronged marketplace of West Cheap, stopping to enquire from the beadles of any news in the city, but they shook their heads.

'Nothing, sir.' was the reply. 'A house was broken into in Three Needle Street, two rogues armed with catapults broke a window in Lothbury and a student from Oxford became drunk and played the bagpipes in Bishopsgate.'

Corbett smiled his thanks and moved on across into Wood Street then Gracechurch Street, dodging and moving aside as the timber merchants opened their stalls and prepared for a brisk day's business. He asked directions from a loud-mouthed apprentice, the boy shook his head, shouting that he didn't know where any Frenchman lived. A maid, carrying buckets of fresh water up from the Conduit, showed him the house de Craon had rented, a small, two-storied building, tightly wedged between two shops, dishevelled and rather crumbling. Corbett grinned to himself, the bells of the church were still ringing for the first Mass of the day and he hoped he was early enough to rouse de Craon from a peaceful sleep. He lifted the great brass door-knocker and brought it down with a crash then quickly repeated the action. He heard footsteps, the door was thrown open and de Craon appeared, fully dressed in a dark red cote-hardie and leather breeches pushed into soft black riding boots. His cunning, foxlike face gave Corbett the falsest of smiles.

'My dear Hugh, we have been waiting for you.' He clasped Corbett's hand, holding it tightly between his. 'Hugh, you look tired. Or should it be Lord Corbett?' The Frenchman's close-set, green eyes glittered with amused malice. 'Oh, yes, we've heard the news. Come in! Come in!'

Corbett followed the man, who would love to kill him, into a small, downstairs chamber. The room was shabby; the rushes on the floor were dirty, the fire a pile of cold ash, the walls cracked and peeled and the chair de Craon pulled out from a table looked splintered and wobbled dangerously.

'Sit down! Sit down!'

Corbett, ever watchful, accepted de Craon's invitation whilst the Frenchman sat on the corner of a table swinging his legs. The clerk just wished the Frenchman would wipe that sly malicious smile off his face. De Craon clapped his hands.

'Well, Hugh, is this a courtesy call? Oh,' he leaned forward and touched Corbett on the hand, 'I have met the Lady Maeve. Your daughter, she is beautiful. She takes after her mother. You want some wine?'

'No!'

De Craon's smile faded. 'Fine, Corbett, what do you want?'

'Why are you here, de Craon?'

'I bring messages of courtesy and friendship from my master, the King of France.'

'That's a lie!'

De Craon glared at Corbett. 'One of these days, Hugh,' he said in a mock whisper. 'One of these days I'll make you choke on your insults!'

Now Corbett smiled. 'Promises, promises, de Craon! You still haven't told me why you are in England and why you tarry in London.'

De Craon stood up and walked to the other side of the table.

'We have French merchants living here, they have interests which affect King Philip. You English are known for being hostile to foreigners.'

'Then, de Craon, you should be careful!'

'Oh, Hugh, I am and so should you. Where's your shadow, Ranulf?'

'At the top of the street,' Corbett lied. 'Sitting in a tavern with a group of royal archers waiting for me to return.'

De Craon cocked his head to one side. 'You were in Winchester, now you are in London. Why should the King send his most trusted clerk and Keeper of the Secret Seal back to the city?' De Craon held a finger to his lips. 'There are the murders,' he continued, as if talking to himself. 'I know the fat ones in the city do not want their secret sins brought to light. There's the death of Lady Somerville and, of course, the mysterious fire at the house of the King's old chaplain, Father Benedict.' De Craon preened himself, running a hand through his thinning red hair. 'Now what else could there be?' he asked in mock wonderment.

'Richard Puddlicott.'

De Craon's mouth opened and closed. 'Ah, yes, Puddlicott.'

'You know Puddlicott?'

'Of course.' The Frenchman smiled. 'A well-known English criminal. What do you call his type, a confidence trickster? He is wanted in Paris by our Provost as he is in London by your Sheriff.'

'For what reason?'

'For the same reasons as in London.'

'Then why?' Corbett asked slowly, 'was Puddlicott seen being entertained by your King's closest counsellor, Master William Nogaret?'

De Craon refused to be flustered. 'Puddlicott is a criminal but a valuable one. He sells secrets to us. What he thinks is valuable information, just as surely as your master buys secrets from traitorous Frenchmen.'

Corbett heard a sound and stood up. He felt nervous in this silent, dusty house. He turned, staring at the doorway, just as a stranger slipped like a shadow into the room.

'Ah, Raoul.' De Craon went round the table. 'Master Corbett, or rather Sir Hugh Corbett, can I present Raoul, Vicomte de Nevers, King Philip's special envoy to Flanders and the Low Countries.'

De Nevers shook Corbett's hand warmly and the clerk took an immediate liking to him. In looks he resembled Maltote but was thinner, leaner, his hair was blond, his features regular, rather boyish, though Corbett noted the shrewd eyes and the firm set to mouth and chin. He could see why Maeve had liked him. He had a lazy charm and a frank, open demeanour which contrasted sharply with de Craon's subtle falseness.

'Before you ask why Raoul is in England, de Craon murmured, 'I'll be honest. Next spring King Philip intends to move into Flanders. He has certain rights there which—'

'Which King Edward does not recognise,' Corbett interrupted.

'True! True!' de Nevers replied in broken English. 'But our master wishes to keep an eye on Flemish merchants. We know they come to London. We watch their movements and we bring messages for your King, how ill advised he would be to give these merchants any solace or comfort.'

Corbett stared at both men. They could be telling the truth, he thought, or at least part of it and de Nevers made more sense than de Craon. English envoys watched Scottish merchants in Paris, so why shouldn't the French watch Flemish merchants in London? Corbett picked up his cloak.

'Monsieur de Craon, Monsieur de Nevers, I wish you a safe stay in London but I also bring warnings from my master. You are protected by letters of safe conduct. Monsieur de Craon, you know the rules of the game. If you are found interfering in anything you shouldn't be, then I will personally escort you to the nearest port and send you packing back to France.' Corbett sketched a bow at both men and, before they could answer, made his own way out of the house.

Corbett stood in the street and breathed a sigh of relief. He was pleased that he had surprised both de Craon and his companion for he was sure that they were involved in some villainy, but only time would reveal what it was. He picked his way round the mounds of refuse and stared curiously at the empty dung cart, a tired-looking horse between the shafts, which stood on the other side of the street. He looked back at de Craon's house. There was something wrong but he couldn't place it. He'd glimpsed some detail which didn't fit. He shrugged. 'Only time will tell,' he muttered.

Staring up and down the street, he noticed the mounds of refuse piled high on either side of the sewer, then he walked gingerly down the street, keeping a wary eye as windows above were suddenly opened and the contents of night pots thrown out to drench the cobbles and passers-by with their filth. He stopped at a cookshop on the corner of Wood Street and bought a pie but then threw it into a sewer when his teeth crunched on something hard.

'Bastard officials!' he grumbled. He wished the beadles and Guild members would take as much care on what was sold in the streets as they did about their precious reputations. He turned and went back up the Shambles, stopping for a while to watch a man, dressed completely in black, the whitened bones of a skeleton painted garishly on his garb, dance a macabre jig whilst his companion tapped a drum and a boy on a reedy flute blew an eerie death march. Corbett pushed his way through the crowds round the butchers' stalls, keeping one hand on his purse and a wary eye on the rubbish underfoot. Outside Newgate a crowd had gathered to greet the death carts taking felons up to the scaffold at Smithfield or down the city to the Elms. He remembered the mad beggar man the night before and, shivering, he hurried on.

Corbett now wished Ranulf was with him. At the corner of Cock Lane, the blowsy harridans and common whores were already touting for business, the white paint on their faces so thick it cracked in places, their shaven heads covered with red or orange wigs.

'A penny for a tumble!' one shrieked at Corbett.

'Tuppence and you can do anything you like!'

'Don't worry,' another cackled. 'It won't take long!'

Corbett went over to the group. He smiled, trying to hide his disgust at the sour smell from their clothes, ignoring the black paint round their eyes which was beginning to run and stain their painted cheeks.

'Good morning, ladies,' he greeted the group.

The women looked at each other speechlessly before bursting into shrieks of laughter.

'Oh, good morning, sir!' they chorused back, flouncing their bright red skirts and bowing in mock curtseys.

'What do you want?' A large fat woman, round as a barrel of lard, pushed her way forward, her lips, parted in a false smile, showing blackened stumps of teeth.

'Which one of us takes your fancy?' She turned and grinned at her companions. 'For a shilling you can have the lot of us, a good baker's dozen!

More shrieks of laughter greeted her sally. Corbett tried to hide his embarrassment and looked away.

'My lady,' he murmured, 'I'd probably exhaust you.' He smiled at the rest. 'I mean all of you.'

The laughter and the catcalls died as a silver coin appeared between Corbett's fingers. 'For the moment, my beauties, accept my profound apologies for being unable to give you my custom, but this silver piece,' he gazed round the group, 'this silver piece is for anyone who can provide information about the death of Agnes. You know, the girl killed in the church near Greyfriars.'

The whores now shrank back like a group of frightened children.

'I mean no harm,' Corbett continued gently. 'I am the King's man. I work with the under-sheriff, Alexander Cade.'

'You mean Big Lance!' the tub of lard shouted back.

Corbett stared at her curiously.

'Oh, yes, that's what we call him. A good jouster, Master Cade. I can tell you.'

A young girl, no more than fifteen or sixteen summers, her thin bony body dressed in rags, pushed her way to the front. 'I can tell you about Agnes.'

Corbett held the silver coin before her eyes. 'I am waiting, child.'

The girl smiled; her pallid, white face suddenly looked pathetic and vulnerable. For a few seconds her eyes lost their watchful hardness.

'Down there,' the girl pointed. 'Next to the apothecary. Agnes had a garret.' She wiped her runny nose on the back of her hands. 'She always claimed to be better than any of us. Oh, yes, a regular lady with her own chamber and her fine gowns.'

'What else do you know?'

'Agnes became frightened. She said she had seen something.' The girl's mouth became slack and she shook her head. 'I don't know what but it was after one of the other girls was killed. Anyway, she refused to go out. She paid one of the boys, an urchin, to watch the door.' She shrugged. 'That's all I know.' Her grimy hand came out. 'Please, sir,' she whispered eagerly. 'May I have the coin?'

Corbett pressed it into her hand, and, unsheathing his dagger, he walked away down the darkened alleyway. At the shop next to the apothecary's he stopped and stared up at the rotting wood and crumbling plaster, before knocking on the door. A toothless old hag answered, her eyes small black buttons in a yellowing, lined face. A regular nightbird, Corbett thought, one of the old hags who rented out chambers to street-walkers, took their money and turned a blind eye to what they did. Of course, at first, the old hag knew nothing but, when coins changed hands, she suddenly remembered everything. Corbett listened to her chatter. The hag told him nothing he hadn't already learnt from the whore but, for another coin, she showed Corbett Agnes's chamber. There was nothing there; the dead girl's possessions, together with every stick of furniture, had been moved and the clerk realised the old woman was just playing him like a landed fish.

Outside in the street, Corbett leaned against the wall of the house and stared around. The place was filthy. He glimpsed things in the sewer, floating on top of the greenish water, which made his stomach turn and he pinched his nose at the terrible smell from the refuse piled high against the walls. He felt sure he was being watched and glanced cautiously up the narrow alleyways which fed into Cock Lane. He walked a little way up the street, his hand against the wall of the house, pulling it away quickly as his fingers touched something warm and furry. He turned, muttering a curse at the rat which scuttled between the crevices, then walked back to the apothecary's. Yes, he had seen it: the small shadow in one of the alleyways.

'This is going to be an expensive morning,' he murmured. He took another coin out of his purse and held it up. 'I know you are there, boy!' he called out. 'You still watch the house don't you? I mean no harm.' He spoke softly, wishing to avoid the prostitutes still gathered at the mouth of Cock Lane and the hungry-eyed faces which peered down from the casement windows. 'Come here, boy!' Corbett urged. 'You will be well rewarded.'

The beggar lad crept out of the alleyway. He was barefoot, his face so thin his large eyes made him look like some baby owl frightened by the light. He nervously plucked at the rough sacking which served as a cloak. He thrust his little hand forward.

'Thank you, sir.'

The voice was reedy and Corbett recognised the professional beggar. The poor child was probably despatched on to the streets by his parents to beg for alms. Corbett crouched in the doorway of the apothecary's shop and waved the lad forward. The boy, wary of the dangers of the street, edged cautiously near, his eyes glued on the silver piece. Corbett quickly reached out, seized the boy's thin arm and felt a twinge of compassion. All skin and bone; how long, he thought, would this child last in the next severe winter?

'Come on!' he urged swiftly. 'I mean you no harm. Look, here's a silver piece. I'll give you another if you tell me the truth.'

The boy sucked the knuckle of his free hand.

'You knew Agnes, the girl who died?'

The boy nodded.

'What was she frightened of?'

'I don't know.'

'Why did she stay in her room?'

'I don't know.'

'What do you know?'

'A man came.'

'What kind of man?'

'A priest, a brother. He was tall and wore a cowl, but he left very quickly.'

'And what else happened?'

'Agnes gave me a message.'

'What was it?'

'Just a scrap of parchment, sir. I was to take it to Westminster.'

'To whom?'

'I don't know.' The large eyes welled with tears. 'I did something wrong. I didn't mean to but I was hungry. I dropped the message in a sewer and spent the money the girl gave me at a bread shop.'

Corbett smiled. 'Can you read?'

'No, but Agnes could write. She was clever. She could read a few words and write some. She said if I kept guarding her door she would teach me one day.'

'But you don't know to whom the message was to be sent?'

'I think it was to a woman?'

'Why?'

'Because Agnes told me to take it to the Chapter House late in the afternoon.' The boy screwed his face up. 'Agnes said she would know.'

'Is that all?'

'Yes, Master, honestly. Please,' the boy whined, 'let go my wrist. You promised me a coin.'

Corbett handed it over, the boy scampered away.

'If you are ever hungry,' Corbett called out, watching the pathetic stick-like legs, 'come to Corbett's house in Bread Street. Tell the servants the master sent you.'

The boy turned, running like the wind up one of the dark runnels.

Corbett got to his feet and walked back, stopping at a small tavern near the bridge over Holborn. He went inside, ordered a jug of ale and sat beneath the room's only window. In the far corner a group of tinkers were baiting a huge, slavering bull mastiff, enraging it by offering it meat, then pulling it away so the dog's sharp teeth narrowly missed their darting fingers. Corbett watched their cruelty and thought about the beggar boy, Agnes's dreadful death and the hideous awfulness of the whores in Cock Lane. Was Brother Thomas right? he reflected. Did the stinking rottenness of the city spawn some of the evil which stalked the streets? He sipped at the blackjack, trying to close his mind to the growling of the dog and the taunts of the tinkers. So, Agnes had seen something? She had hidden away in her chamber and been visited by a man dressed like a monk or priest. Was that the killer? If so, why hadn't he struck then? Because the house was being watched? But surely Agnes would refuse to open the door?

The latter was the most logical, he concluded. So why had the man gone to that house in Cock Lane? Of course, Corbett put the tankard down, Agnes had been lured to her death; the killer had probably slipped her a message, perhaps in someone else's name, telling her to meet him in that church near Greyfriars. Corbett ran his fingers round the rim of the tankard and tried to sketch out the bare details behind the murder. Agnes had known something so she had hidden away, sending messages to someone who would help, one of the Sisters of St Martha, Lady Fitzwarren or maybe de Lacey but the boy had dropped it. He closed his eyes, what next? Somehow the killer had known that Agnes posed danger so he had visited her chamber. The message he had left had been cryptic; the poor girl, barely literate, was not skilled enough to distinguish different handwriting and the rest would be simple. Agnes would have gone to the church looking for salvation and the killer would have been waiting.

Corbett suddenly looked up at the screams and yells coming from the far corner of the tap room. He smiled to himself. Sometimes justice was done, for the bull mastiff had broken loose, seized one of his tormenter's arms and the tap-room door was already splattered with blood. Corbett drained his blackjack and left the noisy confusion behind. He had one further call to make and followed the street up through the city limits round by the Priory of St John of Jerusalem to the other side of Smithfield. Here he asked directions from a water tippler for the whereabouts of Somerville's House. The fellow knew it well and Corbett, keeping well away from the crowds thronging down to Smithfield, crossed Aldersgate into Barbican Street.

The Somerville House was a splendid building though its windows were now all shuttered and great folds of black lawn had been nailed to the wooden beams as a sign of mourning. A tearful maid opened the door and ushered him up to a small but opulently furnished solar on the second floor. The room reminded Corbett of how Maeve had beautified his own house in Bread Street though this chamber looked unkempt as if it hadn't been cleaned for days. Wine stains marked the table and some of the tapestry-covered chairs. The hangings on the wall looked dusty and dishevelled whilst the fire had not been lit or the grate cleaned.

'You wanted to see me?'

Corbett turned and stared at the young man standing in the doorway.

'My name is Gilbert Somerville. The maid said you were Sir Hugh Corbett, King's Emissary.'

The young man offered a limp handshake. Corbett stared at the black, dishevelled hair, the white puffy cheeks, red-rimmed eyes and slack mouth and jaw. A wine toper, Corbett concluded. A son grieving for his mother but someone who loved his claret to the exclusion of everything else.

'I am sorry.' The young man tugged at his fur-lined robe as he ushered Corbett to a seat. 'I slept late. Please sit down.' The young man scratched his stubbled cheek. 'My mother's funeral was yesterday,' he murmured. 'The house is still not clean, I . . .' his voice trailed away.

'My condolences, Master Gilbert.'

'*Sir* Gilbert,' the young man interrupted.

'My condolences on your mother's death, Sir Gilbert. But I believe you returned in the early hours of Tuesday, May twelfth, found your mother not in her chamber and organised a search?'

'Yes. The servants found her near the scaffold at Smithfield.'

'Before her death did your mother act, or speak, out of character?'

'My mother hardly ever spoke to me so I left her alone.'

Corbett saw the anger and the hurt in the young man's eyes.

'She's gone now,' Corbett replied gently. 'Why such a discord between a mother and her only son?'

'In her eyes I was not my father.'

No, no, you're not, Corbett thought. He had vague recollections of the elder Somerville. A tall, brisk fighting man who had given the kingdom good service in the closing years of the Welsh wars. Corbett vaguely remembered seeing him, striding through the chancery offices, or arm-in-arm with the King in some camp, or walking the corridors of a castle or palace.

'Does the proverb "The cowl does not make the monk" mean anything to you?'

Somerville pulled a wry mouth. 'Nothing at all.'

'Did your mother have any confidants here in her household?'

The young man looked sourly at Corbett. 'No, she did not, she was of the old school, Master Corbett.'

'*Sir Hugh* Corbett!'

'Touché!' the young man replied. 'No, Sir Hugh, my mother kept herself to herself, the only people she spoke to were the Sisters of the Order of St Martha.'

Corbett stared at the young man. 'So, you have no idea about the who, why or how of your mother's murder?'

'No, I do not.'

Corbett chilled at this arrogant young man's curt dismissal of his mother's violent death and stared around the chamber.

'Did your mother have any private papers?'

'Yes, she did but I have been through them. There's nothing there.'

'Don't you want vengeance for your mother's death?'

The young man shrugged one shoulder. 'Of course, but you are Sir Hugh Corbett, Keeper of the King's Secrets. I have every confidence in you, Clerk. You will find the killer. You resemble my father. You scurry about like the King's whippet, fetching this or carrying that. The killer will be found and I shall take a flagon of wine down to the Elms to watch the bastard hang.'

Corbett rose, kicking over the stool behind him.

'Sir Gilbert, I bid you adieu.' He turned and walked towards the door.

'Corbett!'

The clerk carried on walking, he reached the foot of the stairs before Somerville caught up with him.

'Sir Hugh, please.'

Corbett turned. 'I am sorry your mother's dead,' he said quietly. 'But, Sir, I find your conduct disgraceful.'

The young man's eyes slid away. 'You don't understand,' he murmured. 'Father did this! Father did that! Yes, my mother's dead. So what, clerk? In her eyes *I* was always dead.'

Corbett gazed at the young man and idly wondered if he had enough hate to commit murder. The young man's bleary eyes caught his.

'Oh, no!' he muttered. 'I can guess what you're thinking, Master Clerk. In my eyes my mother didn't exist so why should I kill her? But wait, I have something for you.' He ran up the stairs and returned a few minutes later with a scrap of parchment in his hands. 'Take this,' he mumbled. 'Study it and use it whatever way you wish. There's no further reason for you to stay or return.'

Corbett sketched a bow, closed the door behind him and left.

He reached St Martin's Lane before he stopped to examine the scrap of parchment. It was a list of clothing, probably drawn up by Lady Somerville in connection with her work at the abbey, but she had roughly etched crude drawings of monks with the hands joined as if in prayer. They were childish and clumsy except, now and again, instead of drawing the tonsured head of a monk, Lady Somerville had drawn the face of a crow, a fox, a pig or a dog. But what really fascinated him was that in the centre of this group, taller than the rest, was a figure dressed in a monk's habit and cowl, the hood pushed back to reveal the slavering jaws of a fierce wolf. Corbett studied the piece of parchment and tried to follow the logic of the dead woman's thoughts. Had she been listing items from the laundry and this had jolted a memory? Corbett shook his head.

'Whatever it is,' he mumbled, 'the Lady Somerville's perception of our brothers at Westminster left a great deal to be desired.'

'What's that? What's that?'

Corbett stared as a small beggar woman, holding a battered wooden doll, jumped up and down in front of him.

'What's that? What's that?' she repeated. 'Do you like my baby?'

Corbett gazed around and realised the crowds were thronging about him. He tossed a penny at the beggar woman and walked briskly back to Bread Street.

Corbett sensed the confusion as soon as he entered his house. He heard the shrieks from the solar, recognising the clear but powerful voice of Ranulf's young son. Griffin dolefully confirmed the news: Ranulf and Maltote were busy playing with the young boy and were supposed to be looking after baby Eleanor whilst Lady Maeve was in the garden. Corbett followed him out. Maeve was busy amongst the lilies and marigolds, roses and gillyflowers. He stood and watched her. She was busy talking to the maid Anna and, in the dying sunlight, Corbett stood under the porch and admired how Maeve had transformed an overgrown moorland into a beautiful garden with gravel paths, sapling apple trees and climbing vines along a wall which caught the sun. Further down, beyond where a small orchard would grow, Maeve had directed the builders to erect a great white-washed dovecote next to a long row of beehives. Maeve turned as if she sensed his presence.

'Hugh! Hugh! Come here! Look!' She pointed towards the ground. 'The herbs have lasted.'

Corbett gazed at the mustard, parsley, sage, garlic, fennel, hyssop and borage she had planted the previous year.

'You see!' Maeve cried triumphantly. 'They have grown.' She turned, her beautiful face flushed with the heat and exertions from her work. 'If all goes well, at Michaelmas we'll have more than salt to flavour the meat.' She narrowed her eyes. 'You look tired, Hugh?' Maeve took off the thick woollen gloves she was using and handed a small trowel to Anna who had been helping her weed amongst the sprouting herb beds. 'Come.' She wiped her brow on the back of her hand. 'A cool tankard of ale. Anna and I have prepared supper.'

By the time he had washed and refreshed himself, Corbett felt better though the evening meal was a riotous one. Young Ranulf shouted all the way through and baby Eleanor, supposedly asleep in her cot, gurgled with laughter at his antics before bawling for her own food, pieces of sugar-loaf soaked in milk. Any conversation was impossible, for Ranulf had regained his good humour – too quickly, Corbett thought suspiciously – and insisted on telling everyone about Maltote's recent clumsiness with a dagger. At last the meal ended, Corbett snapping that Maeve and Ranulf should join him in the solar.

'Your day went well, Ranulf?' he asked innocently, closing the door behind him.

'Yes, yes, it did.'

Corbett gazed round the beautiful room. Maeve stared at him curiously as if she failed to understand her husband's irritation and bad temper.

'I am sorry,' Corbett muttered. 'But this problem seems to pose few solutions. The killer could be anyone. All I have established is that he wears a hood and a cowl.'

'So it could be a monk?' Ranulf interrupted.

'For God's sake, Ranulf!' Corbett snapped back. 'Every man in the city possesses a hood and cowl!' He settled himself on a stool. 'And what have you done?'

Ranulf grinned from ear to ear. Corbett groaned to himself.

'I used my initiative, Master. You may remember Lady Fitzwarren said we were welcome to view her work? Well, I paid a courtesy visit to the Lady Mary Neville.'

Maeve covered her mouth with her hand. Corbett stared down at the floor.

'The day is not yet done, Master. Lady Fitzwarren has issued an invitation for you to join her at the hospital of St Katherine by the Tower. Who knows,' Ranulf beamed, 'we might find out more.'

Corbett covered his face with his hands.

Chapter 8

Corbett raised his head and gazed furiously at Ranulf.

'I do not wish,' he roared, 'to be travelling round the city at the dead of night!' He glared at Maeve who stood behind Ranulf, pushing the cuff of her sleeve into her mouth to stop her laughter.

'But, Master, I thought it would help? We need to question both ladies, particularly Lady Mary. After all, she was the last person to see the Somerville woman alive.'

Corbett scuffed the toe of his boot on the carpet. Below, in the small hall, he could still hear Eleanor bawling and young Ranulf's shrieks of delight. He glared at Ranulf and then at Maeve. Perhaps, he thought, it was best if they left; the house was in turmoil; Maeve had her mind set on her uncle's imminent arrival and both children were in full voice. Corbett would have no peace and there were pressing matters to attend to.

'Fine,' he agreed. 'But send Maltote ahead of us. Before we visit the Sisters of St Martha, I wish to meet the following: William of Senche, Brother Adam Warfield and his fat friend, Brother Richard. Tell these three redoubtable characters from Westminster that they are to meet me at The Three Cranes tavern in The Vintry. They will object, they will make excuses, they will inform you about what duties they have to perform, they may even be drunk. Tell them I don't give a sod! They are summoned on the King's authority and either they come or they spend the next two weeks in the Fleet, be they priest, monk or parish official!'

Ranulf, grinning from ear to ear, scampered off. In his chamber he washed carefully, changed his robes and preened himself in the metal disc which served as a mirror. 'So far, so good,' he murmured. He could not forget the Lady Mary and she had been so welcoming when he had paid her a courtesy visit on behalf of his master earlier in the day. Of course, Ranulf had told Lady Mary that Corbett had sent him. He only hoped his master didn't interrogate the lady too closely, but, even in her dark house-gown, Lady Mary had been a vision of loveliness. She had sat opposite him in her small parlour serving him a cup of chilled Alsace wine and offering him sugared marzipan on a silver dish. Ranulf had acted his part, telling her how he was the son of a knight who had fallen on hard times. How he was now well placed in the Chancery, earned good fees and that he placed his good services entirely at her disposal. The Lady Mary had fluttered her eyelashes and he had trotted back to Bread Street like Galahad returning to Camelot.

Ranulf now pressed his damp hair into place and liberally sprinkled his doublet with rose water. He clambered downstairs to kiss his offspring good night and hustle a complaining Maltote out of the door and across to the tavern for their horses.

Corbett left the house an hour later, still disgruntled at Maeve's total absorption with her uncle's visit and nursing a sore elbow where young Ranulf, who had inveigled him into a short game in the buttery, had thrown his toy sword at him. 'A sad day,' Corbett grumbled, 'when a man can't find peace in his own home.'

Still muttering curses, he pulled his cloak around him and made his way across Trinity through the darkened streets to Old Fish Street and into The Vintry and the welcoming warmth of The Three Cranes tavern. He must have been there an hour, sitting in a darkened recess beside the great open hearth, before Ranulf and Maltote joined him, leading his three disgruntled visitors: William the Steward was half-drunk whilst the two monks looked peeved and red-faced at being unceremoniously dragged away from their evening meal. Corbett made them welcome and ordered tankards of watered ale for, by the looks of William's flushed face, bleary eyes and fiery red nose, if the steward took any more wine he would fall into a drunken stupor. The sacristan was the only one of the three who appeared to have his wits about him.

'We have been summoned here,' he drew his dark robes about him, 'without good cause or reason.'

Corbett made a face. 'Monk, the King has summoned you here. So, if you object, take it up with him.'

'What do you want?'

'Honest answers to honest questions.'

'I *have* answered your questions.'

'What's been happening at Westminster Abbey and Palace?'

'What do you mean?'

Corbett drew Somerville's drawing from his purse and tossed it at the sacristan, pushing the thick tallow candle closer so the monk could study it.

'What do you make of that, Adam of Warfield?'

The sacristan studied it. 'A crude drawing,' he snapped.

Corbett saw he was blustering and sensed his fear. Brother Richard leaned over and, bleary-eyed, also examined the drawing.

'Scandalous!' he mumbled. 'Whoever drew this offends the Church.'

'Lady Somerville drew it,' Corbett replied. 'A high-ranking member of the Sisters of St Martha. She worked in the vestry and laundry of the abbey. What did she discover, this widow of good repute, this pious noblewoman? What did she see which made her draw such a cruel parody of so-called "men of God"? Master William, perhaps you can help?'

The steward shook his head and Ranulf, sitting behind Corbett's visitors, smirked from ear to ear. He always enjoyed such occasions, when the so-called 'pious', the self-seeking, high and mighty, were brought to account. Corbett was forever quoting St Augustine: '*Quis custodiet custodes*?' 'Who shall guard the guards?' Ranulf was forever repeating it and he couldn't resist choosing this occasion to murmur it into the ear of Adam of Warfield. The monk turned, his lip curling like a dog.

'Shut up, knave!' he snarled.

'Enough!' Corbett ordered. 'Brother Adam, Brother Richard, Master William, did you know any of the whores recently murdered in the city?'

'No!' they chorused in unison.

'Do the names Agnes or Isabeau mean anything to you?'

Adam of Warfield shot to his feet. 'We are men of God!' he snapped. 'We are priests, monks bound by chastity. Why should we have anything to do with whores, prostitutes and courtesans?' He leaned over the table, his eyes glaring with hatred. 'Do you have any more questions, clerk?'

Corbett made a face. 'No,' he said slowly. 'But you still haven't answered the ones I have asked.'

'We don't know any whores.'

'And you know nothing about Lady Somerville's death?'

'No, we do not!' the monk shouted, disturbing the other drinkers.

'Or what she meant by "The cowl does not make the monk"?'

'Master Corbett, I am leaving. Master William, Brother Richard?'

The monk swept towards the door, his two tipsy companions staggering behind him. As the monk's robe swirled about him, Corbett caught a glimpse of his high-heeled, costly Spanish leather riding boots and the beautiful gilded spurs attached to the heels.

'Monk!' Corbett bellowed, now rising.

'What is it, clerk?'

'You also took a vow of poverty. You have eaten and drunk well before you came. Your companion, Brother Richard, is tipsy and you wear boots even the King himself would envy.'

'My business, clerk.'

Corbett waited until the priest was almost at the door.

'One last question, Adam of Warfield!'

The sacristan turned and leaned against the lintel, a smug smile on his face. After all, he had come to see this clerk, he had answered his questions and the matter was now ended.

'For God's sake, clerk, what is it?'

Corbett walked across the quiet tap room and grasped the half-open door. He pushed his face close to the monk's. 'Do you,' he hissed, 'know anyone called Richard Puddlicott?'

'No, I do not.' Warfield turned and walked into the tavern yard, slamming the door behind him.

Corbett rejoined his companions. Ranulf still smirking, Maltote, as usual, sitting, mouth half-open, he was still unused to his strange master dealing so brusquely with the great ones of the land. Corbett sat down and leaned back against the bench.

'You learnt nothing, Master?' Ranulf taunted slyly.

'No, I learnt three things. First, Adam of Warfield and his companions, or at least one of them, knew the dead whores. You see, Ranulf, although he was angry, Brother Adam never queried *why* I asked him. I never actually told him that Agnes and Isabeau were two whores, so why did he reach that conclusion?'

Ranulf's smile faded. 'Yes, yes, he did. And what else?'

'Secondly, something is going on in the abbey. I don't know what. Again, Adam of Warfield didn't ask me the reason for that question. Like any guilty man he wanted to keep his answers short and brief.'

'In other words,' Maltote interrupted like some schoolboy solving a problem, 'least said soonest mended!'

'Exactly!'

'What else?' Ranulf asked crossly, glaring at Maltote.

'More importantly . . .' Corbett looked across the tavern at a slattern in the corner clearing a table. 'Girl, come here!'

The serving girl hurried over. Corbett slipped a penny into the pocket of her dirty apron.

'Tell me, girl, do you know Richard Puddlicott?'

'No, sir, who is he?'

'It does not matter,' Corbett replied. 'I just wondered. You see,' Corbett murmured as the girl walked away, 'when I asked her about Puddlicott, she immediately answered my question with another one. Our good sacristan never did that about the whores, about their names, about what might be going on in the abbey and, most importantly, why I should be asking about a complete stranger named Richard Puddlicott.' Corbett drained his tankard, picked up his cloak and got to his feet. 'At last we have made some progress,' he murmured. 'But God knows where it will lead us.'

Corbett, Ranulf and Maltote hired a wherry from Queenshithe and made their way up river, disembarking at the Custom House near the Wool Quay. They walked along the riverside, past the darkening mass of the great Tower and out through open fields to where the lights of the hospital of St Katherine beckoned. Ranulf kept silent, sulking, for he always loved to catch his master out and matters were not helped by Maltote openly preening himself. At St Katherine's a porter let them through and took them across to the small church which stood next to the main hospital building.

'The Sisters always meet here,' he announced. 'I believe they've arrived already.'

Corbett pulled open the door and walked into the porch. The church was simple enough; a long, narrow, vaulted nave under a soaring hammer-beamed roof, a chancel screen at the far end and fat rounded pillars down each side of the nave. Most of the Sisters were already assembled. At first, Corbett and his companions were ignored as the ladies scurried around, lighting braziers, pushing long trestle tables together. On these they piled clean clothes and cut up long loaves of bread, putting out bowls of salt, dishes of dried meat and bowls of apples and pears sliced and covered with sugar. Lady Fitzwarren came in through a side door, smiled and waved at them. Behind her, Lady Mary looked coyly at Ranulf.

'You have come to watch, Sir Hugh?'

'Aye, Madam. But also to ask you some questions.'

Fitzwarren's smile faded. 'When I'm ready! When I'm ready!' she snapped. 'The wine jug's not yet out! I think the weather will change and we could have a busy night.'

Corbett and his companions had to sit on a bench and kick their heels before Fitzwarren and Lady Mary joined them.

'Well, Sir Hugh, what questions do you still have?'

Corbett caught the exasperation in her voice.

'First, Lady Mary, you were with Lady Somerville the night she died?'

The woman nodded.

'And you left St Bartholomew's, when?'

'About a quarter of an hour after Lady Somerville.'

'And you noticed nothing untoward?'

'Nothing at all. It was pitch dark. I hired a boy to carry a torch and made my way home to Farringdon.'

'Lady Fitzwarren, did you know any of the girls who died?'

'Some, but you must remember the victims were all petty courtesans. We tend to meet the most degraded.'

'Did you know Agnes, the girl killed in the church near Greyfriars?'

'Yes, I did, and strange you mention her name. After her death I had a garbled message from someone who knew her that she wanted to speak to me.'

'Who gave the message?'

Lady Fitzwarren shook her head. 'I meet so many girls, it was one of them.'

'So you never met Agnes?'

'Of course not!'

'Is there anything else, Lady Catherine?'

'Such as what?'

'Well, you meet in Westminster Chapter House. Have you noticed anything untoward in the abbey or palace?'

'Well, they're fairly deserted,' Lady Mary interrupted. 'The old abbot is ill and they have no prior, the King should really return to Westminster.'

Lady Fitzwarren stared at her companion, then back at Corbett.

'Sir Hugh, I think there is something you should know,' the woman lowered her voice as Lady de Lacey swept into the church as briskly as a March breeze. 'Over a year ago,' Lady Fitzwarren continued in a half-whisper, 'just after these terrible murders began, Lady Mary, here, heard a rumour, a story quite common amongst the street-walkers and courtesans, how certain girls had been taken to the abbey, or rather the palace, for parties and roistering which lasted all night.' The woman shrugged. 'You know how it is, Sir Hugh. A common occurrence. Royal palaces are often left deserted, especially in time of war. The stewards and officials become lazy and decide to amuse themselves at the expense of their betters.' She smiled thinly. 'I believe even Christ told parables about it.' Fitzwarren looked over her shoulder and waved at Lady de Lacey who was shouting for her attention. 'That's all I know, Sir Hugh. But, tell me, do you have any idea of who is responsible for these terrible murders?'

'No, my Lady, but I hope to prevent any more.'

'In which case I wish you well, Master Clerk.'

'Oh, Lady Catherine?'

'Yes?'

'Do you or the Lady Mary know anything about the French envoy, Sir Amaury de Craon? Or a man known as Richard Puddlicott?'

Both women shook their heads.

'De Craon means nothing to me,' Lady Fitzwarren answered quickly. 'But I have heard of Puddlicott. He's a villain, a trickster. Some of the street-girls talk about him with as much awe and respect as I would the King.'

Corbett nodded and watched the two women walk away. He sat down on the bench and glanced at Ranulf who appeared to be blind and deaf to everything except the Lady Mary Neville. Corbett blinked and looked away. He had seen Ranulf drunk, angry, sad, lecherous and maudlin but never lovelorn and he still found it difficult to accept that Ranulf was so love-struck. Corbett sighed and diverted his mind to what he had just learnt. Everything pointed to something amiss at Westminster. Lady Fitzwarren was right: it was quite common for officials in deserted royal palaces to spend their time roistering – on one occasion he had acted as a marshal of the royal household in bringing such malefactors to judgement – but did the solution to these terrible murders lie in such roistering? Had the monks of Westminster become involved in these all-night revelries? Had something happened and the murders been committed to silence clacking tongues and scandalous whispers?

The door of the hospital opened slowly and Corbett gazed speechlessly at the two harridans who staggered into the church; their clothes were mere rags around their emaciated bodies, their hair was thin and straggly, they looked like twin witches with their hooked noses, rheumy eyes and slack, slavering mouths. They chattered and cackled like half-wits, crawling towards the tables, snatching mouthfuls of bread and slurping noisily from pewter wine cups. The stench of their unwashed bodies drew even Ranulf from his reverie.

'Sweet Lord!' he muttered. 'We needn't wait until death, Master, to see visions of hell!'

Lady de Lacey noticed their revulsion and strode over.

'Master Corbett, how old would you say those women were?'

'They are ancient crones.'

'No, no. Both have yet to reach their thirty-fifth year. They are street-walkers raddled and ageing, rotting with disease, the discarded objects of men's lust.'

Corbett shook his head. 'I disagree.'

'What do you mean? Men have exploited them!'

'And they have exploited men – though, I suspect, where men had the choice, they had none.'

De Lacey stared at him shrewdly.

'So-called "good men" used these women,' Corbett continued. 'Upright citizens, burgesses who sit on the council, walk in the Guild processions, who go to Mass on Sundays, arm-in-arm with their wives, their children running before them.' Corbett shrugged. 'And such men are liars and their marriages are empty.'

'Most marriages are,' de Lacey retorted. 'A wife is like a chattel, a piece of land, a possession, a horse, a cow, a stretch of river.'

Corbett thought of Maeve and grinned. 'Not all wives.'

'The Church says so: Gratian wrote that women are subject to their husbands. They are their property!'

'The law of England,' Corbett replied, 'also says that a man guilty of treason should be hanged, drawn and quartered but that does not mean it is right.' He smiled at de Lacey. 'You should read St Bonaventure, my Lady. He says "between husband and wife there should be the most singular friendship in the world".'

De Lacey's harsh face broke into a genuine smile. 'Ah,'

she replied as she turned away, 'and if pigs flew, there would be plenty of pork in the trees!'

Corbett watched her go over and talk gently to one of the old crones.

'She's formidable,' Ranulf muttered.

'Most saints are, Ranulf. Come, let us go.'

Later that night Corbett lay beside a sleeping Maeve in their great four-poster bed, staring up at the dark tapestry awning above him. He had chased the problems facing him round and round his tired mind but, though he had suspicions, there were no firm conclusions, nothing he could really grasp. He remembered the sights at St Katherine's, the two ancient street-walkers, Lady de Lacey's gentle care and his remarks that a man and wife should be the best of friends. He glanced at Maeve sleeping quietly beside him. Was this true? he wondered. Strange; he kept remembering Mary, his first wife, and the memories had become more distinct after his meeting with the Lady Neville. Corbett closed his eyes, he couldn't go down that path, the past was best left alone. He chewed his lip and wondered what to do when this business was over. He had seen the filth, the degradation of the street-walkers. Perhaps he should do something and not just turn up his nose and walk on the other side of the street. In France, he thought, at least they tried to control the situation, an official known as the King of Riddles imposed some sort of order and afforded a little protection to the ladies of the night. In Florence, action was more drastic, brothels were controlled by the city authorities who actually appointed clerks to work in what was termed 'the Office of the Night'. But surely the Church could do something apart from just condemn? Hospitals, refuges? He must advise the King that something should be done, but what? Corbett's mind drifted sleepily over the possibilities.

At the very moment their master was slipping into sleep, Maltote and Ranulf, with rags wrapped round their boots to muffle their footsteps, stole downstairs, unlocked the side door and crept out into the darkened street. Ranulf ordered Maltote to keep his mutterings and curses to himself as they slipped along Bread Street where Ranulf had hidden a nosegay of roses in a small crevice in the alleyway. He had stolen these earlier from a merchant's garden in West Cheap. Ranulf sighed with relief, the flowers were undisturbed, and they continued on up the alleyways, passages and runnels to the old city wall, past the Fleet prison and into Shoe Lane where Lady Mary Neville lived. Ranulf refused to let Maltote even whisper, keeping a wary eye on the watch and one hand on his dagger against the footpads, cutpurses and sturdy beggars who prowled the night looking for prey.

Outside the darkened house, Ranulf stopped and, using his old skills as a burglar, carefully edged up the wall, securing footholds in the white lathed plaster and on the rim of the supporting black beams; hissing and muttering, he told Maltote to climb on a lower window sill and hand up the roses the young messenger was forlornly holding. Ranulf worked expertly, using the many holds and gaps in the plaster around the window sill of what he guessed to be Lady Mary's bedchamber, until the whole area was circled by a garland of roses. Some would fall but Ranulf had taken enough to intrigue and fascinate this only love of his life. He then jumped down, laughing softly and, with Maltote in tow, hurried back to Bread Street.

In another part of the city, Hawisa, a young courtesan, recently arrived in London from Worcester, tripped along Monkwell Street near Cripplegate. She had spent the evening comforting an elderly merchant in the room behind his shop whilst his wife and family had gone on a pilgrimage to St Thomas of Canterbury. Hawisa lifted the hem of her murrey skirt, taking great care as she picked her way round the mounds of refuse, jumping and giggling with fright as the rats scurried back to their holes. At last she reached the end house built against the old crumbling city wall and the basement cellar the wool merchant had bought for her. Hawisa was tired and so glad to be home in a chamber which she had decorated and furnished to suit her own comfort. She put the key in the lock, turned it, then froze as she heard a sound behind her. Another rat? Or someone else? She stopped, certain it was a footfall she had heard in the street above her. She stepped out of the porch and looked back up the darkened steps. Nothing. She went back and fumbled with her key then started as she felt a light touch on her shoulder.

'Hawisa,' the voice whispered, 'I have been waiting for you!'

Hawisa smiled, face up, just as the killer's knife swept towards her neck, ripping it in one long, bloody gash.

Chapter 9

Corbett was breaking his fast in the buttery early next morning when the entire house was disturbed by a pounding at the door. He anticipated the news even as he swung the door open and saw the under-sheriff, Alexander Cade, dishevelled and unshaven, standing there.

'There's been another murder, hasn't there?' Corbett said softly.

'Yes, about four hours ago. A prostitute named Hawisa was killed outside her own tenement.'

Corbett waved him in. 'The dead will wait for a while,' he murmured. 'You have broken your fast?'

Cade shook his head. Corbett led him into the kitchen and seated him at a table, pushing a bowl of wine and a trancher of dried meat and fresh brown loaves towards him. Cade ate and drank voraciously, wolfing the food down whilst Corbett watched him curiously: despite his hunger, the under-sheriff seemed upset.

'Did you know Hawisa?' Corbett asked as a bleary-eyed Ranulf and Maltote slipped into the buttery. The under-sheriff looked up, his half-open mouth full of bread and meat. Corbett knew he had caught him unawares. 'You did know her, didn't you?'

Cade nodded. 'Yes,' he mumbled. 'I knew the girl, but that's my business!'

Ranulf and Maltote sat on the bench beside him.

'Master Cade, a moment. Ranulf, I must speak to you.'

Outside in the passageway Corbett grasped Ranulf by the front of his jerkin. 'You left the house last night, didn't you?'

'Yes, Master. But, as Master Cade said, that's my business!'

'When you leave the door off the latch, you make it mine!' Corbett snarled. 'I have enough enemies in this city without extending a public invitation to every felon and footpad, not to mention some red-handed killer of the night!' He pushed Ranulf against the wall. 'Where did you go? The Lady Mary Neville's?'

'Yes, I did!' Ranulf glared back.

'She's a Lady and a widow!'

'And what am I?' Ranulf snapped. 'Some commoner? Am I to know my true station in life, Master?' Ranulf stepped closer. 'Or would you like her for yourself, Master? Is that it? I have seen the way you look at her.'

Corbett's hand flew to his dagger and Ranulf grasped the hilt of his.

'I have served you long, Master,' Ranulf continued quietly. 'And I have served you well. God knows who my father was whilst my mother was the daughter of a peasant farmer. She had aspirations but not the talent to match. Believe me, I have both. One day I will kneel in front of the King.' Ranulf jutted his chin forward. 'I shall be knighted!'

Corbett let his hands fall away and leaned against the wall of the passageway. 'God save us, Ranulf!' he murmured. 'Here we are, hands on daggers! Do what you wish. We have other business at hand.'

They collected Cade and a half-sleeping Maltote from the buttery and walked down a deserted Bread Street and up into Cheapside. The great thoroughfare was empty, only a lonely friar, a chasuble across his shoulder, and a sleepy-eyed boy carrying a lighted taper, hurried along with the viaticum for the sick. Dogs and cats fought over mounds of litter. Two members of the city watch staggered by as drunk as the roisterers they hunted. Corbett stared up at the grey sky.

'Where is the girl's corpse, Master Cade?'

'It's already been moved to St Lawrence Jewry. We put it on one of the dung carts.'

'Who found it?'

'A member of the watch.' Cade looked away and spat. 'He heard the dogs snarling and bickering over the body.' Cade tightened his lips to stop himself retching. 'God save us!' he whispered. 'The curs were licking and drinking her blood!'

Corbett breathed a silent prayer. 'There's little point in going to the place,' he said. 'Was the girl killed in her room?'

'Oh, no, just outside. She had the key in the lock when the killer struck.'

'Shall we go to St Lawrence Jewry?'

'Master Corbett, I have to attend to other matters first. Would you wait?' Cade tapped his pouch hopefully. 'I asked my clerk to make a search of the records. He has drawn up a memorandum on what we know about Puddlicott.'

Corbett smiled. 'Let's attend to your business first, Master Cade.'

The under-sheriff took him up to the Great Stocks near the Conduit where soldiers wearing the blue and mustard livery of the city, had assembled the felons and night-walkers in order to carry out the day's punishments. As Corbett arrived, a cleric caught in the arms of a burgess's wife was being led away, preceded by a man playing the bagpipes.

'He's to walk six times to Newgate and back, bare-arsed,' Cade explained. 'His breeches round his ankles!'

The soldiers roared with laughter as the poor unfortunate was led away. Cade had to see to the ordering of other punishments. A counterfeit man who had purchased two satin cloaks for five pounds; on the excuse of taking one away to show a friend, the man had paid a quarter of a noble, offering as a deposit fifteen similar coins tied up in a purse. The shopkeeper had accepted this, and only when the fellow had gone did he find the coins were mere counters. Another, a cobbler had claimed he could find stolen goods by using a loaf with knives pressed in each side. Now the knives dangled round the man's neck and, as he was clasped into the pillory, the loaf, soaked in horse's urine, was rubbed into his face. The punishments continued. A blasphemer had to carry three pounds of wax to a church in Southwark. A man pretending to be dumb, so he could beg for alms, had the tip of his tongue burnt with a red-hot poker. Corbett got tired of the summary punishments and walked away.

He had to wait almost an hour in a nearby tavern until Cade's duties were done then they all made their way to St Lawrence Jewry. Maltote, now fully awake, eagerly whispered with Ranulf how pleased the Lady Mary would be when she woke up and found the roses. Corbett overheard them and hoped she would, otherwise Ranulf could find himself alongside the felons they had just left in the stocks. He stole a glance at Cade who was still quiet and rather nervous.

'I must ask you some questions, Alexander,' Corbett whispered so that Ranulf and Maltote could not overhear.

'Such as?'

'Did you know any more of the girls who were killed?'

Cade shook his head and stared away.

When they reached St Lawrence Jewry, Cade summoned the fat little priest who, protesting at the early hour, opened the small death house, grumbling that he was tired of having to bury one whore after another. He only shut up when Cade brutally reminded him that the city paid him good silver for his services. Corbett took one quick look at the corpse inside, the great purple slash across her neck, the horrible mutilations in the groin, and walked back into the fresh air.

'I agree with you, Priest!' he called out, 'Having to look at seventeen such corpses would try the patience of a saint!'

The priest, still wary of Corbett since their last meeting, shook his head.

'Sixteen!' he squeaked. 'She is the sixteenth!'

Corbett noticed Cade's face suddenly pale.

'No, no,' Corbett queried. 'She is the seventeenth victim, or eighteenth if we include the Lady Somerville.'

The priest shrugged and waddled back into his house; he returned, carrying a huge, purple-dyed ledger.

'This is the church's burial book,' he explained, opening the yellowing pages. He turned to the back. 'Here are those given a pauper's grave. I have starred the names of the victims – the whores killed over the last few months.'

Corbett took the book and scanned the pathetic entries. An old man who had died in the stocks; a young boy who had fallen from a belfry; a tinker killed in Floodgate Lane. Interspersed with these, each with a star next to the name, were the prostitutes who had been killed. Corbett walked away, ignoring the priest's protests. He placed the book on top of a crumbling tombstone, took from his wallet the list of victims provided by the under-sheriff and compared the two. Cade now stood far away with his back turned, whilst Maltote and Ranulf lounged against the wall watching the sun rise. Corbett scrutinised both lists carefully. He then closed the book and gave it back to the priest.

'Thank you, Father. You will probably never know how valuable that book is. Ranulf! Maltote!' he called. 'Stay where you are! Master Cade, come with me!'

Whilst the priest scurried away Corbett led Cade around to the back of the church. Once alone, Corbett pushed the under-sheriff against the wall, one hand grasping Cade's throat, the other pushing a dagger tip into the soft part of the under-sheriff's neck just under his right ear.

'Now, Master Cade,' Corbett whispered. 'No lies, no fables. What's gone on here? Eh? According to your list, a whore named Judith, living in Floodgate Lane, was supposed to have been killed six weeks ago!'

The under-sheriff's mouth opened and closed. Corbett banged his head gently against the wall.

'Don't lie, Master Cade. You are responsible for all burials. What happened to this woman's corpse?' Corbett smiled thinly. 'Oh, by the way, you're well known by the prostitutes in the city.'

Cade gasped. 'I'll tell you,' he grated. 'Take your hand away and sheath your knife, Sir Hugh. Sooner or later the truth would be out.'

Corbett sheathed his knife and put it away as Maltote and Ranulf suddenly appeared.

'I told you to wait!' Corbett shouted. 'Now, go back!'

The under-sheriff, rubbing his neck, crouched on a stone plinth jutting out from the church wall.

'Yes, yes,' he began. 'I knew some of the murdered girls.

I am a bachelor, Sir Hugh. All I have are the clothes on my back and the fees of my office. I take no bribes, I never look the other way but, like any man, I get lonely. The blood boils within me and a fair face and a soft body, any face, any body will be solace enough. I knew the last girl, Hawisa, as well as others, Mabel, Rosamund, Gennora, but Judith was my favourite. You see, Master Corbett, she was attacked but not killed. I took care of her but put her name on that list to protect her.'

'You what?' Corbett gasped. 'You mean to say there is a girl still living who survived an attack by this insane killer?'

'She saw very little,' the under-sheriff muttered. 'She was frightened. She threatened she would tell others what she knew about me and other city officials unless she was protected.'

'So where is she now?'

'I lodged her at the Friars Minoresses near the Tower. The good sisters agreed to look after her.' Cade wiped his mouth on the back of his hand. 'That is until I raise enough money to send her south to one of the Cinque Ports.'

'Well, Master Cade, we'd best go there.'

They collected a mystified Ranulf and Maltote and made their way down to the Guildhall where they borrowed horses to continue their journey through the half-waking streets to Aldersgate and out into open countryside. They turned south through lush fields, past dairy farms to where the grey flagstoned building of the Friars Minoresses lay nestling amongst woods and fields.

The Sisters, who followed the rule of St Clare, were welcoming enough, always eager to see visitors, especially males. They fussed and clucked round Corbett's party like a group of mother hens. The clerk had to pay the usual courtesies of joining them in the small refectory for bread and ale before Cade asked to see 'his dear sister, Judith', in one of the guest rooms.

The good Sisters agreed but Corbett caught their coy glances and hidden smiles. Whatever the under-sheriff claimed, the nuns were not as innocent as they seemed and had more than a vague idea of Judith's true calling. A young novice was immediately despatched to prepare the girl. Ranulf and Maltote were left in the cloister gardens with strict orders to behave themselves and Corbett and Cade went to the white-washed cell where Judith was waiting. She was a plump, red-headed, pleasant-looking girl, dressed in a dark brown smock, tied closely at the neck. She greeted Cade warmly, kissing him on both cheeks and pressing his hand, but the dark rings round her eyes betrayed her anxiety.

'The nuns still think I am your sister,' she said pertly.

'And why do they think you are here?' Corbett asked.

'You know who I am, sir, but who are you?' she retorted archly.

Corbett smiled, apologised and introduced himself.

'And now my question?' he repeated.

'The nuns,' Cade intervened, 'think Judith is my sister who was attacked by a house breaker.'

'And the truth?'

The girl smiled and looked away. 'I am Master Cade's doxy,' she replied. 'I had a chamber above a shop in Floodgate Lane. Master Cade used to visit me there. I had,' she continued, her voice rising, betraying a faint sing-song accent, 'I had other friends. I lived a good life. I heard of the murders but I thought someone was settling a grudge.' She sat down on the room's one and only stool. 'Then one night,' she continued, 'I came back late and climbed the outside stairs to my chamber. I often left my door open for my pet cat. I went in and lit a candle.

I had a large cupboard, a gift from a carpenter, where I hung my gowns. I heard a sound and, because I couldn't see the cat, thought the poor animal had got trapped inside.' Judith stopped speaking and laced her fingers together. 'I'll never forget it,' she whispered. 'I picked up the candle and opened the cupboard door. I think it was the candle which saved me. I saw a dark figure, the glint of steel and, as I stepped back, the knife cut me.' The girl undid the lacing at the neck of her dress and pulled it low to reveal a long, angry red welt which ran from shoulder to shoulder beneath her neck. 'I screamed even as the blood pumped out, then I swooned. Someone must have heard me. Master Cade was sent for.' She glanced up at Corbett. 'I think you know the rest?'

'I thought it best if the killer believed she had died,' Cade added.

'So you must have seen something?' Corbett asked.

The girl made a face. 'Who would believe me?'

'What did you see?'

'I only caught a glimpse but I thought it was a monk.'

'Why's that?'

'The figure was cloaked, cowled and hooded but you see, Sir Hugh,' the girl smiled primly, 'when I held the candle up I caught a glimpse of the attacker's sleeve. It was the dark brown of a monk. I also saw something else.'

'Come on, girl, tell me!'

'As I drew away and the candle fell, I am sure I saw a white tasselled cord.' She looked up. 'Only a monk wears that.'

Corbett looked accusingly at Cade. 'That's why you were quiet when we went to Westminster Abbey and met the sacristan and his bosom friend. Only Benedictines wear brown habits. Don't you realise, Cade, the killer *must* be a monk!'

Cade banged his fist against the wall. 'Of course I realised!' he retorted. 'But who would believe a prostitute?' He looked at Judith's sad eyes. 'I am sorry,' Cade muttered, 'but that's what they'd say, a prostitute's word against a monk's and what proof would she have, Sir Hugh, except her own assessment? Any monk accused of a crime would have his brethren swearing mighty oaths that Brother So-and-So and Father This-or-That were elsewhere at the time of the attack.'

'You've never put it like that before,' the girl interrupted. 'You always said you had me here to protect me. You were protecting yourself!' She looked at Corbett. 'Before the under-sheriff continues,' she added, 'and asks me what motive a monk would have in attacking a whore, well I'll tell you, Sir Hugh. You will be the only person I have spoken to about it.'

Corbett crouched before the girl and held her fingers lightly.

'Tell me the truth,' he insisted. 'Tell me everything you know and I will catch the man who attacked you. I will give you protection, the King's own writ and a substantial reward. Yes,' he added as he saw the hopeful gleam in the girl's eyes. 'Good silver to go elsewhere and begin a new life. A small dowry, perhaps you can return to your village, marry and settle down.'

The girl gripped Corbett's fingers.

'You promise?'

Corbett raised his other hand. 'I swear by the King and by the sacrament, and my oath is a solemn one. You will be protected and rewarded.'

'About a year ago,' Judith began, 'in the late summer and early autumn, I and other girls were hired to go to the empty Palace of Westminster. We were paid good silver and taken down river by barge. We were led up

King's Stairs and into one of the chambers of the deserted palace. We went there at least a dozen times, indulging in the most riotous revelries. I have never seen anything like it. Wine poured like water, food stacked high on platters,' she smiled. 'But the light was always poor. We would be joined by men. One I recognised, I think he was Steward or Bailiff of the Palace, he was always drunk.'

'And who else?'

'Well, as I have said, the wine would flow like water. We'd take our clothes off, there'd be music and dancing. Our companions were always masked but I am sure,' the girl paused, 'I am sure some of them were monks from the nearby abbey.'

Corbett whistled through his teeth and glanced up at Cade. 'Hell's teeth, Cade! I've heard rumours of these revelries. Does anyone else in the city know about them?'

The under-sheriff had paled. 'There have been rumours,' he mumbled.

'When the King hears this,' Corbett continued, 'his rage can only be imagined.' He smiled at the girl and tightened his grip. 'Oh, not you, Judith. The King will have bigger fish to fry than you. You'll be safe.' He stared into the girl's frightened eyes. 'Who was the leader, the organiser of these parties?'

'I don't know. At first I thought it was the steward but he was a born toper. He was so drunk he couldn't do anything with the girls. No, there was another man. Tall, well built, his body muscular but he always wore a satyr's mask. It was he who made sure the rooms were in darkness, that the food was served, the wine poured and, most importantly, that by dawn we were out of the palace and back in some barge being rowed up river.'

'Do you know who he was?'

'No, he was always called "the Seigneur".'

'How do you know monks were involved?'

The girl laughed. 'Sir Hugh, I may be ignorant but if you work the streets of London you soon learn enough about men to fill a thousand pieces of parchment.' She shrugged. 'I know it was dark but the men's bodies were pampered, well fed. Anyway,' she chuckled, 'only monks have tonsures!'

Corbett grinned. 'So, they would be drinking, eating, dancing and—'

'Yes,' the girl interrupted with a smile. 'And the other. We'd separate into pairs, then a horn would be blown, fresh meats and full cups served and the revelry would go on until the early hours.'

'You said a year ago. Why did it suddenly stop?'

'I didn't say it did. All I think happened is that the Seigneur chose a different group of girls.'

'Ah!' Corbett got to his feet. 'Of course, just in case you or your companions became too knowing.'

'But why,' Cade interrupted, 'didn't anyone report this to the authorities?'

The girl looked at him pityingly. 'Alexander,' she replied. 'You are a good man but you're such a fool. Who was going to tell? The Seigneur and his coven? The girls? And so be deprived of good silver, food and drink? Who would dare?' She tossed her head. 'And, as you said, Alexander, who would believe us, whores and prostitutes!'

Corbett went to stand near the small casement window. He stared out at Ranulf and Maltote who sat in the green cloister garden warming themselves in the early morning sun, laughing and chuckling over their exploits of the previous evening.

'What you say, Judith,' he concluded, 'makes sense.

You think some monks from the abbey were involved in these all-night revelries. Perhaps one of them began to feel concerned, even threatened, and decided to remove the evidence?'

The girl nodded. 'I suppose so,' she replied. 'But there may be more than one killer, Sir Hugh. The deaths have occurred throughout the city.'

'Perhaps,' Corbett replied. 'But everything you say, Judith, fits the puzzle. First, Lady Somerville.' He glanced at the girl. 'She was one of the members of the Sisters of St Martha, brutally murdered at Smithfield. You have heard of the good Sisters?'

Judith nodded.

'Well,' Corbett continued, 'she had a very low opinion of monks. She was always quoting a proverb that the "cowl does not make the monk" and she drew some rather crude caricatures of them. Perhaps she knew about this debauchery and had to be silenced? Secondly, what has always puzzled me is how the killer could slip unobserved around the city and, of course, who would stop and question a monk? Thirdly, a monk was seen entering the house where one of the victims was found. Finally, everyone trusts a monk, which is why the victims always allowed their killer to get close.'

Corbett stared out of the window at the sunlit cloister garth. Of course, he thought, it also fits in with what Brother Thomas had said: perhaps the monk killed these girls, not only to silence them but because he felt guilty at what he had done and believed he was atoning for his sin by spilling their blood. What the old, mad beggar had said now also made sense: the gnarled toes of the devil were really the bare sandalled feet of the monk. And, of course, Lady Somerville would stop in the dark and greet a monk hurrying behind her.

'Father Benedict's death!' Cade interrupted excitedly. 'The old priest died because he saw or knew something about the midnight revelries of these monks. That's why he wanted to see me. And that's why he was murdered!'

Corbett leaned against the wall and nodded. But why, he thought, were these illicit parties organised? Who was this Seigneur? The girl admitted it was not William of Senche. Perhaps it was the sacristan Adam of Warfield? But why, why, why? Corbett stared at the grass, the dew twinkling like diamonds, and he suddenly went cold.

'Of course!' he shouted. 'Of course!'

He strode back to the girl and gripped her tightly by the wrist. 'Is there anything else you can tell me?'

'No, sir. No, I have told you all I can.'

'Good, then you will stay here. Cade, follow me!'

Corbett walked briskly out to where Ranulf and Maltote still sat in the cloisters.

'Ranulf! Maltote! Come on! Don't sit there like two love-lorn squires when there's treason and murder afoot!'

The two men scampered after him like rabbits. Corbett bade a swift farewell to a surprised Mother Superior, collected his horse and cantered out of the convent gates as if the devil himself was driving him.

They rode through the winding lanes, not pausing till they entered the narrow warren of streets in Petty Wales round the Tower where they stopped and dismounted at The Golden Turk tavern.

'No drinks for you, Master Cade, you have work to do!' Corbett drew a warrant from his wallet. 'Take this to the Constable of the Tower. Give him the compliments of Sir Hugh Corbett, Keeper of the King's Seal, and tell him in an hour I want three barges assembled at the Wool Quay. One for us, the other two full of royal archers. I want veterans; good men who will carry out any order I give them. No.' He shook his head at the under-sheriff's face. 'No explanations now. Just do it and come back here when everything is ready.'

He stood and watched Cade stride away.

'Master, what's wrong?'

'For the moment, Ranulf, nothing. I am hungry. I want to eat. You are welcome to join me.'

Inside the tavern, Corbett told Ranulf and Maltote to look after themselves but asked the greasy-aproned, bald-headed landlord for a chamber for himself.

'I want to be alone!' he declared. 'Bring me a cup of wine!' He sniffed the fragrant appetising aroma from the kitchen. 'What are you cooking, Master Taverner?'

'Meat pies.'

'Two of those!' Corbett nodded at a surprised Ranulf and followed the landlord upstairs.

The small bedchamber was clean, neat and well swept. For a while Corbett lay on the small truckle bed staring at the ceiling. The landlord returned with a tray bearing food and wine. Corbett ate and drank hungrily, trying to curb his own excitement for, at last, he had found a way forward. He unrolled the parchment Cade had given him and studied the information provided by the clerks on Richard Puddlicott. According to this, Puddlicott had had a fairly long and varied criminal career. He had been born in Norwich and had so excelled himself as a scholar, he had entered one of the Halls of Cambridge where he had taken a degree, as well as minor orders. He had then abandoned the life of a clerk for a more profitable calling as a trader in wool, cheese and butter. For a while he travelled abroad, visiting Ghent and Bruges but there his fortunes had changed for the worse. The English were forced to renege on loans from the Bruges merchants and Puddlicott had been one of those Englishmen seized in retaliation and forced to kick his heels in a Flemish gaol. At last he had escaped, killing two guards, with a festering grievance against Edward of England.

Puddlicott had returned to London and embarked upon a life of crime. He swindled certain goldsmiths in Cheapside; he defrauded a Lombard banker and stole valuables from churches. Yet his real skill was as a confidence trickster, being able to pose as whoever he wanted to in order to gain money through fales pretences. On a number of occasions law officers had laid him by the heels but Puddlicott, a master of disguise, had always escaped. Corbett sipped the wine and marvelled at this confidence trickster's prowess. No one was safe. Shrewd merchants, hardened officials, dewy-eyed widows, cunning soldiers, grasping tenant farmers, all had been victims of Puddlicott's fraudulent ways.

Corbett tensed as he looked at the list of dates. A government spy had heard of Puddlicott being in England the previous autumn. There were similar reports of fresh sightings in the spring, followed by the English spy's most recent communication of Puddlicott being seen in Paris. Corbett put the parchment down and lay back on the bed. Was it possible? he wondered. Was the Seigneur whom Judith had described, the master of nightly revels at Westminster Palace, none other than Richard Puddlicott? But why? The rogue might be showing his contempt of authority by debauching monks, consorting with whores? Corbett had a vague idea of the truth and there was only one way of establishing that. He heard a crashing on the stairs and Ranulf hammered on the door.

'Master! Master! Cade has returned, the barges are ready!'

Corbett rose, drained his wine cup, and made his way downstairs. He settled his bill with the landlord and strode out into the yard where Cade, still looking rather sheepish, waited, his great hands nervously clenching and unclenching.

'Everything ready, Master Cade?'

'Yes, Sir Hugh. They wait at the Wool Quay.'

'It's Westminster isn't it?' Ranulf shouted. He clapped his hands. 'It's those mischievous monks.' He nudged Maltote playfully. 'Now the fun begins,' he whispered. 'Wait until old Master "Long Face" exerts his power.'

Master 'Long Face', however, as Ranulf secretly described Corbett, was already striding down the alleyway towards the riverside. At the Wool Quay the three great barges were pulled in, waiting. An officer of the Tower garrison came forward to greet them.

'Sir Hugh, my name is Peter Limmer, sergeant-at-arms.' He waved at the barges full of archers dressed in leather sallets, steel conical helmets on their heads. Each was armed with sword, dirk and heavy crossbow.

'Good!' Corbett murmured. 'We go to Westminster and you will do exactly as I say.'

The lanky, crop-haired officer nodded. They clambered aboard. Orders rang out and the barges pulled out into mid-stream.

Chapter 10

The journey was a peaceful one, broken only by the sound of splashing oars, the creak of leather and the clink of armour. A heavy mist still hung over the river so Corbett felt cut off from the busy life of the city. Now and again they passed the occasional boat or ship. The silence was shattered when Limmer roared out orders to pull towards the centre of the arches under London Bridge which provided wider space to shoot through. Here the water frothed around the great starlings built to protect the river craft from the massive stone columns of the bridge. Oars were pulled in and the barges shot under the bridge and into calmer waters. The mist still hung heavy as they turned the bend to go down towards Westminster. The oarsmen feverishly pulled to one side when the great gilt-edged prow of a Venetian galley suddenly broke through the mist bearing down on them. Otherwise, the journey was uneventful. They rowed to the northern bank, the mist now thinning, and they glimpsed the tower and turrets of Westminster.

They disembarked at King's Stairs; orders rang out and the archers, organised in two columns, marched behind Corbett and his companions. They swung through the gardens, surprising the odd, sleepy-eyed servant, and across the palace yard into the abbey grounds. A side door to the abbey was open. Corbett, leaving the military escort outside, walked into the deserted side of the nave. It was dark and cold.

'Bring benches!' he ordered Limmer, pointing further down the aisle towards the south transept. 'I want a bench placed up there against the wall and a chair opposite. I then want the following brought: Master William of Senche, he'll probably be drunk.' Corbett sniffed the still fragrant scent of incense. 'Then go to the abbey refectory. And, whatever they say, arrest Adam of Warfield the sacristan and Brother Richard and bring them here. I want an armed guard left outside and all entrances to the abbey and palace sealed. No one is to leave or enter without my permission.'

'William of Senche will be easy,' the officer replied. 'But the monks may accuse us of blasphemy; trespassing on church property and violation of their clerical orders.' The soldier grinned sourly. 'I don't want some priest shouting Thomas à Becket's martyrdom is being re-enacted, nor do I want my men being cursed and excommunicated by bell, book and candle!'

'Nothing will happen,' Corbett replied. 'This is no clash between Church and King, but between law officers and proven criminals.'

'They are monks.'

'They are still criminals and, Master Limmer, I shall prove that. I assure you, when this business is over and the King knows your part in it, you will be praised and rewarded. As for Holy Mother Church, she will be only too pleased to see justice done and be too busy looking after her own affairs.'

The officer grinned and hurried out, shouting orders at his men.

'And us, Master?'

'You, Ranulf, together with Maltote, stay here near the side door. Only approach me if any of those I interrogate use violence, or threaten to, though I don't suppose they will.'

Corbett walked up the aisle into the south transept where archers had already rearranged the bench and dragged a chair from the Lady Chapel for Corbett. The clerk sat down and breathed a silent prayer that he'd be proven right. Despite his brave words to the soldier, Corbett felt nervous and uneasy. If his allegations were proved false and his theory collapsed, then he would have a great deal of explaining to do, both to the bishops as well as to the King.

Corbett heard shouting and muttered oaths outside the abbey. The door crashed open and a group of archers entered, led by Limmer, with three struggling figures held fast by the arms. Corbett got to his feet. Adam of Warfield seemed on the verge of apoplexy. His sallow face had tinges of anger high in his cheeks, his eyes blazed with fury and Corbett saw traces of white froth at the sides of his mouth.

'You will answer for this, clerk!' the monk roared. 'I will see you excommunicated by our Order! By the hierarchy of England, by the Pope himself!' He struggled and broke free of the grinning archers on either side of him and turned to face his tormentors. 'All of you!' he bellowed. 'All of you are damned! This is sacred property, the King's own abbey! And this man,' he turned, flinging out an accusing finger at Corbett, 'is a limb of Satan!'

Corbett glanced at Brother Richard and took heart at what he saw. The little, fat monk seemed apprehensive, his eyes constantly shifting, his small, pink tongue popping in and out of his mouth, licking his lips. Next to him, the steward William of Senche had been frightened into sobriety. At last Adam stopped shouting and stood, chest heaving, hands hanging down by his side. Corbett stared at the brown cowl and garb he wore, and the white tasselled cord round his waist. He'd seen the man's fury, the foaming at the mouth, the demonic anger. Was this the killer stalking poor prostitutes in the alleyways of London? he wondered. The sacristan drew in his breath for a second tirade. Corbett knew that if the monk was allowed to continue he might lose the support of his military escort, some of whom were already worried at the terrible curses uttered by the priest. Corbett stepped closer and, bringing his hand back, gave Adam a stinging slap across the face. The monk yelped and stepped back, holding his cheek.

'You blasphemer!' he hissed.

'There are courts,' Corbett replied softly, 'where I will answer for what I do as there are courts, Adam of Warfield, where you will answer for the terrible things that have happened here. I, Sir Hugh Corbett, Keeper of the Secret Seal, do arrest you Adam of Warfield, Brother Richard of Westminster and William of Senche, Steward of the Palace for the terrible crimes of blasphemy, sacrilege, misprision of treason and corroboration with the King's enemies.'

Adam of Warfield lost some of his pompous arrogance. His chin sagged, his eyes became more watchful.

'What do you mean?' he muttered and glared at Brother Richard, moaning softly, whilst Corbett noticed to his disgust, the small pool of urine between William of Senche's feet.

'Oh, yes,' Corbett continued. 'The charges I have listed are only the beginning. All three of you will sit on that bench. All three of you, on your allegiance to the King, will answer my questions. And, when I have finished, I shall produce the proof of the charges against you.'

'I will answer nothing!' Warfield screamed.

Corbett hit him again. 'All three of you will answer,' he repeated. 'Or you will be taken to the Tower. If you offer further violence, either by word or action, or attempt to escape, Master Limmer has orders to kill you! Now, sit down!'

The three prisoners were hustled to the bench.

'Sir Hugh, you will be safe?'

'Oh, yes.' Corbett took his seat opposite the three men. 'I am sure I will, Master Limmer. Please stand back. I shall call you forward if I need you. Your men, their crossbows are loaded?'

Limmer nodded.

'Good!' Corbett turned to his three prisoners. 'So, let us begin.'

He waited until the archers were out of earshot before leaning forward, his hand half raised.

'I swear by all that is holy that I know what has gone on here. The midnight revelry, the eating and the drinking, the debauchery, consorting with prostitutes from the city.' He looked at William of Senche who was now quivering with fright. 'You, sir, will answer to the King and your best hope is to throw yourself on the King's mercy.'

Adam of Warfield looked as if he was going to brazen it out but Brother Richard suddenly got to his feet.

'It's all true,' he confessed. The monk glared at the sacristan. 'For God's sake, Adam, can't you see he knows? Master William, the clerk speaks the truth. I am not going to lie. I will confess to breaking my monastic vows. I'll confess to the abuse of royal property.' He turned and smiled bleakly at Corbett. 'So what, Master Clerk? I'll take my punishment, bread and water for three years, the performance of the most menial tasks in the abbey. Perhaps a stay in a public pillory. But what's so terrible about that?'

Corbett stared at this small fat monk, then back at Adam, who now sat head bowed.

'Oh, you're clever, Brother Richard,' Corbett answered. 'You think it's a matter of vows. I accept your confession but I suspect your companions know there is more to my tale than monks who fornicate, become drunk and involve themselves in midnight debauchery.'

Brother Richard looked at his companions. 'What is he saying?' the monk stammered. He grabbed the sacristan by the shoulders and shook him. 'In God's name, Adam, what more is there?'

The sacristan refused to look up.

'Sit down, Brother Richard!' Corbett ordered. 'Now, Warfield, the name of the Master of Revels, the seigneur who organised the activities? By what name was he called?'

'I don't know,' the monk murmured without looking up.

'He was called Richard,' William bleated, his eyes almost popping out of his head with fright. 'He only called himself Richard.'

'Shut up!' the sacristan snarled, his white face twisted in a mixture of fear and rage.

'No, I won't!' the steward yelled.

'What did he look like?'

'I don't know.' The steward rubbed his face between his hands. 'I really don't know,' he bleated. 'He always came in the evening and kept in the shadows. He thought it was best like that. He always dressed like a monk in robes and cowl with the hood pulled well over his head and at the revelries he wore a satyr's mask.'

'He had a beard?'

'Yes, he had a beard. I think his hair was black.'

Corbett got up and stood over the three men. 'I think

Brother Adam of Warfield may know his true identity. Yes, Master William, your Master of Revels was called Richard. His full name is Richard Puddlicott, a well-known criminal. Didn't you ever ask yourself why a man, a complete stranger, was so interested in providing revelry and ribaldry?'

'He came to the palace one evening,' the steward stammered. 'I told him I was bored. He suggested some fun.' The steward glanced sideways at the sacristan. 'Then one day Adam of Warfield found out.' The fellow shrugged. 'You know the rest. Some of the monks joined us.' He looked pitifully at Corbett. 'We did no wrong,' he wailed. 'We meant no harm.'

'Until someone decided the parties must end and the prostitutes you had invited be silenced.'

Both the steward and Brother Richard moaned in terror.

'You are not saying,' Brother Richard's voice rose to a scream. 'You are not saying we are involved in the terrible deaths of those girls in the city?'

'I am, and not only those but perhaps the deaths of Father Benedict, who found out about your midnight feastings, and Lady Somerville who had her own suspicions.'

Adam of Warfield sprang to his feet and Corbett stepped back. The monk's face was now pallid and tense, covered in a fine sheen of sweat. His eyes glowed with the fury burning within him.

'Never!' he rasped. 'I had . . . we had no part in that!'

Corbett sat down in his chair and shook his head.

'I have witnesses,' he said. 'A number of sightings of the killer. All of these point to a man dressed in the garb of a Benedictine monk, very similar to what you are wearing now!' Corbett eased his dagger out of the sheath. 'I suggest you sit down, Master Sacristan.'

The monk crouched between his two companions, his eyes never leaving Corbett.

'You can't prove that,' he muttered.

'Not now, but soon, perhaps.'

The monk stared and suddenly his face twisted in a malicious smile.

'No, you can't, clerk,' he repeated. 'All you can prove is that we broke our vows. Wrong? Yes, I admit we were wrong. But you did say in the presence of witnesses that we were charged with treason. I am no jurist, Master Corbett, but if fornication is now treasonable, then every man in this bloody city should be under arrest!'

Corbett got back to his feet. 'I *shall* prove my charges. Master Limmer, Ranulf, Maltote! You will join us now! Outside the treasury door!' The clerk smiled bleakly at Warfield. He was pleased to see all the bombast and pretence drain from the monk's face. He looked weak like some broken old man.

'What are you going to do?' he whispered.

Corbett snapped his fingers and strode off, the three prisoners and their escort trailing behind. They entered the south transept and stopped before the great reinforced door. Corbett grasped his dagger and, despite the protests and worried exclamations of his companions, slashed through each of the seals.

'What is the use?' Ranulf murmured. 'We do not have keys!'

'Of course,' Corbett cursed softly, in his excitement he had forgotten. 'Master Limmer, I want four of your men. They are to bring one of the heavy benches. I want that door smashed down!'

The officer was about to protest but Corbett clapped his hands.

'On the King's authority!' he shouted. 'I want that door clean off its hinges!'

Limmer hurried off.

'And some others had better bring a ladder!' Corbett called. 'The longest they can find!'

Corbett stood, looking at the treasury door waiting for the soldiers to return. Behind him, Ranulf and Maltote muttered dark warnings, William of Senche was gibbering with fright. Brother Richard lounged against the wall, arms folded, whilst the sacristan just stood like a sleep-walker drained of all emotion.

The soldiers returned. Six carried a very heavy church bench and behind them two more held a long thin ladder. Corbett stepped aside; Limmer pushed the three prisoners away; and the archers, thoroughly enjoying their task, drove their battering ram against the great door. Backwards and forwards they swung the heavy bench until the crashes reverberated through the empty abbey like the tolling of a bell. At first the door withstood the attack but then Limmer told them to concentrate on the far edge where the hinges fitted into the wall. Again the soldiers attacked and Corbett began to hear the wood creak and groan. One of the hinges broke loose and the soldiers stopped for a rest, panting and sweating before resuming their task. At last the door began to buckle. With another crash, followed by an ear-splitting crack, the door creaked and snapped free of its hinges. The archers heaved it to one side, snapping the heavy bolts and lock, and Corbett stepped into the low, dark stone-vaulted passage. A candle was brought and having ordered the sconce torches on the wall to be lit, Corbett grasped one.

'Limmer, leave two, no, three archers to guard the prisoners, the rest follow me but walk carefully! The passageway is steep and ends in stairs but they have been smashed away. Take care!' He turned. 'Oh, by the way, where is Cade?' Corbett realised how the under-sheriff had kept very much in the background.

'He's outside,' Ranulf muttered.

'Then bring him in!'

They waited until Ranulf returned with Cade, who stood astounded at the broken treasury door.

'Sweet Lord, Master Clerk!' he whispered. 'I hope you know what you're doing!'

'Sweet Lord!' Corbett mimicked. 'I think I am the only one who does!'

They went down the passageway, the flames of the torches making their shadows dance on the walls; their footsteps sounded hollow and echoed like the beating of some ghostly drum. Corbett stopped abruptly and pushed the torch forward. Suddenly the passageway ended, and he edged forward gingerly, crouching and waving the torch above the darkened crypt below. The staircase was there – well, at least the first four steps – then it fell away into darkness. The ladder was brought, lowered and, once it was secured, Corbett carefully descended, with one hand on the rung, the other holding the torch away from his face and hair. He looked up, where the others were ringed in a pool of light.

'Leave two archers there!' he called. 'And come down. Bring as many torches as you can!'

He reached the bottom and waited while the archers, with a great deal of muttering and cursing, came to join him. More torches were lit and as their eyes became accustomed to the light they glanced around. The crypt was a huge, empty cavern, the only break being the central column which, Corbett deduced, was the lower part of the great pillar rising to support the high soaring vaults of the Chapter House above. He sucked in his breath. Was he going to be right? Then he glimpsed it: the precious glint of gold and silver plate from half-open coffers, chests and caskets.

'Surely, they should be locked?' Cade muttered, seeing them at the same time as Corbett did. He ran across to one. 'Yes! Yes!' he said excitedly. 'The padlocks have been broken!' He held his torch lower. 'Look, Sir Hugh, there's candle grease on the ground.' He edged towards a white blob of wax. 'It's fairly recent!' he cried.

The others dispersed, examining the various caskets and chests. Some of them had their locks broken, others had been smashed with an iron crowbar or axe, and the contents had been rifled. But none was empty.

'The crypt has been plundered!' Corbett announced. 'Some plate has been taken! But that is bulky, cumbersome and unwieldy and very difficult to sell. Look!'

He pulled from a chest a small silver dish encrusted round the rim with red rubies. He held it close to the flame of his torch. 'This is engraved with the goldsmith's hallmark and the arms of the royal household. Only a fool would try to sell this. And our thief is no fool.'

He went back to stare at the great pillar and noticed that portions of the column had been cut away by a stone mason to form a series of neatly made recesses. Corbett put his hand into one of these and drew out a tattered empty sack. 'By all the saints!' he muttered. 'Everyone. Here!' He held up the tattered remnants of the bag. 'Our thief did not come for the plate but for the newly minted coins of gold and silver. I suspect these recesses were once full of bags of coins and now they have all gone. These sacks were the thief's quarry.'

'But how did he get in?' Cade asked.

Corbett walked over to the grey mildewed wall of the crypt, built with great slabs of granite.

'Well,' Corbett murmured, his words echoing through the darkened vault. 'We know the thief could not come from above. He certainly didn't come through the door.' He tapped his boot on the hard concrete floor. 'From below is impossible, so he must have burrowed through the wall.'

'That would take months,' Limmer answered.

'You've been at a siege?' Corbett asked.

The soldier nodded.

'These walls are thirteen feet thick. No different from many castles. How would a commander breach such a wall?'

'Well, a battering ram would be useless. He would probably try and dig a hole, a tunnel beginning at the far side of the wall under the foundations and up.'

'And if that didn't work?'

'He would attack the wall itself. But that would take a long time.'

'I think our thief had plenty of time,' Corbett muttered. 'I want you to examine the wall with your torches. If the flame flutters from a violent draught, that's the place.'

It took only a few minutes before Ranulf's excited yell, from behind some overturned chests, attracted their attention. Corbett and the others examined the place, and Ranulf pushed against the stone.

'It's loose!' he said. 'Look!' He pointed to the mounds of dusty plaster around the foot of the wall.

'Oh, Lord!' Corbett whispered. 'I know what he's done.' He tapped the wall. 'On the other side of this is what?'

'The old cemetery.'

'Let's go there.'

They rescaled the ladder. Corbett ordered the archers to guard it whilst, outside the door, the three prisoners stood silent and forlorn, their hands and feet quickly bound. Corbett and the others, at a half-run, went out of the abbey and into the old cemetery. They had to wade through the waist-high hempen coarse grass and other shrubs before they stood before the walls of the crypt. Here the signs of an intruder were more apparent: a broken spade, a rusting mattock, pieces of old sacking and Ranulf even found a silver noble shining amongst the weeds. Corbett tried to visualise the inside of the crypt and pointed to a fallen, battered headstone.

'Pick that up!' he said.

The stone was easily shifted to one side, revealing a hole large enough for a man to go down. Corbett looked round and grinned to hide his own nervousness. He could not stand such enclosed spaces and knew what terrors would assail him if he got stuck or was unable to turn. He shrugged uneasily.

'I have a fear of such places,' he whispered.

Ranulf needed no second bidding but, on hands and knees, wriggled down the hole, Corbett heard him scuffling down the tunnel like some fox returning to its earth. After a few tense minutes Ranulf returned, covered in dirt, but smiling from ear to ear.

'The tunnel gets wider as you approach the base of the wall.'

'And the wall itself?'

'Nothing but a hole. Apparently our thief simply hacked his way through, crumbling the stone by lighting a small fire then bringing it out in sacking and scattering it amongst the graves.'

'It would take months!' Limmer repeated unbelievingly.

'It can be done,' Corbett replied. 'I have seen miners in the King's army perform a similar feat against castle walls. Remember, it's not natural rock but man-made slabs of stone. Once cracked, it's a matter of scooping it out.'

'And the final stone?' Cade said. 'The one Ranulf disturbed in the crypt?'

'The tunnel ends there,' Ranulf replied. 'But if you brace yourself and thrust with your feet, the stone simply slides in and out. Our thief even fashioned a great hook to pull it back. Once pushed away there's a natural door into the crypt and the King's treasure.'

Corbett stared round the forlorn cemetery. 'So, we have a man probably working at night. He begins here, digs through the soft clay until he reaches the base of the wall. He then hacks through the brickwork, probably weakened by fire, bringing out the results of his handiwork in sacks. The final stone is also attacked, weakened and an iron hook and ring placed in it so it can be pushed in and out. The thief helps himself to some of the royal plate, though his real quarry are those sacks of coins.' He stared round. 'And now they have gone.'

Corbett rubbed the side of his face with his hand. He'd felt pleased that his theory had proved correct. But two problems remained. First, the thief? He had no doubt it was Puddlicott but where the hell was the man? And, more importantly, where were his ill-gotten gains? Corbett squeezed his lips between his fingers. Secondly, although the secret life of these monks had been revealed in the full glare of day, he still had no evidence to link them to the murders. Nothing except the scribblings of an old woman and the eyewitness account of a beggar boy and a common prostitute. Corbett sighed and looked up at the blue sky.

'Of course,' he muttered. 'There's a final problem. Who will tell the King . . . ? We have done what we can here,' he continued loudly. 'Master Cade, you are to take the archers and secure the treasury room, fill in the stone, bring masons and carpenters from the city and do what you can. Master Limmer, I want you to forget the law! Our three prisoners are to be taken to the Tower and, short of loss of life or limb, they are to be interrogated until the full story is known.'

The soldier, nervous at what he was being involved in, spat and shook his head.

'Sir Hugh, two of them are priests!'

'I don't give a damn if they are bishops!' Corbett snarled. 'Take them and do what you have to. This is treason, man. They have robbed a royal treasury. You would soon object if the King could not pay your wages.'

'How do we know they were involved?' Cade interrupted.

'Oh, you will,' Corbett replied. 'Master William perhaps, Brother Richard maybe, but Adam of Warfield definitely. I also suggest you search the latter's chamber. I am sure you will find more than an expensive pair of riding boots.' Corbett clapped his hands. 'Now, come on, there's yet more to be done.'

Limmer and Cade hurried away. Corbett slapped Maltote on the shoulder and the young messenger, who was staring open-mouthed at the hole in the ground, jumped and blinked.

'Yes, Master?'

'Take two horses, Maltote. The fastest we have. You are to ride to Winchester and tell the King exactly what you have seen here. You are to ask His Grace to return with all speed to London. Do you understand? You have money?'

The young man nodded.

'Then go now!'

Maltote hurried off and Corbett grasped Ranulf by the arm.

'Take your care whilst you can, Ranulf,' he murmured. 'For, when the King returns, the city will buzz like an overturned beehive!'

They waited until Limmer sent archers round to guard the secret tunnel, then Corbett and Ranulf walked back through the abbey grounds.

'What shall we do, Master?'

Corbett watched Limmer's archers now hurrying backwards and forwards and noted with relief that fresh troops, men-at-arms, had also arrived from the Tower. Some of the abbey lay-brothers, officials, scullions and servants from the kitchens wandered about asking questions, whilst at the gates, archers with drawn swords were pushing back a small crowd of curious bystanders.

'Master, I asked, what shall we do?'

Corbett looked at his dishevelled manservant.

'Well, you need a wash and I need something to eat and drink. So, for a while, it's back to The Golden Turk to sit and take stock.' He squeezed his servant's arm. 'Oh, by the way, I am grateful for you going down the tunnel. I may have gone in but I doubt if I would have returned.'

Ranulf was about to make some mischievous reply when, suddenly, Lady Mary Neville appeared, her black hair falling loose under her blue veil as she ran breathlessly towards them.

'Sir Hugh, Master Ranulf, what is the matter?'

The young widow stopped in front of them, her face slightly red, her eyes sparkling with excitement.

'What is happening?' she repeated. 'There are soldiers all over the abbey. They say some of the brothers have been arrested! Have you found the killer, Sir Hugh?'

Corbett took the young woman's small, white hand in his, lifted it and brushed it softly with his lips.

'Oh, more than that, Lady Mary. But for the moment,

let the gossips have their way.' He bowed and moved on, Ranulf trotting enviously behind him.

'Oh, Master Ranulf!'

Corbett deliberately walked on as Ranulf stopped and returned to Lady Neville.

'Yes, Lady Mary?'

The young widow looked at him coyly. She lifted her hand and Ranulf, with a flourish which would have been the envy of any courtier, caught it and raised it to his lips. The young woman laughed, withdrew her hand, turned and walked swiftly away. Only then did Ranulf realise she had pressed a small gold amulet into his hand with the phrase 'Amor vincit omnia – Love conquers all' inscribed on it. Ranulf gazed after her, speechless with amazement, until the roars of Master 'Long Face' shook him from his golden reverie.

Chapter 11

After their journey down river, Corbett went into the tavern whilst Ranulf stayed to wash himself in the water butts near the horse trough. By the time he rejoined his master, the landlord was serving two bowls of hot spiced lamb and chunks of meat, roasted on a spit, floating in a thick gravy with onions, leeks and other vegetables. Corbett had bought a small jug of wine, the best the house could provide, and as he filled their cups commended Ranulf for his bravery, until his servant blushed crimson with embarrassment.

'Do you think we've reached the end of the story, Master?' Ranulf said trying to divert the conversation away from his own achievements.

'I don't know. What do we have here, Ranulf? Mischievous monks and a subtle thief who has stolen the royal treasure. These things we can prove but what is more difficult, is to make the logical leap and link the debauchery in the abbey with the robbery of the royal treasure house and then with the deaths of those poor prostitutes in London, not to mention the murder of poor Lady Somerville and Father Benedict.' Corbett scraped his bowl clean with his horn spoon, then wrapped the spoon in a napkin and put it back in his pouch. 'Everything we know seems to prove there is a link, but a good lawyer would demonstrate we have fashioned a net with as many holes as it has cords. Moreover, we do not know who the thief is.'

'It must be Puddlicott?'

'Oh, yes, we think it is; we *know* it is. You know; I know. We are all very knowledgeable,' Corbett retorted. 'Yet we have no proof. Who is Puddlicott, where is Puddlicott? We can't even answer these questions.' He picked up his wine cup and held it, gently rocking it to and fro. 'Above all, we do not know who the *murderer* is.' He took a generous swig of wine, and his servant glanced at him curiously – Corbett was known for his sobriety.

'You are anxious, Master?'

'Yes, Ranulf, I am anxious because when the King asks me to account, I'll describe the problems but offer few solutions.'

'You discovered the treasury was robbed.'

'The king won't give a fig for that. He will be more interested in getting his treasure back and hanging the bastard who stole it. No, no.' Corbett loosened his tunic round his neck. 'It's the murders which fascinate me and I have two nightmares, Ranulf. First, are the murders connected to the abbey? And, secondly, are we talking of two or even three murderers? The prostitutes' killer, the murderer of Lady Somerville and the silent assassin of Father Benedict.'

'You have forgotten one thing, Master. Amaury de Craon, that cunning bastard must have some hand in all this dirt.'

Corbett looked sharply at Ranulf. His servant's words jogged a memory and he realised he had forgotten all about his French opponent.

'Of course,' he breathed. 'Amaury de Craon. Look,

Ranulf, have you finished? Good! Then go to Cock Lane.' He shook his head at the smile on his manservant's face. 'No, no, keep your lusts to yourself. I want you to stand outside the apothecary's shop and search out a little beggar boy dressed in rough sacking. Take him to Gracechurch Street and tell him to keep a sharp eye on the house of the Frenchman. If anything untoward happens, such as an unexpected visitor or busy preparations for departure, the boy is to come and leave a message at my house in Bread Street.'

Ranulf agreed and hurried off. Corbett finished the rest of the wine and, feeling rather flushed and slightly sleepy, left the tavern and made his way to the main gateway of the Tower. He showed his warrants to the guards on duty, crossed the moat, went under successive arches and into the inner wards which surrounded the four-square central donjons, or White Tower. The clerk was challenged as he approached each gateway but, on producing the King's writ, was allowed to proceed. At last he reached the inner bailey, quiet in the early summer heat though Corbett could see that building works in the Tower were now underway again as the King feared a French landing in Essex or even on the Thames estuary. Bricks were stacked around huge kilns, sand and gravel were piled high, and thick oaken beams lay in lopsided heaps.

The Tower was a village in itself, with rows of stables, dovecotes, open-fronted kitchens, barns and hen coops all huddled along the inner walls. A small orchard stood in one corner next to the wooden and plaster houses of the Officers of the Tower. Corbett passed huge mangonels and battering rams being prepared and was half-way across the green to the White Tower when he was challenged by a burly-faced officer. The fellow was still trying to read

Corbett's warrant when Limmer suddenly appeared and hurriedly intervened.

'Sir Hugh,' he announced, 'the interrogation has begun.' He shook his head. 'But, so far, we have learnt little.'

He beckoned Corbett forward, leading him down a steep row of steps cut into the side of the White Tower and into a dungeon at the base of one of the turrets. Corbett shivered: the place was low-roofed, cold and damp and, despite the daylight, torches had been lit and were now spluttering against the darkness. He could smell the damp earth beneath his feet mingling with the stench of smoke, charcoal, sweat and fear. The chamber was bare of all furniture except for great iron braziers clustered together at each end. Chains and manacles hung on the walls but the clerk's eyes were drawn to a small recess and the macabre group standing there. As Corbett approached, he glimpsed the torturers: men stripped to their waists, scraps of cloth wrapped around their foreheads to keep the sweat from running into their eyes. Their bodies glistened as if covered in oil and they lovingly stood over the braziers, pushing in and out long rods of iron, the handles wrapped in cloth to protect their hands. One of the torturers lifted a rod out, blew the red hot tip and moved to the shadowy recess. The fellow muttered something then Corbett heard a scream. He moved closer and saw that Adam of Warfield, Brother Richard and William the Steward had all been stripped of everything except their breeches, their outstretched hands being manacled to the wall. The torturer whispered something, then grunted and the iron was placed on a body that jerked in terror, the chains drumming against the wall. Another iron was placed, more whispers from a scribe sitting on a small stool keeping a faithful record of what was said. A curse, a scream, a cry, and so the questioning continued. Corbett turned away.

'Stop it, Limmer!' he hissed. 'Stop it now! And tell the scribe to join us outside.'

Corbett walked back into the open air. 'Christ,' he gasped. 'From such terrors deliver me!'

He sat on one of the wooden beams and wished he hadn't drunk the wine for his throat was dry and he found it difficult to reconcile sitting on green grass under a clear blue sky with the terrors he had just witnessed. Limmer and the scribe joined him. The latter was a chubby, bald, red-faced man who seemed to enjoy his work and viewed the horrors he had to witness as one of the gruesome necessities of life.

'Have the prisoners confessed?' Corbett asked.

Limmer shrugged.

'Yes and no,' the scribe replied thinly.

'What do you mean?'

'Well, Sir Hugh, we must draw a line. Brother Richard is guilty of nothing except drinking too much wine and the violation of his monastic vows. He has been terrified but not tortured. I strongly recommend that he be released.'

Corbett stared at the scribe's hard blue eyes and nodded.

'Agreed. But he is to be kept until even-tide, then released into the custody of the Bishop of London. What else?'

'The steward, William of Senche, is guilty of gross misdemeanours against the King.'

'Nothing else?'

'Patience, Sir Hugh. He also confessed to knowing a well-known criminal, Richard Puddlicott. Master William has some knowledge of thieves for his brother is Keeper of Newgate Gaol. Now William of Senche was approached by Puddlicott and, together, he and Puddlicott planned to enrich themselves at everybody's expense.' The scribe licked his lips. 'According to William's confession, Richard Puddlicott – and before you ask, Sir Hugh, we have no clear description of the villain except talk of black hair and black beard, and of Puddlicott being constantly cowled and hooded.' The fellow shrugged. 'You can believe that if you wish – anyway, according to the confession, one day the steward and the rogue were wandering through the abbey cloisters. They greedily noticed the rich stores of silver plate carried in and out of the refectory by the servants who wait on the brethren at meals.' The scribe laughed softly. 'The happy idea struck them that such silver could be theirs. One night they put a ladder against the wall of the refectory and secured a rich booty of plate which they carried off and sold.'

'And no one noticed it was gone?'

'Well.' The scribe smiled bleakly. 'It's the usual story. A sick, old abbot, no prior.' He glanced up at Corbett. 'Yes, Sir Hugh, the thought also occurred to me. I do wonder if the good prior was helped out of this vale of tears. Anyway, now we come to Adam of Warfield. He noticed the silver was gone. He also heard of the revelries William was holding in the palace, he demanded to be involved in these nefarious goings-on or he would go straight to the King. Master William and Puddlicott agreed. Warfield was given a third of the monies they had made in selling the abbey plate. Then they seized on a brilliant idea of robbing the royal treasury.' The scribe moved the sheafs of parchment in his hand. 'Their schemes were well laid. Sixteen months ago Adam of Warfield declared the cemetery was out of bounds; hempen seed, which grows quickly, was sown in profusion and Puddlicott began his tunnelling. About ten days ago he forced an entry; he did not want the plate, our good sacristan sold that.' The scribe smiled. 'I suspect, Master Corbett, that there are goldsmiths in our city who know full well that the plate they have acquired is stolen property.'

He paused and Corbett whistled through his teeth in disbelief.

'And when did Puddlicott dig his tunnel?'

'According to Warfield, at night, but because the cemetery was deserted, sometimes even during the day.'

Corbett's hand flew to his mouth. 'Good God!' he breathed.

'Sir Hugh,' Limmer asked. 'What is the matter?'

Corbett just shook his head. He did not want to confess that he had probably seen Puddlicott, for he remembered his first visit to the abbey and the old gardener, hooded, with his back to him. No gardener, Corbett thought bitterly, but Master Puddlicott in one of his clever disguises.

'What else?' he asked sharply. 'Could they tell us anything about Puddlicott?'

'No, the rogue was a master of the shadows. He always contacted them and never told them where he stayed. He was either late or very early and would disappear without a word to anyone. Sometimes he would be a regular visitor, at other times he would be absent for weeks.'

'And the gold and silver which was stolen?'

'They received their share but, naturally, Puddlicott took the lion's portion.'

'And the murderers?'

'Ah.' The scribe shook his head. 'They deny any involvement in anyone's death, be it Lady Somerville, Father Benedict or the whores in the city.' The scribe plucked a quill from behind his ear and tapped the parchment. 'However,' he added hopefully, 'Warfield is a killer. He is no more a man of God, Sir Hugh, than the creatures in the royal menagerie. I have attended many interrogations,'

Corbett looked into the flint-like eyes and could well believe it.

'I have attended many similar interrogations,' the scribe continued firmly. 'Warfield is a murderer, he has killed once. I am sure he had a hand in the death of the prior. You know the way of the world, Sir Hugh? A man who kills once will always kill again.' The scribe rolled the parchment up. 'More than that,' he concluded flatly, 'I can tell you nothing.' He smiled bleakly. 'Of course, we still have further business with Brother Adam.'

Corbett thanked him and the little man waddled off, back to his duties.

'What further can we do?' Limmer asked.

'As I have said, release Brother Richard into the hands of the church. Interrogate Warfield. I also want a message taken to the Sheriffs and Guildmasters. On the King's authority, they are to make a thorough search of the city. They are to look for plate bearing the royal insignia and report any influx of freshly minted coins. The sheriffs are to hand over a summary of their findings to me at my lodgings in Bread Street. Do you understand that?'

Corbett waited until the soldier faithfully repeated his instructions, bade him adieu and left the Tower.

By the time he had reached Bread Street, Ranulf had returned from his errand. Maeve was absent, taking her small daughter and the maid Anna to one of the stalls at Cornhill. So Corbett, feeling tired and dejected, went upstairs to his bedchamber. He kicked off his boots and lay down on the red and white silk cover. He drifted in and out of sleep, his mind plagued by horrible nightmares, peopled by torturers, the walking corpses of young girls, their throats slashed from ear to ear, Adam of Warfield's hate-filled eyes and the roars of wrath of his royal master. Corbett woke and stared at a hanging on the wall, depicting

Salome's dance before Herod. Why had Maeve hung it there? he wondered. He tossed and turned and thought about the death of the last whore, Hawisa. Why had she been killed at the time she had? Corbett had expected the next murder to have occurred sometime in the middle of June. He thought of the Lady Mary Neville and her same sweet smile as his first wife. Corbett drifted into a calmer sleep and was awoken by Maeve, bending over him, shaking him by the shoulder.

'Hugh! Hugh! Supper is ready!'

Corbett yawned and swung his feet to the floor.

'Come on, clerk!' Maeve teased with mock severeness. 'You stay in bed and there's work to be done. More importantly, the table has been laid and the meal is ready.'

Maeve's teasing eventually drew Corbett out of his dark depression. Moreover, his wife was determined that he now attend to certain household duties. Letters had come from the bailiffs of their manor at Leighton in Essex. She wished to discuss preparation arrangements about Lord Morgan's stay. Would Hugh be free of his duties? So Corbett, at his wife's insistence, spent the next few days in his own house. He played with baby Eleanor. He sat in the garden with his steward Griffin going through household accounts and, once again, tried to advise the impetuous Ranulf against his love tryst with the Lady Mary Neville. However, Ranulf was totally smitten and Corbett sensed the change; his manservant's red hair was now groomed and carefully covered in oil, his doublet, hose and boots were the very best Cheapside could provide and Corbett secretly smiled at the richly perfumed oils Ranulf rubbed into his skin. Maeve enjoyed every minute of it and, when Ranulf hired a troupe of musicians to serenade the Lady Mary, she collapsed in a fit of giggles.

Such domesticity, however, was shattered by Maltote's

return from Winchester. He looked ashen-faced and highly nervous when Corbett and Ranulf met him in the clerk's private chancery office.

'You gave the King my news?'

'Yes, Master.'

'And his reaction?'

'He drew his dagger and, if the Lord de Warrenne hadn't been there, he would have thrown it at me!'

'What happened then?'

'Most of the furniture in the chamber was ruined. The King took a great mace from the wall and smashed everything in sight. Master, I thought he had fallen into a fit! He cursed and ranted. He said he would hang every bloody monk in the abbey.'

'And me?'

'You'll be exiled to the Island of Lundy, stripped of all offices and made to fast on bread and water.'

Corbett groaned and sat down on the chair. The King's rages were terrible and Edward probably meant every word he uttered, at least until he calmed down.

'And what now?'

'I left Winchester the same evening. The King was in the palace yard screaming at the porters, grooms, men-at-arms and household officials. The chests were to be packed, sumpter ponies to be loaded and messengers sent out. He will be at Sheen tomorrow morning and demands your presence there.'

Corbett caught Ranulf's evil grin.

'You will be with me, Ranulf!' he snapped. 'Sweet Lord!' Corbett muttered. 'Tomorrow the King; the next day Lord Morgan! Believe me, Ranulf, Holy Mother Church is right when she says marriage is a state only the foolish will rush into!'

'What shall we do, Master?'

Ranulf's glee at hearing about the consternation amongst the great ones of the land faded now. Moreover, he always kept a wary eye on the King and, if he thought 'Master Long Face's' career might be in jeopardy, became ever so solicitous. Corbett stared out of the window. The sun was setting and he could hear the bells of the city faintly tolling for vespers.

'We shall go out,' he said. 'We shall act like three roisterers, drink ale and sack and come home singing. For, as they used to say in ancient Rome, when you are about to die you should enjoy yourselves.'

Ranulf glanced at Maltote and pulled a face. They both had plans to visit Lady Mary in Farringdon but Corbett was insistent so, seizing cloaks and belts, they slipped out of the house and up into a now deserted Cheapside. Corbett walked fast as if the exercise would clear the foreboding in his mind about his imminent meeting with the King. They entered the Three Roses tavern in Cornhill and, whilst Ranulf and Maltote talked about everything under the sun, Corbett drank as his mind probed the problems which faced him. The more he drank the greater grew his despair as he realised he had only proven two things. Firstly, the monks at Westminster had broken their vows and, secondly, the royal treasury had been plundered by the greatest thief in the kingdom.

Three hours later, a fully depressed Corbett, aided and abetted by Ranulf and Maltote, staggered out of the tavern and began the long walk home through the black, deserted streets. Ranulf believed 'Master Long Face' was not drunk but slightly in his cups for he had spent the last hour lecturing Ranulf: how marriages between social unequals were never successful; how the Lady Mary Neville may be playing with him, just teasing his affections. Now Corbett had fallen silent for he suddenly remembered de Craon and was trying to recall what had been amiss when he visited the Frenchman. They reached the bottom of Walbrook and turned up Budge Row. They crossed the stream covered by a loose grating and were preparing to go down a narrow alleyway which ran alongside St Stephen's church. Maltote was ahead of them, singing some silly song when the hooded men launched their attack. They had expected Corbett and Ranulf to be walking alongside the young messenger and, because they weren't, Maltote bore the first brunt of their surprise attack and the scalding fistfuls of lime. Maltote screamed in agony as the burning fire turned his eyes to searing pain and he collapsed into the mud. The rest of the lime hit Corbett's hair and the side of his face as it did that of Ranulf but it missed both their eyes. Now the hooded men, four in number, each carrying shield and sword, slipped further out of the shadows towards the surprised clerk and his companions. They ignored Maltote, screaming on his knees that he couldn't see. Surprised and befuddled, both Corbett and Ranulf stepped back. Then the savagery of the attack dawned on Ranulf and, drawing both sword and dagger, he hit his assailants like a berserker. These were rifflers and roaring boys, used to the strange dance of street fights, not Ranulf's foolish courage. He smashed into their leader, sending him winded and sprawling to the ground. Another took Ranulf's dagger in his shoulder, he clutched the hot spurting wound and staggered back up the alleyway, whilst Ranulf attacked the third. By the time the fourth attacker regained his wits, Corbett, his mind cleared of the wine fumes, also joined the fray. The fight swirled to and fro. Corbett and Ranulf edged closer, fighting back to back, their swords and daggers flickering out until the dark alleyway rang with the clash of metal, the scrape of boots and the gasping grunts of struggling men. Once again

Ranulf launched himself furiously into the fray, aware that Maltote, still clutching his eyes, desperately needed their aid. The attackers had enough and, like shadows, just faded away. Ranulf re-sheathed his sword whilst Corbett staggered after their wounded but still active opponents. Cursing and yelling at them, the clerk suddenly realised the futility of his temper and returned to where Ranulf sat squatting in the mud, cradling Maltote in his arms as he struggled to take the young man's fingers away from his eyes.

'The poor bugger's blinded!' Ranulf yelled. 'It's your fault, you bloody clerk! You and your maudlin moods. We should have gone to Farringdon!'

'Shut up!' Corbett rasped back.

Corbett knelt beside Maltote and dragged the young man's hands away from his face. In the poor light of the alleyway he could see how the skin round the eyes looked as if it had been marked by falling cinders, whilst the eyes themselves were inflamed and running with water. Corbett ran back up the Walbrook, banging on the doors until a householder, braver than the rest, opened up. Maltote was dragged into a lighted doorway, the damage to his eyes now more apparent as Corbett desperately poured jug after jug of cold water to clear the lime from them. The watch, four soldiers and an alderman, alerted by the noise of the commotion, entered the Walbrook. Corbett told them to piss off and not be officious unless they wanted to help. The alderman managed to secure two horses. Maltote was helped up and, with Ranulf trotting behind him, Corbett rode as fast as his wounded companion would allow, up Budge Row into West Cheap and along the Shambles to Newgate. The city guards let them through a postern gate, Maltote moaning and groaning, Ranulf running beside him, screaming at him not to touch his eyes.

They never stopped until they arrived at St Bartholomew's, bathed in sweat and covered in dirt as they banged on the gate, screaming for Father Thomas. They were given entrance and lay-brothers helped Maltote down from the saddle. Father Thomas, who had been in church, hurried out and took the young messenger away. Corbett and Ranulf were left to kick their heels in the long, empty corridor. Behind the sturdy, locked door they could hear Maltote's screams interspersed with Father Thomas's calm voice and the quiet reassurance of lay-brothers who hurried in carrying bowls of water and trays of herbal remedies and ointment. Corbett grew tired of Ranulf's lectures and lay down on the bench to snatch an hour's sleep whilst his servant paced restlessly up and down. The clerk awoke, revived and refreshed. He sent a lay-brother with messages to Bread Street and waited for Father Thomas to finish working on Maltote's eyes. Just after dawn the physician came out.

'No, you can't see him.' he announced wearily. 'He has had a cup of drugged wine and will sleep till mid-day.'

'His eyes?' Ranulf shouted, grabbing the priest by the sleeve. 'Has he lost his eyesight?'

The physician gently prised himself free.

'I don't know,' he murmured. 'The water you threw over his face saved him from further injury. I have cleaned his skin and the lime from his eyes; for the moment, that's all I can do.'

'His eyes?' Ranulf repeated. 'Will he go blind?'

'I don't know. Only time will tell. He may lose the sight of one eye or yes, Ranulf, he could be blinded for life.'

Ranulf turned and pounded his fists on the passageway wall.

'Corbett,' Brother Thomas continued. 'I must go. I will keep you informed.'

Corbett shook him warmly by the hand, seized Ranulf's arm and pushed him, still mouthing protests and curses, out of the hospital.

At the gate they met the lay-brother returning from Bread Street.

'I told the Lady Maeve,' he announced. 'She is worried. She wishes you to return now.'

Corbett thanked him and walked on. They were half-way down the street, going back towards Newgate when Corbett heard the lay-brother behind him.

'Oh, Sir Hugh! Sir Hugh!'

'What is it, Brother?'

'Well, as I left your house a little urchin stopped me, jumping up and down like some imp from hell. He said he had a message for the Lord Corbett.'

'What was it?'

'He said the Frenchman was ready to move with all his baggage.'

'Is that all?'

'Yes, Sir Hugh.'

The lay-brother hurried off. Ranulf, now sullen and withdrawn, though the fury of their recent battle still glowed in his face and eyes. He picked up a stone and threw it as far as he could down the street.

'What's that all about, Master?'

Corbett just stood, staring after the lay-brother.

'Master, I asked a question!'

'I know you did, Ranulf, but keep your bloody temper to yourself. Those attackers were probably stalking us all evening. If you'd gone to Farringdon they would have been waiting for you there. For all I know, if we'd stayed within doors, they may even have attacked the house itself.'

'Well, who sent the bastards?'

Corbett smiled thinly. 'Maltote's in good hands. The

Lady Maeve knows where we are. Let's break our fast.' He pointed towards a small tavern, The Fletcher's Table which opened early to serve the butchers and slaughterers who worked in the Shambles. 'A little food and some watered ale?'

'Maltote's lying half-dead!' Ranulf retorted evilly.

'Yes, I know,' Corbett replied. 'But we need to think. The message the lay-brother brought; de Craon is preparing to leave. I suspect he sent those attackers.'

Ranulf shrugged and allowed Corbett to usher him across the street and into the still silent taproom. Sleepy-eyed scullions and black-faced cook boys served them fresh pies and jugs of ale. Corbett told Ranulf to stop moaning and sat eating and drinking, trying to recall every detail of his meeting with de Craon. At last Ranulf grew more amenable.

'Master, what makes you think de Craon was behind the attack?'

'Ranulf, you visited the Frenchman's house, or at least saw it in Gracechurch Street. Did you notice anything untoward?'

'Rather dirty, ramshackle. I thought it was a strange residence for an envoy of a French king. I mean, Master, the streets outside were littered with piles of refuse yet the dung carts were empty.'

Corbett half-choked on the piece of pie he was eating.

'Of course,' he whispered. Images flashed into his mind: the meeting with de Craon and de Nevers, the old gardener in the cemetery at Westminster Abbey, the silent street, the empty, deserted dung cart, Puddlicott in Paris then in London.

'Listen, Ranulf, quickly, do two things. You are to hire a horse and ride as if Maltote himself was with you to the Guildhall. Cade will be there. You are to tell him that the

Harbour Masters on the Thames are to stop all shipping. Also every soldier in the city is to muster at the corner of Thames Street. They are to be there within the hour.' He grabbed the tankard from Ranulf's hand. 'Go on, man! We may not be able to do anything about Maltote's eyes but we might seize the men who hired his attackers!'

After Ranulf had left, Corbett sat and cursed his own stupidity. He had established that the treasury had been robbed, the wall being finely breached within the last few days. Puddlicott must have worked on that tunnel like a farmer clearing a field, slowly, regularly over a number of months. Now, most of the plate hadn't been touched, being too bulky and obvious to move and sell immediately. Perhaps the robbers had decided to divide their loot, Warfield taking the plate and Puddlicott the coins. Corbett gnawed on his lip and rose slowly to his feet. But, he wondered, didn't the same apply to sacks of coin? Puddlicott could move them but if he started using them, surely he'd be traced? Where would such a flow of coins pass unnoticed . . . ? Of course! Corbett groaned, seized his cloak and hurried out of the tavern.

Chapter 12

Corbett ensconced himself in one of the many taverns along Thames Street as he waited for Ranulf and Cade to arrive. He also hired five fishermen, who had been celebrating a successful night's catch, to hunt amongst the wharves and docks for a French ship preparing to leave on the morning tide. Over an hour passed before his spies returned, saying there was a French cog, the *Grace à Dieu*, berthed at Queenshithe, which was a veritable hive of activity. One of the fishermen accurately described de Craon, and Corbett became alarmed when another reported how the ship was well manned, bore armaments and was guarded by soldiers.

'Supposedly a wine vessel,' the fellow concluded sourly. 'But you know the French, Master? It's a merchant ship turned man-of-war.'

Corbett cursed, and paid the fellows their due. If the ship slipped its mooring he did not want it to become involved in some sea fight on the Thames or, even worse, out in the Narrow Sea where it might give any pursuer the slip and make a quick dash for Dieppe or Boulogne. He left the tavern and paced restlessly up and down. By all rights he should be on the way to Sheen, but the King would have to wait. Corbett just hoped his guess would prove correct.

At last Ranulf returned with Cade, one of the sheriffs and troops of city archers and men-at-arms. They thronged the streets and narrow alleyways causing consternation amongst the early morning shoppers, seamen, traders, hucksters and costermongers. The under-sheriff, still looked peakish and nervous, realising his dishonesty about Judith had not yet been fully resolved.

'Any news from the Tower, Master Cade?'

The under-sheriff shook his head.

'Brother Richard has been released and Adam of Warfield keeps repeating his story but what's this fracas about, Sir Hugh?'

'This fracas,' Corbett snapped, 'is about treason!' He looked at Ranulf. 'The harbour master has been warned?'

Ranulf nodded.

'Two men-of-war have been alerted,' Cade added. 'The Thames below Westminster has been sealed but a ship on this tide could force its way through and make a run for the open sea. I take it that our quarry is a ship?'

Corbett nodded. 'A French merchant ship turned man-of-war, the *Grace à Dieu*. It's berthed at Queenshithe. I want no nonsense. Forget about protests, protocol and diplomatic ties. I want the ship seized, the soldiers disarmed and the place searched from poop to stern.'

Cade blanched. 'Sir Hugh, I hope you know what you are doing? If you are wrong, and I suspect we are looking for the stolen treasure, the King's cup of wrath will spill over on us all!'

'And if I am right,' Corbett soothingly replied, 'then we shall all dance round the maypole.'

He led the archers and men-at-arms into the narrow alleyway leading down to the wharves and quays. Instructions were whispered and, at last, they reached the riverside. Corbett glimpsed the *Grace à Dieu*; its ramps were still down but the sailors were already scaling the masts to prepare the ship for sail.

'Now!' Corbett shouted.

He, Cade and Ranulf led the charge across the cobbled stones. The ramps were stormed. Two men-at-arms, wearing the royal livery of France, tried to block their progress but were knocked aside as English archers and men-at-arms swarmed all over the ship. Sailors caught unawares in the rigging were ordered down, soldiers found between decks were disarmed.

In a few minutes the ship was secured and the French soldiers reduced to mere bystanders. The door of the small cabin in the poop opened and de Craon, followed by de Nevers, stormed across the deck to where Corbett and Cade stood at the foot of the great mast.

'This is outrageous!' de Craon yelled. 'We are the accredited envoys of King Philip, this is a French ship!' He pointed to the large banner jutting out from the poop. 'We sail under the royal protection of the House of Capet!'

'I don't care if you sail under the direct protection of the Holy Father!' Corbett replied. 'You have been up to mischief again, de Craon. I want the King of England's gold back. Now!'

De Craon's eyes flickered with amusement. 'So, we are thieves?'

'Yes. You are!'

'You'll answer for this!'

'Either way, monsieur, I'll answer!' Corbett turned to Cade. 'Search the ship!'

The under-sheriff turned and rapped out orders and, despite de Craon's protests, the English soldiers fell to with a will. The cabin was ransacked but the searchers came out grim-faced, shaking their heads. A troop was sent down to the hold. Corbett just stared at de Craon, who stood arms crossed, tapping his foot impatiently on the deck. The English clerk deliberately did not look at de Nevers but whispered to Ranulf where to stand. The soldiers came up from below.

'There's nothing,' they said. 'Just cloth and sacks of food stuff.'

Corbett controlled his panic as he sensed the dismay of Cade and the other officers. He knew the gold and silver were on board; but where?

'Master.'

'Shut up, Ranulf!'

Ranulf grabbed Corbett by the arm. 'Master, I used to run along these wharves. This ship is ready for sea, yes? There are sailors in the rigging preparing to sail. They are looking for a speedy departure.'

'So?'

'Master, the ship's anchor is down. It should be up!'

Corbett turned his back on de Craon. 'Ranulf, what are you saying?'

'Master, they haven't raised the anchor!'

Corbett smiled and turned to Cade. 'I want three swimmers to make sure that the anchor of this ship is fine. Perhaps check the hawser chain?'

De Craon's face paled, his jaw fell open. De Nevers began to move to the rail but Corbett seized him by the arm.

'Master Puddlicott,' he hissed. 'I insist you stay!'

'Puddlicott!' de Craon snapped.

'Yes, monsieur, an English criminal wanted by the sheriff of this city and other counties for a list of crimes as long as this river!'

De Nevers tried to break away. Corbett clicked his fingers and indicated to two men-at-arms to hold him fast. Meanwhile, Cade had selected his volunteers. Three archers stripped off their helmets, sallets and sword belts, kicked off their boots and slipped like water rats into the scum-covered river. They dived out of sight and resurfaced, shouting triumphantly.

'Sacks!' one of them yelled, spitting out water and shaking his head. 'There are heavy sacks of coins tied to the anchor chain!'

'Bring a barge round,' Corbett ordered. 'Have the swimmers retrieve the sacks, place a strong guard and order carts to take the sacks to Sheen Palace!'

Cade hurried away, shouting orders. Corbett looked at his opponents.

'Monsieur de Craon, I will leave you now. I will take Master Puddlicott; for it *is* Richard Puddlicott, not Raoul de Nevers, isn't it? He's an English subject owing allegiance to our King and will undoubtedly answer for his terrible crimes.'

De Nevers yelled at de Craon but the Frenchman just shook his head and the white-faced prisoner was hustled away.

'We knew nothing of this,' de Craon protested. 'We accepted de Nevers for what he claimed to be.'

Corbett grinned at the blatant lie and pointed to the anchor chain. 'And I suppose,' he replied, 'as you raised anchor and set sail you would have found sacks tied by strong cords to the chain. Of course, you would claim it was treasure trove and take it home to your royal master as a fresh subsidy for his armies in Flanders. Naturally, when the time was ripe, you would whisper about what you had done and turn Edward of England into a laughing stock, a prince who lost his gold so his enemy could use it to attack his allies.' Corbett shook his head. 'Come, come, monsieur. Our Chancery will lodge objections with yours.

You will protest your innocence but you are still a liar and a bungling fool!'

Corbett, followed by Ranulf, walked to the rail.

'Did you send them?' Corbett shouted back over his shoulder. He turned and stared into the hate-filled eyes of the Frenchman.

'Did I send whom?' De Craon snapped back.

'The assassins who attacked us?'

De Craon smiled and shook his head. 'One day, Corbett, I will!'

Corbett and Ranulf strode down the ramp where their prisoner waited, now securely chained between two guards. Behind him the clerk heard the whistles of the officers ordering their men off the French ship and the hurried cries of the French captain, eager to get the *Grace à Dieu* to sea as swiftly as possible.

'Where shall we take the prisoner, Sir Hugh?'

Corbett looked at the officer, then at Puddlicott.

'Newgate will do, but he is to remain chained between two guards.' Corbett stepped closer and stared into the bland face of this master trickster. 'Puddlicott, the actor,' he whispered and touched the man's blond hair. 'How often was this dyed, eh? Black, red, russet? And the beard? Grown and shaved, then grown again to suit your purposes?'

Puddlicott stared back coolly. 'What proof do you have, Master Corbett?'

'All I need. You know Adam of Warfield has been taken? He puts the blame squarely on you. Oh, I know about the disguises; the beard, the different coloured hair, the cowl and the hood, but they won't save you from the hangman's noose. I take no enjoyment in this, Puddlicott, but you are going to hang.'

The arrogant coolness slipped from Puddlicott's face.

'If you make a confession,' Corbett continued. 'And answer certain questions, then perhaps something can be done.'

'Such as what?' Puddlicott sneered.

'You committed treason. You know the new laws. To be half-hanged, cut down, disembowelled and quartered.'

Corbett flinched at the fear in the prisoner's eyes.

'Well, Master Clerk,' he slurred. 'Perhaps we should talk.'

Corbett stared along the quayside. There was nothing he could do for this man except make his captivity a little easier.

'Bring the prisoner!' he ordered.

The soldiers, with Puddlicott in between them, followed Corbett and Ranulf into a small ale house. Corbett demanded that the room be cleared.

'Release him!' he ordered the soldiers. 'Let him keep his chains. You can guard the door outside.'

The soldiers, disappointed – their hopes of a free meal being dashed – released Puddlicott but rearranged the gyves of his chains so he could shuffle and still use his hands. Corbett pushed the prisoner over to a corner table.

'Make yourself comfortable on that stool. Landlord, your best dish. What is it?'

'Fish pie.'

'Is it fresh?'

'Yesterday the fish were swimming in the sea.'

Corbett smiled. 'The largest portion for my guest here and some white wine.'

Puddlicott, a half-smile on his face, watched the landlord bustle off to serve them as if he was some important guest of state rather than a doomed malefactor. They waited in silence until the landlord returned. Puddlicott ate the food eagerly enough and Corbett had to admire the man's cool nerve. When he had finished, Puddlicott drained his wine cup and held it out for more.

'Make hay whilst the sun shines.' Puddlicott grinned, then he became serious. 'I do have a favour to ask, clerk.'

'I owe you nothing.'

'I have a brother,' Puddlicott persisted. 'He's been witless since birth. The Brothers at St Anthony's hospital look after him. Give me your word he will be well looked after. A royal stipend, and I'll tell you what I know.' He half-raised his cup. 'If I am to die I want it to be quick. Richard Puddlicott was not put on God's earth for the amusement of the London mob!'

'You have my word on both matters. Now, you stole the gold and silver?'

'Of course. Adam of Warfield and William of the palace were involved. William is just a toper but Adam of Warfield is a malicious bastard. I hope he hangs beside me!'

'He will.'

'Good, that will make it all the more enjoyable.' Puddlicott sipped from his cup.

'Eighteen months ago,' he began, 'I was in France after a short stay at Westminster where I helped William of Senche remove some of the abbey treasure from the monk's refectory. Now, I am not a thief,' he continued with a grin, 'I just find it difficult to distinguish between my property and everyone else's. I tried the same ruse in Paris at the house of the Friars Minor. I was arrested and sentenced to hang. I told my gaoler that I knew a way of making the French king rich at the expense of Edward of England.' Puddlicott blew his lips out. 'You know the way of the world, Corbett? When you're in a corner you'll try anything. I thought it would be forgotten but, the day before I was due to hang, de Craon and the Keeper of the King's Secrets, William Nogaret, visited me in the condemned cell. I told them my plan and heigh-ho, I was released.'

'You could have gone back on your word,' Ranulf interrupted. 'Shown them a clean pair of heels.'

'And fled where?' Puddlicott asked. 'To England? As a ragged-arsed beggar? No,' he smiled and shook his head. 'De Craon said if I broke my word he would hunt me down. Moreover, I had my own grudge against Edward of England. Oh, by the way, Corbett, de Craon hates you and one day intends to settle scores.'

'So far, you have told me nothing I didn't know already,' Corbett snapped.

'Ah, well, I returned to England. I grew a beard, dyed my hair black and arranged the festivities at the abbey.'

'Why?'

'Adam of Warfield has his brains between his legs. He has a weakness for whores, heady drink and good food. William of the palace can be bought for a good jug of wine, so I had them both. I told them my plan; the cemetery was declared unuseable; I thickened the undergrowth by sowing hempen seed – it sprouts quickly and covered my activities.'

'You made the tunnel at night?'

'Usually. But sometimes I dug during the day. It was a brilliant plan, Corbett. No one likes cemeteries by night, or day, and, with the protection of Warfield and William, I could make all the progress I wanted.' He shrugged. 'You know the rest. I was after the coins. Warfield took some of the plate, the silly bastard! I moved and hid the sacks in an old dung cart. You guessed that, didn't you?'

'Yes,' Corbett replied. 'Both Ranulf and I saw it there. Yet, strangely, the street seemed no cleaner.'

Puddlicott smiled. 'What else did I do wrong?'

Corbett seized Puddlicott's hands and turned them palm up. 'When I shook your hand in de Craon's lodgings I sensed something was wrong but didn't realise what it was until later. You were a nobleman, Puddlicott, or supposed to be, yet your hands were calloused and rough. The legacy of a misspent youth as well as digging in the abbey graveyard.' Corbett filled his prisoner's wine cup. 'Now the murders.'

Puddlicott sat back. 'What murders?'

'The whores! Father Benedict! Lady Somerville! We believe the whores were killed because of the midnight revelries, whilst Lady Somerville and Father Benedict were murdered because of what they knew.'

Puddlicott threw his head back and laughed. 'Corbett, I am a thief and a rogue. If I thought I could kill you and escape, I would. But some poor girls, an old priest, a grey-haired old lady? Oh, come, come, Master Corbett.' He sipped from the wine cup and his expression hardened. 'A comfortable cell in Newgate and I'll tell you something extra!'

Ranulf snorted with laughter. 'Any more, Master, and he'll be bargaining for his release.'

'I agree to your request,' Corbett snapped. 'But no more. Well, what is it?'

'Something I saw the night Father Benedict died. I was in the abbey grounds resting after hours of digging. I saw a tall, dark form slip through the grounds. I was intrigued so I followed. The figure stopped outside Father Benedict's house, crouching before the keyhole. The figure, nothing more than a mere shadow, came round to the open window and threw something in.

I saw a tinder struck, I guessed what was happening so I fled.'

'And you know nothing more?'

'If I did, I would tell you.'

'Then, Master Puddlicott, I bid you adieu.' Corbett rose and called for the guards even as Puddlicott grabbed the wine cup and drained it.

Corbett stood and watched the soldiers carefully secure Puddlicott's chains to their own wrists.

'Take him to Newgate!' Corbett ordered. 'He is to be lodged there as the King's guest. The most comfortable room, everything he desires. The Exchequer will pay the bill.' And, turning on his heel, Corbett left the tavern with Puddlicott's fond farewell ringing in his ears.

Edward of England knelt on the window seat and stared out over the gardens of Sheen Palace. Corbett and de Warrenne, Earl of Surrey, sat watching him guardedly. Of course, the King had been pleased. The Barons of the Exchequer were already counting the coins from the sacks, and high-ranking clerks had been despatched to the treasure house to carry out a full audit. Searches had been made in the London markets for any of the King's plate, and royal troops were now garrisoned in the abbey grounds. Edward had already sent a note of furious protest to his good brother, the King of France, in which the English King declared that Monsieur Amaury de Craon was *persona non grata* and if he set foot on English soil would face the full rigours of English law. Corbett had been thanked: a silver chain with a gold Celtic cross for Maeve; a silver goblet stuffed with gold pieces for young Eleanor. The King had clapped Corbett on the shoulder, calling him his most loyal and faithful clerk; but Corbett was vigilant. Edward of England was a consummate actor:

the rages, the tears, the false bonhomie, the role of the courageous general and the stern law-giver. All of these were masks that Edward could don and doff to suit his pleasure. Now, Edward was cool, calm and collected and Corbett sensed the genuine fury in what the King saw as treason, breach of faith and blasphemy.

'I could hang Cade,' the King muttered over his shoulder.

'Your Grace, the man is still young and inexperienced.' Corbett said. 'He has proved to be a great asset. He was the only official in London who helped me. A reward rather than a reproof would make him more loyal.'

Edward laughed to himself. 'Agreed. I knew Cade's father. He began life as a yeoman bowman in my households. Cade was his thirteenth son. Do you know that even as a child Cade was forever lifting girls' petticoats? He has to learn the hard way that a royal official must be careful with whom he sleeps, as well as those he does business with.'

'And the girl, Judith?'

'She will have her reward.'

Corbett shuffled his feet and glanced sideways at de Warrenne.

'And Puddlicott and the others?'

'Ah!' Edward turned and Corbett did not like the look on the King's face. 'They will hang!'

'Warfield is a priest, a monk!'

'He's got a neck like any other man.'

'The Church will object.'

'I don't think so. I'll point out that the monks of Westminster not only betrayed their vows but also their King. Can you imagine old Winchelsea of Canterbury?' Edward smiled to himself. 'Good Lord, sometimes I love being King. I am looking forward to telling our venerable

Archbishop of Canterbury and his brother bishops how lax they have been in their pastoral care. They should keep a sharper eye on their vineyards and what they sanctimoniously call "their flock".'

'I gave my word to Puddlicott,' Corbett interrupted. 'That he would hang but die quickly. No mutilation. And there is the business of his brother . . .'

The King slouched in the window seat. 'I have no quarrel with witless men; the lad will be looked after. But Puddlicott . . .' The King shook his head.

'Your Grace, I gave my word.'

The King made a face.

'I gave my word,' Corbett repeated. 'Knowing, your Grace, that you would respect it.'

Edward made a sweeping movement with his hands.

'Agreed! Agreed! Puddlicott will stand trial before the Justices at Westminster. He will be given a fair hearing then he will hang.' The King rubbed his hands together and smiled evilly at de Warrenne. 'A pretty mess, eh, Surrey?'

'As you say, your Grace.' The Earl looked squarely at Corbett. 'But there's the business of the murderer still roaming the streets and not yet laid by the heels. That was your task, Corbett.'

'I was distracted, your Grace!' Corbett snapped back.

'You have no idea?' Edward asked.

'None whatsoever. Vague suspicions, but that's all.'

'And the Sisters of St Martha are being co-operative?'

'Of course.'

The King grinned. 'Especially the Lady Neville?'

'Especially the Lady Neville!'

'And old de Lacey is still frightening the wits out of everyone?'

'I deal more with the Lady Fitzwarren.'

'Ah, yes.' The King narrowed his eyes. 'I remember when her husband died. We were in Wales, near Conway, the Feast of St Martin, pope and martyr. A good man Fitzwarren.' The King rose and clapped his hands. 'Well, in which case, Corbett, it's back to London for you.' Edward extended his hand for Corbett to kiss. 'I shall not forget, Hugh,' he murmured, 'your loyalty and commitment in this matter.'

Edward closed the door behind his clerk and leaned against it, waiting till the footfalls faded. De Warrenne smirked.

'You'll keep your word, Edward?'

'About what?'

'Cade and the woman, Judith.'

Edward shrugged. 'Of course. You know Edward of England's motto. "Keep faith".'

'And Puddlicott?'

'Of course,' Edward smirked, 'I will keep my word. But now I have a task for you, Surrey. You are to join Corbett in London, present my compliments to the Lord Sheriff, publicly praise Cade, supervise Puddlicott's execution, make sure he dies swiftly.'

'And then, your Grace?'

'I want the bastard's body skinned!' the King hissed. 'Do you understand me, de Warrenne? I want the skin peeled off and nailed, like that of a pig, to the abbey door so everyone knows the price for robbing Edward of England!'

Chapter 13

Corbett was relieved to find the Lord Morgan had not yet arrived at Bread Street.

'He has been delayed,' Maeve moaned. 'Matters in Wales are not proving as easy to leave as he had thought.'

He's bloody drunk, more like it, Corbett thought, and still can't get his horse to take him across the drawbridge. However, he kept his unkind sentiments to himself for Maeve worried herself sick over the old rogue's health and well-being.

Ranulf was absent when Corbett arrived but, on his return, declared that Maltote's life was in no danger, though Brother Thomas could not say whether or not he would regain his sight.

Corbett retired to his small, chancery office, idly sifting through letters, memoranda, bills and petitions which the Chancery had sent on to him. Nevertheless, his mind was elsewhere: back in the abbey grounds watching that dark shape, so vividly described by Puddlicott, slip across to Father Benedict's house to begin that dreadful fire.

Maeve came in with baby Eleanor, and Corbett cosseted and teased both until Anna arrived, talking volubly in Welsh. She seized the child, glared at Corbett, and mumbled something about the infant being too excited.

Maeve stayed for a while as Corbett described his recent interview with the King and his frustration at being unable to catch the assassin and trap the murderer of the city whores.

'It could be anyone,' he muttered. 'It could have been Warfield or another of the monks.'

Maeve seized him by the hand. 'You are agitated, Hugh. Come, join me in the kitchen, I am cooking the evening meal.'

Corbett followed her down the passageway and helped prepare the meal, as Maeve chattered about this and that, trying to distract her husband. He always loved to watch her cook: she was so expert, so neat and tidy, and the dishes she served were always fresh and fragrant. After the hard-baked bread and rancid meat of London's taverns and the royal kitchens, Corbett always appreciated whatever she cooked.

She deftly peeled the whitened flesh of a roasted chicken, dicing it with a small knife, scraping the portions into a bowl, mixing in oil and herbs. Then she looked up, startled, as her husband gasped. He stood, mouth open, staring at her.

'Hugh!' she exclaimed. 'What is the matter?'

'Of course!' Corbett murmured, as if in a trance. 'Oh, by Hell's teeth, of course!' He put down the knife he had been holding and moved like a sleep-walker towards the kitchen door.

'Hugh!' Maeve exclaimed again.

He just shook his head, leaving his wife puzzled and exasperated. Outside in the passageway, Corbett stared at the white plaster, so surprised by his own thoughts he leaned his hot face against the wall, relishing its coolness.

'No,' he whispered. 'It can't be, surely?'

Ranulf came running down the passageway. 'Master, are you well?'

'Yes,' Corbett replied absent-mindedly. 'I am glad Maltote's well.' He patted the surprised Ranulf on the shoulder. 'Lady Maeve may need some help.' Corbett shook himself and narrowed his eyes. 'What did I say, Ranulf?'

The manservant just shook his head. 'Have you been drinking, Master?'

'No,' Corbett murmured, striding down the passageway back to his office. 'No,' he repeated. 'But I wish to God I had!' Back in his office, Corbett reached for the Calendar of Saints at the end of a Book of Hours then sat for an hour writing furiously as he developed the idea which had so surprised him in the kitchen. He tried to disprove his own theory but, whatever ploy he used, the conclusion reached was unshakeable and he cursed his own lack of logic.

'So simple,' he murmured to himself, lifting his head to stare out of the window. 'I know the murderer. I can prove the murders, but what else?'

He rose, strode to the door and shouted for Ranulf.

'Come on, man!' Corbett urged. 'We have business to do in the city. You will take the following message to the Lady Mary Neville.'

Corbett went back to his writing tray and scrawled a few words on a piece of parchment which he then deftly folded and sealed.

'Give this to her; and watch her eyes. Then you are to go to the Guildhall and do the following . . .'

Corbett heard Maeve's footsteps coming along the passageway so he quickly whispered his instructions to an even more surprised Ranulf.

'Master, that's foolish.'

'Do as I say, Ranulf. Go now!'

'What is the matter, Hugh?'

Corbett seized his wife and kissed her on the forehead. 'I have been a fool, Maeve, but bear with me.'

He walked back, collected his sword-belt, boots and cloak and, shouting farewells to his wife and daughter, ran into the darkening street. He took a barge from Fish Quay and, ignoring the boatman's chatter, sat, wrapped in his cloak, as the skiff, helped by the pull of the tide, swept him down to the King's Stairs at Westminster. The abbey and palace grounds were now packed with soldiers, men-at-arms and archers. They had constructed their own bothies from branches, cut from the nearby trees, whilst officers had set up their own coarse-clad pavilions.

Corbett was challenged at every turn but, when he showed his warrant, was allowed through the different cordons thrown around the abbey until he reached the Chapter House. An officer, now carrying the keys of the abbey, unlocked the door for him.

'Collect three men and stay outside!' Corbett ordered. 'But allow any visitors in!'

The soldier obeyed and Corbett walked into the long, high-vaulted, deserted room, his footsteps ringing hollow and eerie in the watchful silence. Despite the warmth of a summer evening, the Chapter House was cold and dark so Corbett took a tinder and lit a few of the sconce torches, and wax candles on the table, where he sat in de Lacey's chair and waited for the drama to begin.

Ranulf and Cade came first, the under-sheriff looking haggard and tired.

'Sir Hugh, what is the matter?'

'Sit down, Master Cade. Ranulf, did you deal with the other matter?'

'I did.'

Corbett tapped his fingers on the table top. 'Then let us wait for our guests to arrive.'

They must have sat for half an hour, Cade trying to make desultory conversation, when they heard a knock on the door.

'Come in!' Corbett shouted and Lady Mary Neville slipped into the room.

She had the hood of her cloak well forward, and, as she pushed it back and sat in the chair Corbett offered, he caught the woman's nervousness. Her skin had lost its lustre, she kept licking her lips and her eyes darted to and fro as if she suspected that some great danger threatened.

'You asked to see me, Sir Hugh?'

'Yes, Lady Mary. The night Lady Somerville died, you went to St Bartholomew's hospital?'

'I have told you that.'

'So you did. And who else knew you were going?'

Corbett watched the woman closely as he heard the Chapter House door quietly open. 'I asked you a question, Lady Mary. Who else knew? Or shall I answer it for you?' Corbett looked up and stared at the woman standing just inside the doorway.

'Well, Lady Fitzwarren, can you answer?'

The tall, angular woman swept towards him; her stern face looked harsh, her eyes were like two pieces of hard slate in her angry, drawn face. Corbett saw her hands were tucked into the sleeves of her gown and he did nothing to stop Ranulf drawing his own dagger.

'Master Cade, a seat for our second guest.'

Lady Fitzwarren sat down carefully.

'As I was saying, Lady Mary and her companion went to St Bartholomew's hospital on Monday, May eleventh. Now, I always believed that Lady Somerville's death was some accident, but I have changed my mind. I realise my own mistake, a lack of attention to detail. Only someone who knew Somerville would know she would walk across Smithfield Common by herself.' Corbett smiled at both women. 'Oh, yes, Lady Somerville knew her killer. You see, the murder was witnessed by someone.' He saw Fitzwarren's eyes flicker in fear. 'A mad beggar squatting at the foot of the scaffold saw Lady Somerville stop and wait for her killer, he heard her call out "Oh, it's you!" Now,' Corbett leaned his hands on the table, 'I was far too clever. I should have listened to that beggar man more carefully. He described the killer as tall as the devil with horned feet. I dismissed that as some phantasm of his imagination but, of course, he was talking about you, Lady Catherine. *You* are taller even than most men. And you were dressed in cowl and hood when you carried out your bloody murders.'

Lady Mary recoiled in fright and horror. Fitzwarren pursed her lips.

'You speak gibberish, clerk!'

'Oh, no, I don't. Let's go to another murder. Father Benedict. Someone blocked the keyhole of the poor priest's door, threw a jar of oil through the open window then struck a tinder and flung that in as well. Go and look at the ruins of Father Benedict's house. The window is high in the wall, someone well above average height threw that jar in.'

'They could have stood on a log or a stone,' Lady Mary whispered.

'Yes, that's true, but they didn't. No log or stone was found near the window nor did the ground outside bear any such mark.'

'You still haven't produced any proof,' Fitzwarren challenged.

'Oh, I'll come to that by and by. You see, when I examined the room, I found traces of the oil, clear and pure, of a very high quality. Only the wealthy purchase such oil for their food. I realised that this evening whilst watching my wife prepare our meal. The assassin used that oil because it was free of any reeking odour and, if spilt over dry rushes, would soon catch alight.'

'The assassin could have bought it!' Fitzwarren snapped.

Corbett steeled himself for the next lie to come.

'Ah, yes, but in Newgate there is a man called Puddlicott, lying under sentence of death, who is responsible for the robbery of the King's treasure. You must have heard of that? He was in the abbey grounds the night Father Benedict's house was burnt down. He saw you, Lady Fitzwarren, throw a jar of oil through Father Benedict's window.'

'He's a liar and a rogue!' she hissed. 'Who would believe him?'

'The King, for a start. Puddlicott has no grievance against you. He seeks no reprieve or pardon. Both are out of the question. Lady Fitzwarren, he recognised you.'

The old noblewoman's face lost some of its arrogant hauteur. Corbett leaned towards her, silently praying that his bluff would force a confession.

'Even if Puddlicott's story is rejected,' he continued quietly, 'others saw you. Do you remember the whore Judith? I believe you were hiding in a large cupboard in the garret she used? She opened the door and you lashed out with your knife. You did not stay to mutilate her body because she had screamed but, Lady Fitzwarren, she survived and is now under royal protection. Master Cade will swear to that.'

The under-sheriff, who was staring open-mouthed at Lady Catherine, nodded solemnly.

'She, too, recognised you,' Corbett insisted. 'She caught the fragrance of your perfume, a glimpse of your face. I don't bluff. Judith must have survived for only she or her would-be killer would know about the incident in the cupboard.'

Lady Fitzwarren drew back, hissing and muttering to herself.

'I could go on,' Corbett continued. 'The whore Agnes, the one you killed in a church near Greyfriars, she also glimpsed you leaving the house where her friend had died. I believe she was on the point of sending a note to Lady de Lacey, here at Westminster, but the boy dropped the note down a sewer. Somehow you realised the poor girl posed a danger. She saw you, perhaps you glimpsed her. Anyway, you forged a note, probably in de Lacey's handwriting and, dressed like a monk, you slipped it under her door. The poor girl fell into the trap. She would never dream that her killer was luring her to murder on consecrated ground. She was one of the few not killed on the thirteenth of the month. Because she had seen you leaving the corpse of one victim, Agnes had to be silenced as quickly as possible. Now, as regards Lady Somerville . . .'

'This is impossible,' Lady Mary interrupted. 'Why should the Lady Fitzwarren murder one of her sisters and poor Father Benedict?'

'You are right to think both are connected. You see, our killer dressed as a monk. She carried with her the sandals, cloak, cowl and hood of a Benedictine monk. She took them from the vestry which adjoins this Chapter House. Now, I can only conjecture, but I suspect that Lady Somerville, whilst cleaning and laundering the vestments, came across a monk's cowl, or gown, which bore marks of blood, perhaps traces of a woman's perfume. Naturally, she would be puzzled, hence her constant quotation of the riddle "the cowl does not make the monk". She was not referring to any moral platitude about our monkish brethren, though God knows she may have been right, she was being quite literal. Just because someone dons the cowl and hood, that doesn't make the wearer a monk.'

'And Father Benedict?' Cade asked, reasserting himself.

'Oh, I suspect Lady Somerville talked to him. Perhaps even conveyed her suspicions that the person killing the prostitutes and whores of London was one of her own sisters, someone from the Sisters of St Martha.' Corbett glanced at Lady Mary Neville. 'The shock of what Lady Somerville learnt made her sketch a caricature of what was happening at Westminster. The monks here may have been lax but, in their midst, they harboured a slavering wolf. It also explains why Lady Somerville thought of leaving the Sisters of St Martha.'

'But why would the killer suspect Lady Somerville?' Ranulf asked.

'A matter of speculation, as well as logic. Lady Somerville was muttering mysterious riddles which only the killer could understand and, perhaps, the murderer realised the mistake she had made in returning a blood-stained gown. A gown quite singular because it had been designed for someone very tall in stature. The assassin would watch Lady Somerville and notice where she went. Now, Lady Somerville wouldn't talk to the brothers in the abbey and her story was too incredible to take to any official, she was alienated from her own son so Father Benedict was the logical choice.'

'He's right,' Lady Mary retorted, staring at Fitzwarren. 'He's right.' Her voice rose in anger. 'Lady Somerville and Father Benedict were very close.'

'Yes, yes, they probably were,' Corbett answered.

'Everything else fits the picture,' Ranulf remarked, rising out of his seat to go and stand behind Lady Fitzwarren. 'Our murderer had two advantages: dressed as a monk, she could go anywhere and, being a member of the Sisters of St Martha, she knew which whores were more vulnerable, where they lived, their routine, their personal circumstances. Moreover, no woman would see another as a threat.' Ranulf leaned over the woman's chair and seized her by the wrists.

Fitzwarren struggled, her face snarling like a vixen.

'You bastard!' she hissed. 'Take your hands off me!'

Ranulf drew Lady Catherine's hands out of the sleeves of her gown and looked at Corbett in surprise, for there was no dagger there.

Corbett stared at the ugly, old face, full of venomous hatred. She's mad, he thought. Like all killers she has let some canker, some rot, deep in her soul, poison her whole mind. Fitzwarren stared at him like some spiteful scold being caught in a misdemeanour.

'Finally,' Corbett concluded, 'I became fascinated why the women died on or around the thirteenth of each month. You know the reason why. Your husband, Lady Catherine, died at Martinmas, the Feast of St Martin, pope and martyr, whose mass we celebrate on April thirteenth.'

'But the last one, Hawisa's death, did not follow this sequence,' Cade interrupted.

'Yes, I know,' Corbett replied. 'But that was meant to puzzle us. You see, Master Cade, only a handful of people realised the pattern in the deaths. Ranulf, myself, you and two other people I talked to: Lady Mary Neville and Lady Catherine Fitzwarren.' Corbett smiled weakly. 'I confess, for a while, Master Cade, you were under suspicion. Lady Mary, I also began to wonder about you. However, both Puddlicott and the beggar described the killer as very tall.

Finally, His Grace the King unwittingly told me the date of Lord Fitzwarren's death. You killed that last girl, Lady Catherine, just to muddy the water.' Corbett drummed his fingers on the table top. 'You were always dirtying the water,' he added.

'When we visited you at St Katherine's by the Tower you hinted that the monks of Westminster were involved in some scandal which could be linked to the deaths of the street girls.' Corbett smiled thinly. 'I suspect when the dust settles, everyone will be so knowledgeable. You, however, saw such rumours as a cover for your own murderous activities.'

Fitzwarren preened herself, smiling spitefully. 'All of this is conjecture,' she retorted. 'You have no real proof.'

'Perhaps not, but enough for the King's Justices to try you at Westminster. And what then, Lady Catherine? Public humiliation? Suspicion? You will be regarded as the lowest of the low.' He watched the smile fade from the old woman's face. 'And after conviction? God knows what. If you are found innocent or, more likely, the case not proven, will you ever be able to walk the streets of London? And, if you are found guilty of so many deaths, you will be taken from the Fleet prison, dressed in the scarlet rags of a murderer and burnt at Smithfield, where every whore in the city will gather to laugh at your dying screams.'

Fitzwarren looked down then quickly back at Corbett. 'What other choices are there?' she asked softly.

'The King would wish this matter kept quiet. A full and frank confession and forfeiture of all your goods to make compensation.'

'And me?'

'You will take the veil in a lonely, deserted convent. Perhaps somewhere on the Welsh or Scottish march and live out the rest of your days on bread and water, making reparation for the terrible crimes you have committed.'

The old lady grinned and cocked her head sideways.

'You are a clever, clever boy,' she murmured. 'I should have killed you,' she added softly. 'With your hard face, worried look and cunning eyes.'

'You tried to, didn't you? You hired those killers who attacked us in the Walbrook?'

Fitzwarren wriggled her shoulders and pouted as if Corbett had made some mild criticism.

'You are a clever, clever boy.' Fitzwarren repeated. You see, Corbett,' she moved in her chair, as if she was telling a story to a group of children. 'You see, I loved my husband. He was a noble man. We had no children so I lived for him.' She looked around, her eyes brimming with tears. 'Don't you understand that? Every breath I took, my every thought, my every deed was centred on him. He died a warrior's death fighting for the King in Wales.' Fitzwarren crossed her arms, her face became sad, losing its mask of hatred as she withdrew deeper into the past. 'I really loved my husband,' she repeated. 'In a way, I still do, despite the terrible injury he did me.' Her eyes quickened with malice and she glared at Corbett. 'I joined the Order of St Martha, devoting my life to good works, I pitied these girls and I never dreamt what secrets I would find. One day I was talking to one of them, she was young, with skin as white and smooth as marble and eyes as blue as the summer sky, she looked like some angel, beautiful and innocent.' Fitzwarren tightened her arms. 'That was until she opened her mouth. I tried to reason with her, tried to explain the wrong she was doing. I pointed out how hard my life had been, a Fitzwarren, with a husband who had been a general in the King's army.' Lady Catherine's lips curled. 'The bitch asked my name and I repeated it. She asked me again and again whilst rocking to and fro with peals of laughter.' The old woman stopped speaking and looked down at the table.

'My Lady?' Corbett insisted.

Fitzwarren looked up, her eyes slits of malice, and Corbett sensed her mind was slipping into madness.

'The bitch,' she hissed. 'She plucked up her skirts and showed me her private parts! "See these, my Lady Fitzwarren!" she yelled. "Your husband fondled them, kissed and ploughed me because of the joys you could not give him!"' Fitzwarren rubbed her face in her hands. 'I couldn't believe it,' she whispered. 'But the whore described my husband, his skin, the colour of his hair, his walk, his posture, even his favourite oaths. According to the bitch, my husband used not only her but others of her ilk. I could not deny it for when we were in London my husband was often absent on the King's business, or so he said.'

The old noblewoman laughed abruptly. 'The bitch thought it was so funny. Here was I, serving those who served my husband so well! The girl kept pulling up her skirts, standing on a stool, flouncing her filthy nakedness before me. There was a knife on the table. I don't know what happened. I picked it up and struck. The girl screamed so I yanked her hair back and slit her throat.' Fitzwarren stared at Corbett. 'How could he,' she whispered hoarsely. 'How could he consort with such women and leave me a laughing stock, the butt of every common prostitute's jokes? Oh, I am no fool,' she added. 'The girl's words raised ghosts in my own mind. How my husband neglected me and everything began to fester. Yet I found the whore's death acted like a purge, cleansing my blood, purifying my mind, so I struck again. Each time I used a robe and cowl from the vestry at Westminster.' She smiled. 'Those fat monks never noticed that anything was amiss. I heard the rumours about their late-night revelries and saw them as a marvellous opportunity. I also thought of my dear departed husband and vowed that every month, on the anniversary of his death, a whore would die.' She raised whitened knuckles to her lips. 'Oh, I used to love it. I would prepare carefully, single out my victim and plot her destruction.' Fitzwarren leaned over and tapped Corbett on the hand with her icy fingers. 'Of course, you were right, you clever, clever boy. Now and again things went wrong. The whore Agnes saw me. Silly, silly girl! She thought she was hiding in the shadows but I saw the light glinting on her cheap jewellery, and her stupid face peering through the darkness.' She rubbed the side of her cheek. 'Her death was easy, but Lady Somerville was different. Usually I checked the robe I used, even cleaned it myself, but one day I made a mistake. You know how it is, Corbett? Dark red blood merges so well with brown. Then, of course, the fragrance of my perfume. Anyway, I caught Somerville holding the robe, she just stood and looked at me, and I smiled back.'

'And Father Benedict?' Corbett asked.

'I knew Somerville would go to him,' she spat out. 'For she would find no joy with de Lacey.' She smiled to herself. 'Life became so, so busy. Somerville suspected and was already talking to Father Benedict. I knew he would take some convincing and I had already marked Isabeau down as my next victim.' Fitzwarren gazed into the middle distance, talking as if to herself. 'Somerville had to die and Father Benedict as soon as possible afterwards, before he could gather his dithering wits and realise what was happening. The following evening I visited Isabeau. I didn't dream Agnes would arrive. The rest . . .' Fitzwarren shrugged and put her hand inside her robe as if to scratch her chest, 'well,' she whispered then rose, bringing her hand back in a lightning lunge. Corbett saw the glint of a thin steel dagger in her hand. Yet Fitzwarren's speed made her clumsy, instead of thrusting she tried to hack at his face. Cade jumped up and Lady Mary Neville screamed as Corbett seized Fitzwarren's wrist, squeezing it tightly till his assailant, her face contorted with pain, let the dagger drop. Ranulf sprang forward, grabbed the woman, dragging her arms behind her back and expertly tying her thumbs together with cord from his pouch. Fitzwarren just stood, smirking in satisfaction.

'Clever, clever boy,' she murmured. 'I paid those bastards well but trust a man to bungle matters.' She threw her head back and laughed until Ranulf slapped her across the face. 'Bastard!' she screamed.

Ranulf seized her shoulder and whispered something in her ear. The old noblewoman drew away, her face pale with fright.

'You wouldn't?' she hissed.

'Oh, yes I would,' Ranulf replied quietly.

Corbett just stood and watched this eerie pantomime being played out.

Again Ranulf whispered in the old woman's ear.

'At The Wolfshead tavern, Southwark,' Fitzwarren replied. 'The former hangman, Wormwood.'

Ranulf nodded and stepped away. Corbett snapped his fingers at Cade.

'Take her,' he ordered, 'to some chamber in the White Tower. She is to be held there until the King's wishes are known.' Corbett nodded at Lady Mary Neville, who sat white-faced, eyes staring, mouth half-open. 'Ranulf, see the Lady Neville home.'

Corbett sat down as Cade hustled a now passive Fitzwarren to the door. Ranulf gently helped Lady Mary

Neville to her feet and, with one protective arm around her, left the Chapter House without a backward glance. Corbett watched the door close behind them and leaned back in the chair, hugging his chest. He stared into the dark emptiness. 'It's all over,' he whispered. Yet was it? As in war, victims and wounds remained. He would draw up his report, seal it with the secret signet, and pass on to other matters. But what about Cade and his young doxy Judith? Puddlicott and his brother? Young Maltote? The monks of Westminster? The Sisters of St Martha? All had suffered because of this. Corbett sighed and rose wearily to his feet and wondered what Ranulf had whispered to Lady Fitzwarren.

'He's changing,' Corbett murmured. Lady Mary Neville, he thought, only emphasized these changes more: Ranulf was more cautious, more ruthless in his self-determination and Corbett had glimpsed the burning ambition in his manservant's soul. 'Well, well, well!' Corbett tightened his sword-belt round his waist and then grinned to himself. If Ranulf wants more power, he thought, then he will have to accept the responsibility that goes with it. The clerk's grin widened as he decided Ranulf would be responsible for informing the formidable Lady de Lacey of what had been happening in her Order.

The clerk stared around the gathering shadows. So much had happened here, the chamber seemed to echo with the vibrant passions revealed there. Corbett recalled Fitzwarren's sardonic dismissal of him as a clever boy. He grinned sourly. 'Not so clever!' he muttered. He had always prided himself on his logic and yet that had actually hindered his progress: he had believed that Warfield, Puddlicott, de Craon, the killer and the murder victims were all inter-woven. He should have remembered how logic dictated that all parts do not necessarily make the same whole and that fortune, chance and coincidence defy the laws of logic. The only common factor was Westminster, its deserted abbey and palace. Corbett tapped the table-top absent-mindedly. 'The King must return,' he whispered, 'set his house and church in order!'

Corbett left the Chapter House, walked through the abbey grounds and hired a wherry to take him down river. He was still thinking about Ranulf as he pushed open the door to his house and heard the commotion from the solar above: baby Eleanor's shrieks, the shouting and thumping of feet and, above all, the beautiful wild singing of Welsh voices. Corbett leaned against the wall and covered his face with his hands. 'Now,' he groaned, 'my happiness is complete!'

The door at the top of the stairs was flung open and Corbett forced himself to smile as Maeve, leaning on the arm of a stout, long-haired figure, shouted, 'Hugh! Hugh! You'll be ever so pleased! Uncle Morgan has just arrived!'

Ranulf left the Lady Mary Neville on the corner of her street in Farringdon. He gently kissed her fragrant fingers, nodded perceptibly as she murmured how grateful she was for his protection, and watched the beautiful young widow walk down to the door of her own house. She stopped, her hand on the latch and looked back up the street to where Ranulf stood, legs apart, thumbs thrust into his sword-belt. She pulled her hood back, shook her hair free and, raising her fingers, blew him the sweetest of kisses. Ranulf waited until she had gone in and smiled, fighting hard to control his own elation which wanted to make him shout and cry for joy.

Yet Ranulf had decided that the day's business was

still unfinished. He walked back into the city, visiting a fletcher's shop just off West Cheap, before hurrying as fast as he could down to Thames Street and the barges waiting at Queenshithe. He would have liked to have stopped at Bread Street or even visited Maltote in St Bartholomew's but Ranulf was determined to carry through what he had decided. If his master knew, or even suspected, Corbett would use all his power to hinder and impede his plans. Ranulf drew his cowl over his head, wrapped his cloak more tightly about him and clambered into a two-oared wherry. He kept his face hidden, curtly informing the boatman to drop him in Southwark just beneath London Bridge. So, whilst a powerful oarsman pulled his little craft across a choppy Thames, Ranulf clutched his sword and carefully plotted how to carry out his plan. He only hoped the Fitzwarren hag had told the truth. Ranulf had threatened that if she did not give him the information, he would tell every whore in London about her. Yet her confession was the easy part. Southwark at night was regarded as London's own entrance to Hell and Ranulf knew that The Wolfshead tavern had a worse reputation than the devil himself.

The wherryman, intrigued at Ranulf's silence, thought his passenger was going to visit one of the notorious Southwark brothels and refused to let him land until he had given him stark advice on how to get his money's worth at The Golden Bell tavern where the bawds rutted like stoats for a penny and would do anything for two. Ranulf thought of the poor pathetic corpses he had seen, smiled bleakly and, once ashore, headed into the warren of alleyways which led off from the riverside. No lamps or torches flared here. The tenements and hovels huddled together and Ranulf felt he was picking his way through a darkened maze. Yet he knew Southwark came to life at night: cut-throats, pickpockets, pimps, vagabonds and outlaws roamed the alleyways looking for prey amongst the weak and unarmed. The runnels were cluttered with filth of every kind which reeked like the rotting decay of a charnel house. As Ranulf moved deeper into the darkness, dark forms emerged from narrow doorways but then slunk back as soon as they saw the hilt of Ranulf's dagger and sword.

At last he found The Wolfshead, a small, dingy tavern with narrow slit windows out of which poured the sounds of violent roistering. Ranulf pushed the rickety door open and stepped into the stale, noisy half-light. As he entered, the din fell away. Ranulf pulled his cloak aside, the sword and dagger were noted and the hum of conversation continued. A greasy, fat-faced tapster hurried up, bobbing and curtseying as if Ranulf were the King. His greedy little eyes took in the fine fabric of Ranulf's cloak and the leather, well-heeled boots.

'Some ale? Some wine, Master?' he whined. 'A girl? Perhaps two?'

Ranulf beckoned him closer and grabbed the man by his food-stained jerkin.

'I want Wormwood!' he muttered. 'And don't lie, you slob of lard! He and his companions always meet here. They can be hired, yes?'

The fat tapster licked his lips, his eyes darting like those of a trapped rat. 'Don't look!' he hissed. 'But in the far corner, Wormwood and his companions. They are here. What is it you want, Master? A game of hazard?'

Ranulf pushed him away. 'Yes. Yes,' he muttered. 'A game of hazard.'

He shoved the man aside, walked over to the corner and stared down at the four gamblers rolling cracked dice from a dirty cup. At first they ignored him but then the one-eyed man in the corner looked up; his face was narrow, thin and made all the more vicious by the rat-trap mouth and the dagger wound under his good eye; his greasy hair was parted in the middle and fell in straggling locks down to his shoulders.

'What is it you want, bucko?'

'You are Wormwood?'

'I am. And who are you?'

'Someone recommended you!'

'For what?' Wormwood's hands went beneath the table as did those of his three companions.

Ranulf beamed at all of them. They looked what they were: footpads, cut-throats, men who would slit a baby's throat for a groat. Unshaven faces, sly glittering eyes; Ranulf saw that one of them nursed a wound in his shoulder and knew that he had found his prey.

'I want to hire you,' Ranulf announced. 'But first I'd like to gamble some of my gold.'

Wormwood's hands, as did those of his companions, came back from under the table. Ranulf noticed the rags tied round their fingers and saw the lime stains. He knew how professional assassins had their own hallmark. Some would use the garrotte, others the crossbow, whilst these beauties used lime to blind their victim before striking with dagger and sword. Wormwood spread his rag-covered hands.

'So, you wish to hire us but first you want to dice?' He smirked at his companions. 'Mother Fortune, my dear brothers, is smiling on us tonight. Landlord!' he called out. 'Bring a stool for our friend. A jug of your best wine and five cups! He'll pay!'

The landlord hurried up but kept his face hidden as if he suspected what was to come. A stool was brought and the wine served. Wormwood shook the dice in the cup.

'Come, Master, guests first!'

Ranulf shook the dice and threw a ten then passed the cup to the fellow sitting to his left. Each had their throw and, slurping their wine and shouting abuse, they all threw less than Ranulf. The dice cup came round again.

'The best of three!' Wormwood announced angrily. 'And we'll see the colour of your gold just in case you lose!'

Ranulf slipped a piece on to the table and his companions gazed greedily at it. Ranulf picked up the dice cup.

'Strange!' Wormwood exclaimed.

'What is?' Ranulf smiled back.

'We have seen your gold but what are we gambling for?'

Ranulf put the cup back down on the table. 'Oh, didn't I tell you?' He smiled sweetly. 'Your lives!'

Wormwood's hands fell away but, before the rest could regain their wits, Ranulf leapt to his feet, kicking the stool behind him. The small crossbow concealed beneath his cloak was brought up and a barbed-edged quarrel hit Wormwood in the chest even before the footpad's hand could reach his dagger. His companions were too slow or fuddled with drink. One sprang up and almost fell on Ranulf's dagger. He backed away, screaming, his hands clutching the blood-spurting split in his belly. The other two fared no better, Ranulf, moving lithely, pushed the table with his boot, wedging one against the wall. He stepped back and drew his sword as another footpad, clutching his dagger and mouthing drunken curses, lurched towards him. Ranulf feinted, the man tottered by him then screamed in pain, crashing to the floor as Ranulf brought his sword back, slashing deep into the small of the man's back. The fourth assassin, still jammed between table and wall, struggled to free himself. Ranulf picked the small sack from the belt tied to one of the fallen. He opened its neck, poured the lime into his hands then threw it into the seated man's face. The fellow shot back, screaming, drumming his feet on the floor. Ranulf turned and stared round the now silent taproom.

'Justice has been done!' he bellowed. 'Is there any man here who wishes words with me?'

No one answered. Ranulf plucked his dagger out of the dead assassin and edged towards the door. The only sound was the scraping of stools and the muttered curses of Wormwood's remaining companion moaning for water. Ranulf slipped into the night and hurried back along the darkened alleyways to the riverside. There he cleaned his weapons, re-sheathed them and walked along the quayside to hire a wherry. He paid his coin and clambered in. As the oarsman pulled away, Ranulf gazed across the fast-flowing river. He felt no scruples about what he had done. Those men had attacked him for no cause except they had been hired by the Fitzwarren bitch. They had almost killed him and his master and caused God knows what damage to poor Maltote's eyes. Ranulf leaned back in the stern. When the time was right, he would tell Corbett what he had done. Ranulf thought of the Lady Mary Neville and smiled. Perhaps it was time that he told a little more to Master 'Long Face'? Above him a gull shrieked but Ranulf hardly stirred. He recalled his boast to Corbett: he, Ranulf-atte-Newgate, was as good a man as any; he would kneel before the King, be dubbed knight, be given high office and bed the Lady Mary Neville as his wife. And what could Master 'Long Face' do about that? Ranulf closed his eyes and dreamed of future glories.

By the time he reached the steps of Fish Wharf, Ranulf was so lost in his reverie that the boatman had to shout and give him a vigorous shake. Absent-mindedly, Ranulf tossed a few coins into the fellow's hands and stood looking along the quayside, remembering Corbett's conversation with Puddlicott. The trickster, now lodged in the Fleet, had failed to resolve one small mystery; something Master 'Long Face' Corbett had overlooked, a minor detail which had puzzled Ranulf. He recalled his ambitious dreams and wondered if now was the time to take the first step to realise them. Or should he just go home? He looked up the alleyway towards Thames Street. A wet-tailed rat scurried across his boot. Ranulf lashed out angrily but also took it as a sign. He was growing tired of scampering around in the dark on his master's errands. Yes, he concluded, now it was time Ranulf-atte-Newgate took care of his own future. As he walked briskly up the alleyway, two dark forms slipped out of a doorway. Ranulf threw back his cloak and drew his sword.

'Piss off!' he shouted.

The figures slipped away and Ranulf strode on, threading his way along the alleyways until he reached Carter Lane then across Bowyers Row and up Old Deans Lane which ran under the darkened mass of St Paul's. Ranulf, his curiosity whetted, stopped and edged his way up the cathedral's high cemetery wall. As usual, the old graveyard beyond was a hive of activity; Ranulf caught the smell of cooking and saw dark figures huddled around the fires and battered stalls selling trinkets and other gewgaws which, even at night, never closed. St Paul's was the refuge of the sanctuary men, the wolfs-heads, who fled there beyond the jurisdiction of the city officials or the King's law officers. Ranulf stood, silently staring into the night; if his master had not plucked him from Newgate prison, then this would have been the best his future could have offered him. More determined than ever, he climbed down, cleaned his hands and went up into Newgate. He bribed a sleepy-eyed guard to let him through the postern door and made his way across Smithfield Common to St Bartholomew's Priory. He stopped near the scaffold; the rotting, dangling cadavers did not concern him.

'Are you there, Ragwort?' he called softly.

'Old Ragwort's not there and he's not here either,' the mad beggar replied angrily.

Ranulf smiled, flicked a penny in the direction of the gibbet and went to hammer on the priory door. A few minutes later a lay-brother ushered him into the hospital. For a while Ranulf stood in a draughty passageway wondering what news awaited him.

'Ranulf, Ranulf,' Father Thomas came hurrying towards him. 'You come about Maltote?'

'I was passing this way, Father. I hate to bother you.'

'No trouble, Ranulf. I do my best work at night.'

'Well,' Ranulf asked hastily, 'is Maltote blind?'

Father Thomas took him gently by the arm and guided him to a bench.

'Maltote will be fine,' Father Thomas answered, sitting down beside him. 'His eyes will hurt and smart for some time but the lime was either washed or cleaned out very quickly. The side of his face will be slightly pitted but he is young and his body will mend quickly.'

Ranulf stared at him anxiously. 'So, what's the problem, Father?'

'It's his spirt I'm worried about.'

'What do you mean?'

'He might have a horror of violence, particularly weapons.'

Ranulf bit his lip. 'Go on, Father.'

'Well, we gave him a knife to cut his meat. He did more damage to his fingers than he did to his food.'

Ranulf leaned back and laughed in sheer relief, patting

Father Thomas gently on the hand. The apothecary sat puzzled by Ranulf's outburst.

'Oh, I'm sorry, Father. I must apologise. Didn't you know?'

Father Thomas shook his head.

'Never give Maltote a knife, a spade, anything which will cut. He will only harm himself and everyone else in St Bartholomew's! Yet, Father, I do thank you for your care.'

'Don't you wish to see him?'

'He's sleeping?'

'Yes, yes, he is.'

'Then let him be, Father. I have other business to tend to.'

Once outside St Bartholomew's, Ranulf strode back across the common and, covering his face against the terrible smells from the city ditch, followed the winding cobbled alleyway down to the entrance to Fleet prison. The porter was not too accommodating; only after silver had changed hands was Ranulf allowed into the grim, stinking entrance hall. A burly gaoler with greasy spiked hair and a drink-drenched face accosted him.

'What do you want?' the fellow asked, wiping his hands on a stained leather jerkin.

'A word with Puddlicott.'

The gaoler's thick lips parted in a smile.

'Ah, the plunderer of the King's treasure! We have orders to allow no one near him.'

'Whose orders?'

'Sir Hugh Corbett, Keeper of the Secret Seal.'

Ranulf fished in his wallet and took out a warrant bearing Corbett's seal. 'My master sent me! Do as I say!'

Naturally, the fellow could not read but he was impressed by the seal and even more so by the silver piece Ranulf placed on top of the warrant.

'You'd better come with me. He's nice and safe now. Comfortable lodgings he has, well away from the rest of the scum.'

The gaoler led him through a cavernous chamber where the common felons crouched, chained to the wall. The manacles were long enough for the prisoners to stand up and walk about but now they huddled under threadbare blankets, moaning and whimpering in their sleep. Ranulf looked with distaste at the long common table covered in greasy dirt where mice, impervious to their presence, still gnawed at the dirty scraps of food and globules of fat strewn there. A few of the prisoners woke and staggered towards them; dirty, fetid men and women clothed mostly in rags, their bare skin showing terrible sores and purple bruises. A guard shouted at them and the prisoners slunk away.

Ranulf and the gaoler left the hall, crossed a stone-flagged corridor past grated windows where felons awaiting the death cart shook begging bowls through the bars, cried or shouted abuse. They climbed slimy, cracked steps into a long, torch-lit corridor containing a number of cells. Ranulf immediately knew where Puddlicott was lodged, by the two guards crouching outside. They hardly stirred as the gaoler unlocked the door and ushered Ranulf in.

'Puddlicott, my lad!' the gaoler shouted. 'You poor benighted bastard! You've got a visitor!'

Ranulf peered through the gloom. The cell was a perfect square, clean and swept. There was a privy in the corner, which evidently drained down to the city ditch, and even some furniture: a small table, a broken stool and a long bed with a straw-filled mattress on which Puddlicott now half sat, his face heavy with sleep. At last he shook himself awake, stretched and yawned. Ranulf had to admire his coolness. The prisoner smiled at him.

'There's a candle on the table but I have no flint.'

Ranulf took his own and the candle sparked into light. Puddlicott went to piss in the privy, plucked up his cloak and came back to sit on the edge of the bed.

'So, Corbett has sent you again, eh? Has he missed something out?'

Ranulf sat on the table. 'Not really, we now know what happened. You apparently slipped in and out of the country when you wished, and moved sacks of coin to Gracechurch Street down to the docks by using a dung cart.'

Ranulf leaned back and stared at the ceiling. He and Corbett had made one mistake: never once had they asked why an important envoy like de Craon had not chosen a better lodgings. Yet, there again, accredited envoys had every right to choose where they stayed.

'Didn't you wonder,' Ranulf abruptly asked, 'why some of the whores invited to the abbey were murdered? Some of your girls must have been amongst the victims?'

Puddlicott shrugged his shoulders and pulled his gown tighter. 'You know the way of the world. It's Ranulf, isn't it?'

His visitor nodded.

'Men die violently, as do women and children, so why shouldn't whores.' Puddlicott stretched his legs. 'Your master will keep his word about my brother?'

'Yes,' Ranulf answered. 'And if you tell me more, you have my oath that twice a year I shall go to St Anthony's to make sure all is well.'

Puddlicott got to his feet and went to stand over Ranulf. 'Corbett didn't send you. You've come here on your own. I have told you what I know and, although I think all law officers are bastards, you are not here to gloat. So what is it? The slayer of the prostitutes?'

'No,' Ranulf answered defensively. 'We have our own thoughts on that.'

'What then?'

'Information!'

'For Corbett?'

'No, for myself.'

Puddlicott roared with laughter and went back to sit on his bed. 'So, that's your game, Master Ranulf? The servant competing with the master? Why do you think I have more information?'

Ranulf leaned forward. 'I accept,' he began, 'that de Craon would come to England to take the treasure home. I also understand why he would hide away but, what I can't understand, Master Puddlicott, is why you, digging away at the foundations of the crypt, had to leave such an important task and go back and forth to France!' Ranulf looked at the prisoner. 'That's the only loose thread. Why didn't you stay in London? What was so important that you had to journey backwards and forwards to Paris. We know you did; your accomplices stated how you would disappear for weeks. So, what else were you up to?'

Puddlicott waggled a finger at him. 'You're very sharp, Master Ranulf. Corbett didn't ask me that.'

'Perhaps he thought you were going back for fresh instructions.'

Puddlicott shrugged. 'So?'

'So,' Ranulf replied. 'Will you tell me the real reason?'

Puddlicott lay back on his bed, crossing his hands behind his head.

'You've got nothing to lose.'

'I've got nothing to gain,' Puddlicott snapped.

'There's your brother, and, as you know, Puddlicott, the hangman has his own way of easing pain. I am also sure our good friend the gaoler could provide a deep-bowled cup of spiced wine before your last ride in the death cart.'

Puddlicott lay whistling softly through his teeth.

'Agreed,' he said sharply and swung himself off the bed. 'I am a dying man, Ranulf. You know any oath made to me is sacred.'

'I'll keep it.'

Puddlicott tapped his feet on the ground. 'Would you like to look on the face of Christ?' he asked suddenly.

'What?'

'Would you like to look on the face of Christ?'

'Of course. What do you mean?'

'You know the Order of the Templars?'

'Of course!' Ranulf snapped.

'Well,' Puddlicott drew in his breath. 'I don't know the full story but sometimes de Craon babbled in his cups. His master, Philip of France, is desperate for money; the roads of northern France are clogged with men-at-arms as Philip assembles his armies for all-out war against Flanders.' Puddlicott held a hand up. 'I realise you know that. Anyway, Philip has heard of a precious relic, the Shroud of Christ held by the Templars.'

'And now he wants it so he can sell it abroad?'

Puddlicott made a face. 'Ah, but there's more. You see, I had three tasks: breaking into the crypt was one, the others were to collect information about the Templars in England as well as the whereabouts of their famous relic.'

'Why this information?'

'Ah.' Puddlicott rose and whispered in Ranulf's ear. He then stood back, enjoying the amazement on Ranulf's face.

'You are telling the truth?' he asked.

Puddlicott nodded. 'The breaking into the crypt is nothing compared to Philip's plans for the future. Only four others now know what you do.' Puddlicott held up his fingers. 'Philip of France, Master Nogaret, de Craon and myself.' Puddlicott shrugged. 'I'll soon be dead. Let's face it, that bastard de Craon did nothing to save me.'

Ranulf eased himself off the table and hammered on the cell door.

'You'll keep your word?' Puddlicott pleaded.

Ranulf looked over his shoulder. 'Of course, provided what you have told me is the truth!'

In the porter's lodge, Ranulf dug deep into his purse and slipped some silver coins into the gaoler's palm.

'You'll do what I say?' Ranulf asked.

'I understand, Master,' the fellow replied. 'On the morning he dies, Puddlicott will drink deeply and go high up the hangman's ladder.'

Ranulf assured him that he would check that his silver was well spent and, breathing a sigh of relief, stepped out of the prison, the iron-studded door slamming firmly behind him. He stood for a while sucking in the cool night air and staring up at the stars.

'Ranulf-atte-Newgate,' he whispered to himself. 'The

searcher of secrets.' He recalled what Puddlicott had whispered to him. Oh, he would tell Master Long Face but his own quick wits would choose both the time and the place. The revelation of Puddlicott's terrible secret would be the key to Ranulf's fortune.

Author's Note

The events described in this novel actually occurred. Richard Puddlicott was an educated clerk, a master of disguise and a well-known villain with an international reputation. He had been a merchant in the Low Countries and, because of Edward I's economic measures, suffered financial hardship there. Puddlicott returned to England where he, with Adam of Warfield and William of the Palace, plotted the great robbery at the Abbey. The situation at Westminster was as described in this novel; there was no real authority in the deserted palace buildings and the Benedictine monks, lax in the observance of their monastic duties, were easy targets for a man like Richard Puddlicott. Midnight revelries were organised in the deserted palace buildings in which Puddlicott, Adam of Warfield and William of the Palace were the principal protagonists. Prostitutes and courtesans were invited to these revelries and, from midnight feasts, Puddlicott and Warfield moved on to robbery.

The old deserted cemetery was sown with hempen, and Puddlicott, under Warfield's protection, tunnelled his way into the crypt. A great deal of plate was removed as well as freshly minted coins. Fishermen found goblets floating in the Thames, some of the plate turned up at Kentish

Town and even the city goldsmiths, men like William Torel, whose work can still be seen in the Abbey, were happy recipients of the stolen plate. When the robbery was discovered Edward was furious; the monks were committed to prison whilst Richard Puddlicott and William of the Palace paid for their crimes with their lives. The crypt at Westminster can still be visited and I have sat in what used to be the deserted cemetery and reflected on this most daring of robberies which took place almost six hundred and ninety years ago.

Accounts of the robbery, including Puddlicott's confession, are still extant. The chief source is manuscript Chetham No. 6712 which is still preserved in the Chetham Library, Manchester. Indeed, the author of this account may well have been one of the forty-nine monks indicted in the subsequent investigation and sent to cool his heels in the Tower. Puddlicott's cheeky confession, in which he claims full responsibility for everything, can be read in the original (Exchequer Accounts K.R. 322/8 at the Record Office, Chancery Lane), whilst there is even a picture of the supposed robbery in a manuscript of the Cotton Collection Nero D. ii Folio 192D at the British Library. In all these original documents, Puddlicott comes across as an able, quick-witted rogue, a born charmer, and one can only regret the manner of his death. He suffered the supreme penalty for his insolence and there is no doubt that his corpse was flayed and the skin nailed to the Abbey door. Hundreds of years later, archaeologists found traces of this skin still embedded in the old Abbey door. It might have been left there to rot: a powerful testimony of Edward I's violent reaction to the plundering of his treasure.

A survey of the court records for London, during the year mentioned in this novel, shows that a number of prostitutes were killed. I have weaved this list of tragic deaths in with Puddlicott's raid on Westminster Abbey. Puddlicott's links with France are tenuous, to say the least, but what cannot be denied is the increased diplomatic activity by both Philip's and Edward's agents as each king struggled for dominance over the other. Philip IV's economic and financial measures ranged from an attack on the Church to the investigation of whether alchemy did actually work. His designs on the Templars, the famous religious fighting order, later led to one of the greatest scandals in medieval Europe, but that will be the subject of another novel.

Many people have written and asked me whether Hugh Corbett is based on an actual historical person and, perhaps, now it is time I confessed to the truth. He is; and this real clerk was a principal agent in discovering the crime and bringing Puddlicott to justice and the treasure back to the King. His name was John de Droxford and if anyone wants to look at the real Corbett's handwriting then look at Cole's Records (Record Commission 1844) which prints the indenture in which de Droxford specifies the jewels lost and recovered. John de Droxford was also commissioned to empanel the juries to try Puddlicott and was instrumental in resolving this and many other mysterious incidents. Perhaps it is only right and time to give credit where credit is due.